THE NAKED SOUL

The Reverend Jack Mallund knows his SAS regimental reunion party won't be a night for the faint-hearted. When a pornographic film is played to the rowdy former servicemen, he turns away — but not before the face of one of the actors jumps out at him with a familiarity that makes him sick. It is his teenage daughter Alice — currently missing, presumed dead . . . Jack's life is turned upside down all over again. With the police reluctant to reopen the case, Jack must go it alone. As he fights to find Alice, his faith is tested to the extreme, and his conscience pushed to the precipice of insanity . . .

SPECIAL MESSAGE TO READERS

THE ULVERSCROFT FOUNDATION

264873)

unds for
e diseases.
ed by
e:-

rfields Eye

it at Great
Children
eases and
thalmology,

h Group,

e Western

the Royal
gists

oundation
egacy.
d. If you
ation or
ontact:

THE ULVERSCROFT FOUNDATION
**The Green, Bradgate Road, Anstey
Leicester LE7 7FU, England
Tel: (0116) 236 4325**

website: www.foundation.ulverscroft.com

Alexander Lindsay was born in Ayrshire, Scotland. As an international journalist he has lived and worked in the Middle East, New York, Paris, the UK, Ireland and the Greek Islands. Based in Belfast, he covered the Northern Ireland conflict as staff correspondent for the *Sunday Express*, during which time his main claim to fame was being ignominiously blown off the lavatory seat by an IRA bomb at his office, sustaining moderate injuries to his head and major ones to his dignity. He has been a newspaper and magazine editor, newspaper proprietor, restaurant critic, national newspaper theatre critic, feature writer and magazine columnist.

Visit his website at
www.alexanderlindsay.com

ALEXANDER LINDSAY

THE NAKED SOUL

Complete and Unabridged

ULVERSCROFT
Leicester

First published in Great Britain in 2015 by
Robert Hale Limited
London

First Large Print Edition
published 2017
by arrangement with
Robert Hale
an imprint of The Crowood Press
Wiltshire

A catalogue record for this book is available
from the British Library.

ISBN 978–1–4448–3121–4

Published by
F. A. Thorpe (Publishing)
Anstey, Leicestershire

Set by Words & Graphics Ltd.
Anstey, Leicestershire
Printed and bound in Great Britain by
T. J. International Ltd., Padstow, Cornwall

This book is printed on acid-free paper

1

A letter from Hereford. The postmark sent a frisson of dread down his spine even after all these years. Twelve years, in fact, during which there had been blessed silence.

So what could they possibly want with him now?

The Reverend Jack Mallund stuffed the envelope unopened behind the clock on the mantelpiece.

You can sit there and stew until I'm ready, he told it. *I don't jump to the summons anymore.*

He went to the kitchen and brewed a pot of strong tea. He opened a round Cadbury's Roses tin and took out a half-eaten lemon drizzle cake, baked by his parishioner Mrs Sanderson, a comely forty-something widow with her sights on him, the good-looking single vicar. He cut a generous slice and settled down at the kitchen table to eat, thinking of anything but the envelope festering away on the mantelpiece.

He fetched a Bible and a writing pad and set about roughing out his sermon for Sunday:

When we consider the meaning of St Paul's first letter to the Corinthians and compare it to the way we live life in the fast lane today, several glaring issues raise their heads. Firstly, there is the question of . . . What was the question? What issues? His concentration had deserted him. He was stuck. And restless. He loped into the sitting room. The envelope was still there, behind the clock.

Of course it was.

I don't even have to open it at all, he reasoned. *It can sit there behind that clock until Doomsday for all I care. I can be strong and resist the temptation. After all, I'm a man of the cloth, I'm supposed to be good at temptation. But wasn't it Oscar Wilde who said, 'I can resist anything but temptation'?*

He slid his hand behind the clock, extracted the envelope and weighed it in the palm of his right hand, bouncing it up and down. It didn't look too official; that was a good sign. Maybe it was just an innocent missive from somebody in Hereford. What's Hereford noted for? It's the birthplace of Nell Gywnne, the orange seller who became a famous actress and mistress of King Charles II. But it couldn't be from Nell. She died nearly 400 years ago. The city is also the centre of the English cider-brewing industry. But he doesn't drink cider. He was running out of options. *Bite the bullet, Jack,* he urged himself. *You know who it's from.*

Hereford has only one other claim to fame. It is the headquarters of the SAS, the Special Air Service regiment, the elite Special Forces unit that is the envy of the world.

He ripped open the envelope. Sure enough, the first image to emerge on a piece of card was the time-honoured logo: A winged dagger and below it the legend: *Who Dares Wins.*

With it came a surge of painful memories he thought he had buried long ago. Would they never leave him alone? He pulled out the rest of the card . . .

YOU ARE INVITED TO A REUNION

'Well I'll be . . . ' He read the back of the card, recognized the unbridled scrawl of his old mate and comrade Corporal Ben Yates:

Hi, Vicar, thought it was time we all got together to raise Hell — oops! Sorry your Reverendship — and bore the arses — oops! — off each other with our tales of derring-do. I suppose you're too righteous now to be bothered with nose pickers like us from your murky past, but if you don't come, me and the crew will come for YOU. Knives between our teeth, balaclavas, faces blacked up, abseiling through your bedroom window. You will awake in another place with the hangover you so richly deserve.

Ben Yates. Porkhead, to his brothers in arms. Difficult to tell where his head ended and his neck began. Shoulders that could fit between the shafts of an ox cart; legs that could propel that very same cart with the ease of any self-respecting ox. Hands like bears' paws, yet he astounded his mates when he announced he was taking up the violin. Typical Porkhead. Still, he managed a fair tune. Not quite Nicola Benedetti, but a recognizable tune nevertheless. As one wag remarked: 'At least he made a brave fist of it.' Deceptively intelligent, he was an avid reader, devouring any books he could get his hands on. Mallund could never work out why he had remained a corporal with such a keen mind.

Now he was inviting Mallund to a reunion party. Party? More like a testosterone-fuelled celebration of beer, machismo, and chauvinism. No thanks. He had put all that behind him a long time ago. He dropped the invitation into the kitchen bin.

★   ★   ★

The following morning he delved into the bin and fished out the invitation, along with a fistful of soggy tea bags and congealed takeaway chicken tikka masala. He ran the card under the cold tap to remove the mess which had left a rich ruby stain, and put it under the grill to dry. After all, what harm could it do to go to the party? These were men he had shared spine-chilling danger with, their lives dependent on a hive instinct of mutual protection. Friend covering friend's back. All for one and one for all. It would be churlish to let his grudge against the regiment put a damper on their evening. He idly wondered what the lads would make of him drinking orange juice.

*   *   *

The testosterone was so thick in the air you could almost photograph it. The bar and waiting staff were all male, an arrangement the management had made in the light of previous experience. Voices were loud and raucous; battlefield-honed voices, rough and hoarse. Those who couldn't be heard because of the distance from one end of the bar to the other were using a peculiar sign language like that used by bookies at the racecourse. Old habits die hard. Mallund immediately recognized it as the hand signals for silent communication in covert operations. Sweat, spilt beer, muscle punches, and the occasional unclaimed fart. This was the SAS at play.

As Mallund stood by the door weighing up the scene, a swath was opening up in the tight crush of bodies, like the Red Sea parting for Moses. Through it came trundling the immense bulk of Cpl Ben Yates.

'You made it, Sarge! Knew you would.' He embraced Mallund in a crushing male hug.

'Couldn't leave you lot on your own, could I?' Mallund grimaced under the pressure of the hug. 'I'd end up bailing all of you out of jail like the old days.'

'That could still happen.' Yates looked Mallund up and down. Still reasonably fit, he hadn't let himself go. But the dog collar! 'Bloody hell, what do I call you these days?'

'Jack will do, we're all off duty now. Permanently.'

'Permanently.' A hint of wistfulness clouded Yates's eyes; just a second and it was gone.

'I was spooked a bit by the Hereford postmark on your letter. Thought they had come back to haunt me.'

'Oh, that? Forgot to tell you I settled down in the town after I retired from the regiment.'

'But you're a Geordie. Aren't they

6

supposed to go back home to die, like elephants?'

'Well, there wasn't much left for me up there after Irene and I split up and the kids had grown up and gone.'

'Yes, I was sorry to hear about that,' said Mallund.

'I was sorry to hear about yours too.'

'The old occupational hazard, eh?' Mallund's own marriage had also been a casualty of his lifestyle. 'So you chose Hereford of all places to settle down.'

'I've probably got more roots here than anywhere. Still have a pint with serving troopers, although they probably think I'm a boring old fart. And there's a big plus point too: it's great not having to salute the Ruperts in the street anymore!'

Mallund smiled. It was a long time since he had heard the regimental slang for their officers. *Ruperts.* Yes, he'd had a bellyful of them in his time. But better not to go there now. This was a party after all, and old familiar faces were crowding in on him . . .

'Pongo' Williams, whose tinderbox Welsh nature sat ill at ease with his quiet, patient role as a specialist sniper.

'Cleggie' Cleghorn, explosives and demolition. This ebullient Brummie could make a bomb out of the contents of his wife's handbag if put to the test.

'Slippery Sam' Andrews, who once escaped from a Libyan jail dressed in a woman's *burqa*. A good man to be covering your back.

These and others came to shake his hand, each dragging his speciality with him, and making lame jokes about Mallund's dog collar and orange juice.

Soon, Mallund was beginning to relax. He was glad he had come. He made a mental note to keep in touch with the men.

Porkhead Yates's voice cut across the hubbub of the room: 'All right, settle down, ladies, the entertainment is about to start.'

The hubbub continued unabated.

'*Quiet, you miserable dollops of wombat shit!*'

Porkhead now had their attention.

'We have a special entertainment lined up for you, just as soon as Eddie here can get the projector going. A little, shall we say . . . ooh la la.' He tried to mimic a swaying exotic dancer. He failed.

'Is this where I make my excuses and leave?' said Mallund, as Porkhead rejoined him at the bar.

'Just a little titillation for the lads, to round off the evening. Soft porn, nothing too extreme. Nothing you wouldn't have seen before.'

'At least I should step outside until it's over.'

'Naw, what would the lads think? Stay. You don't have to look and it's quite short. Couldn't you just sit and have a quiet prayer or something?'

'Ben, prayer was never intended as a distraction.'

In the end Mallund was persuaded and took his seat at a table with Yates and four others. He sat squirming with embarrassment. He was finding it difficult not to look at the screen. It is one of life's contrary tricks that the more you are trying not to look at something the more your eye will be drawn to it. He had sat staring down at the table, reading the beer mats over and over. This was a bad idea. He decided to get up and leave. As he got to his feet a flicker of the screen caught his eye. The face of one of the players. Just a flicker. But it was enough to stop him in his tracks.

'My God!' He reeled and knocked over the table. 'My God!' He stared at the screen for a few seconds and rushed from the room, sending bodies, chairs and tables flying. Outside, he bent over the balcony and threw up.

Yates was behind him.

'What's up, Jack?'

'She's supposed to be dead.'

'Who's supposed to be dead?'

'The girl on the screen . . . I thought she was dead.'

'You know her then?'

'She's my daughter.'

2

Equatorial Africa, Twelve Years Earlier

'Alpha One Zero, this is Delta Two Zero, do you read?'

The buzz of static was the only reply.

'Alpha One Zero, do you read?'

'Keep trying,' said a whispered voice.

'Alpha One Zero, this is Delta Two Zero, do you read?'

'The buggers aren't answering. They've dropped us, I tell you, Sarge. We don't exist here. What do we do now?' Trooper Cleggie Cleghorn clicked off the radio and stared at his superior in wide-eyed question. His sweat gave the black-up on his face a shiny glow, his eyes and mouth standing out in pinky white.

Sergeant Jack Mallund bit his lower lip in thought. Stuck in the middle of the bloody jungle and HQ has pulled the plug on us. They're probably sitting on their fat arses in some cushy billet trying to think up excuses for why the mission has gone pear-shaped, and why we've been dumped. At times like this he always thought the worst, that way you were never disappointed. He and his three comrades had been trying to contact their mission base for two days, ever since they had sneaked across the border into this strife-torn emergent republic. Radio transmissions had to be kept brief. A sophisticated radio direction finder could pinpoint your position in less than a minute. It could be simply that conditions were not right for radio reception, or there was a glitch in the electronics preventing contact. What he'd give for one of those new satellite phones that were scheduled for service. Then he'd be able to contact base and give them a piece of his mind as if he was calling from the phone box on the corner. Instead, they had to transmit and run; transmit and run, to escape detection. However, Mallund doubted whether this impoverished country could afford such sophisticated detection technology. Impoverished now, perhaps, but sitting on vast mineral deposits that promised a bright future once the bloodshed was over. Which was why Mallund and his team were there. Her Britannic Majesty's Government wanted a piece of any action going whenever peace returned, and was willing to expedite the peace in any way possible. Mallund's patrol was the advance guard, feeling out the lie of the land.

'You'll no doubt find a rather crowded

jungle when you get there,' the briefing officer had warned after a detailed outlining of the mission. 'The Chinese are sure to be sniffing around. The Russians too, not to mention our dear friends from across the pond. But do not engage. Our policy is strictly one of non-interference. Officially, you will not be there. If you get caught we will deny your very existence. You're on your own. Questions?'

'Yes — whose side are we on?' It was Mallund, blunt as ever. 'This is a classic case of rebels versus government forces, and as far as I can see, nobody is quite sure who are the good guys and who are the bad guys.'

'There isn't much reliable news coming out of the country,' said the officer, 'but there are unconfirmed reports of appalling atrocities committed by the rebel forces. We don't officially take sides, Sergeant. But for your, er, guidance, we favour the government. You must not engage with government forces and if it becomes really necessary you might even lend them aid.'

'What kind of aid would that be, Boss?'

'Well, Sergeant, I suppose . . . well, anything you think might have a positive outcome.'

It was clear to Mallund that the officer was floundering — himself a victim of woolly orders from above. The further up the line you got, the more elastic the orders became, as level after level ducked and dodged to cloak themselves in a shroud of deniability. The only certainty was that the buck would stop not at the top, but right down as far as you can go — right down to Jack Mallund and his band of brothers. Mallund muttered under his breath: 'So when the fertilizer hits the fan, it'll be us taking the shit shower.'

'Sorry, Mallund, I didn't hear that.'

'Just thinking aloud, Boss.'

'Very well, then. Good luck. And remember — do nothing to hinder the government forces.'

★ ★ ★

Now, leaving the security of their resting place under a canopy of trees, the SAS team were on the move again.

'So what do we do now, Jack?' repeated Cleggie, hauling the radio on to his back.

'Keep moving and maintain radio silence till the morning. We've been on the air more than is healthy already. Get Slippery Sam to check out what escape and evade corridors we have available in case we have to bug out in a hurry.'

It was just before noon that they came

upon the first of the villages. They slipped into standard formation for an approach. They needn't have bothered. There was no sign of life among the collection of charred huts. Only the signs of death.

The patrol stared in mute horror at the carnage spread all over the clearing. Bodies of men and children lay strewn in the dry dirt. Mutilated and some blackened by fire, they lay where they had died their horrible deaths. Cleggie threw a rock at a wild dog racing past with a child's arm between its teeth.

'Jesus wept!' breathed Porkhead. 'The bastards! They used machetes. Chopped off heads and limbs. The kids. My God, the kids!'

'Probably saving ammo,' said Pongo Williams.

'Notice anything missing?' Mallund was slowly scanning the scene with his eyes from left to right.

'Yup. No women,' said Cleggie. 'Probably took them with them.'

'Bloody rebels — the usual undisciplined rabble. Give them an AK47 and they think they rule the world. Think it gives them the right to do anything they like with anybody.' Porkhead spat into the dust.

'There's nothing we can do here.' Mallund shrugged. 'Move on. And stay alert. They could still be nearby.'

Three hours later they came upon another village. It too had been razed, and bore the same grim legacy of carnage. There were still wisps of smoke curling up from the burnt huts. The four of them picked their way through the mutilated bodies and pushed on. The four-man patrol is the ideal size for an SAS intelligence-gathering reconnaissance mission. It is small enough to be unobtrusive and flexible, yet can pack a good punch of firepower if it comes to the push.

'We're getting warm,' said Mallund. 'It's only a matter of hours since these huts were torched. Keep your eyes peeled and your ears open.'

'What do we do if we find the rebels?' said Cleggie.

'We follow orders and do nothing. Do not engage. Just observe and report back. Remember, we're not here.'

'And how do we report back when the buggers can't or won't acknowledge us, Jack?'

'We'll cross that bridge when we come to it.'

Mallund did not bridle at his subordinate's use of his Christian name when normally a 'sir' or 'sarge' would be expected. Despite its ultra-strict discipline, the SAS tolerates this informality, in the same way as troopers and NCOs are allowed to address their officers as 'Boss'. They are a law unto themselves as opposed to the regular British Army, whom they casually refer to as 'The Green Machine'. They rightly regard themselves as outside the normal rules. As something special. After all, the clue is in the name — *Special* Air Services.

Pressing on, Mallund and his men had already wiped the horrific scenes from their minds. You had to or you would go mad. Yet there was always a lingering prick of conscience. *Should I have done something? Even given them a decent burial? Forget it. What can one man — even four men — do? The scale of the horror is too immense. Press on.*

They did not have long to wait until their next encounter. The screams led them to the village. They crawled on their bellies and selected a concealed spot from which to observe. The bloodshed was in full riot. Fathers were being hacked to death in front of their children. The children would be next. The women were being rounded up and penned in the small corral where they wailed and screamed and threw themselves prostrate on the ground. In the centre of the clearing a man was tied to a stake. Probably the village head man, Mallund guessed. Men were bringing bundles of straw and throwing them at his feet.

'Good Christ! They're going to burn him alive!' Mallund lowered his field glasses and rubbed his eyes.

'And another thing, Jack.' Porkhead grabbed his arm to gain his attention. 'Uniforms . . . they're wearing uniforms. These are no rebels. These are *government* troops. This is fucking genocide!'

Through his glasses Mallund could see what appeared to be the officer, smiling contentedly and smoking a cigarette while his men ran amok.

I'd like to take you out first, you bastard. If only I was allowed to. Mallund subconsciously measured the range in his brain. This was the greatest hurt of all: lying powerless while watching the deed being done. He had seen the aftermath of ethnic cleansing in Bosnia and also in other African countries, but never, never could he have imagined the deed playing before him like this, in slow motion, like some rickety old movie. It tugged at the very root of his humanity, worrying it, like a dog with a bone it won't let go. *Do something, do something,* said a voice from the depth of his soul. But he must stay strong. Orders is orders. My country right or wrong.

But this is very wrong. Very, very wrong.

Follow your orders, or follow your conscience, said the voice, now louder in his head than even the sound of the bloody massacre. *It's up to you and you alone.*

'I count ten of them, including the officer,' he said to Porkhead.

'Don't even think about it, Jack.' Porkhead was slowly shaking his huge head.

'I say again ten, check.'

'Ten, check.'

'You lot stay here. I'm going in for a closer look.'

'Jack — '

'That's an order, Corporal!'

Mallund slipped out from under cover and, bent double, zig-zagged his way towards the clearing. Within fifty metres of the compound he took cover behind a tree. The officer had ambled up to the man tied to the post and casually tossed his cigarette into the straw at his feet. The man was screaming wildly as the straw began to smoke. The women were screaming as soldiers took their pick and dragged them from the corral. Mallund's brain was screaming as he fought the battle with his conscience. So much screaming!

Then he snapped.

His first shot took the officer square in the chest, knocking him backwards and tumbling

19

him into the smoking straw. Four soldiers dragging the women had propped their rifles against a tree. A fatal mistake. One, two, three, four . . . Mallund's automatic assault rifle settled each of the four in as many seconds. The remaining soldiers were frantically scouting around trying to pinpoint where the shots were coming from. They were shooting indiscriminately, spraying the area with automatic fire. Totally undisciplined, Mallund noted, while he calmly picked them off, as relaxed as if he were in a fairground shooting gallery. After three of them went down, the remaining two retreated into the trees and ran for it. Mallund started to give chase, but stopped short. The straw around the village head man's lower half was now alight, and he was squirming and tugging frantically at his bonds. It was only the dead officer's body lying on the straw and muffling the flames that had saved the victim so far. He sprinted across the clearing, pulling out his knife as he went. He gulped in a lungful of air and held his breath while he cut the man free and dragged him clear. The man was badly burned around the legs, but he would live. Mallund's eyes were stinging and watering and he was coughing profusely. Through the mist covering his eyes he could vaguely make out the bulk of Porkhead rushing towards him.

'Get back, Ben,' he croaked. 'We need to bug out sharpish. Some of them got away. Our cover's blown.'

The patrol withdrew into the trees and doubled along to put as much distance between themselves and the village in as short a time as possible. After an hour they flopped down in a hollow dell and slipped into their escape and evade routine. Without needing to be told, Cleggie unpacked the radio and clambered out of the dell and up a hillock to gain some height. Slippery Sam was checking pre-arranged escape corridors and rendezvous. Porkhead backtracked 100 meters and took up a sentry position.

'*Alpha One Zero, this is Delta Two Zero.*'

'*Delta Two Zero, this is Alpha One Zero. Go ahead.*' The voice was faint and crackly.

'*Delta Two Zero. Cover blown request escape RV.*'

With the rendezvous details jotted down, Cleggie slid down the hillock and joined Mallund in the dell. They bent over a rudimentary map of the area.

'This map's about as useful as an ashtray on a motor bike,' said Mallund. 'It looks like it's been drawn by a five-year-old.'

'Still, it gives us a rough idea,' said Cleggie. 'And it's not good news. I make it the RV is about thirty miles from here, in three day's time. Over this terrain we'll be lucky to make it.'

'Then there's no time to lose. Move out, lads!'

It was a harrowing thirty miles across a terrain that threw everything it had at them, from almost impenetrable bush to rugged crags that crumbled under your feet as you tried to scale them; one step forward, two steps back. At the first rest break Porkhead sidled up to Mallund.

'Just to let you know, Jack, me and the boys? We're with you.'

'With me?'

'Back at the village. We're with you. They attacked us, didn't they? We had to defend.'

'No, no, no, Ben.' Mallund was shaking his head. 'This is down to me. I don't want you lot involved. You were following my orders.'

'But you don't know what kind of shit they'll throw at you when you get back. This could cost you big. What the hell came over you, Jack?'

'Dunno. I just snapped. Couldn't watch anymore. Had to do something. Just had to do something. I guess you could call it conscience.'

'Conscience? What's that when it's at home?'

'It's a thing that has been bred out of us in this game. But once in a while it rears up to bite you on the bum.'

They made the rendezvous just in time, staggering out of the bush as the Black Hawk helicopter came wobbling down in a tornado of dust, an airman dangling out of the open door to haul them inside while the machine hovered and flew off without touching the ground.

'You boys have a good holiday then?' said the fresh-faced pilot.

The dark looks of sullen animosity from four worn-out faces was all the answer he would get.

⋆   ⋆   ⋆

Two hours later the Black Hawk touched down at base. The members of the patrol piled out. Last was Mallund. Waiting for him were two heavies.

'Sergeant John Mallund?' Mallund nodded.

'You are under arrest. Come with us.'

3

On the drive home from the reunion party in Hereford, Mallund had to stop less than halfway. His hands were shaking and he had lost all concentration. The shock of seeing the face of his daughter, Alice, in the pornographic movie had blotted out all sensibility. She had been missing for almost a year. He felt as if he was going to throw up again.

I'm just not safe to drive, he decided. He pulled in at a service area and got out of the car to walk around. His head was buzzing with questions.

Could she be alive despite the grim conclusions drawn by everyone — the police, the social services and, reluctantly, he himself? Where is she now?

And how did she come to be in that depraved movie?

The thought of it again made him retch and he threw up in a flower bed.

'Everything all right, sir?' Two constables had got out of their patrol car parked nearby and were approaching with suspicion all over their faces.

'Yes, Officer, just something I ate.' He was

still bent double, his back to them.

'Have you been drinking, sir?'

Mallund straightened up and turned to face them.

'Oh, sorry, Vicar. I didn't realize — '

'It's OK, Officer. I'll be fine in a minute.'

'Is there anything we can do? Perhaps help you get home?'

'No. I can manage. Thank you, Officer.'

He just wanted them to go away, leave him with the pictures that were crowding his head. Pictures of Alice cavorting in that awful, disgusting movie.

Where had it all gone wrong? That time in the jungle? It certainly was a milestone. But the rot had set in long before that. Right back to the day when, resplendent in his dress uniform, he took the hand of his new wife, Jennifer, and walked out of the church door. Confetti rained down on them as they emerged and were engulfed by a mob of friends and well-wishers. A happy, radiant couple.

But within a couple of years it became clear that Jennifer was not suited to the service life. She became resentful of his colleagues and the time they stole from her, monopolizing her husband even when he was home on leave. And then there were his tours of duty when she didn't even know when he would come home, if at all. The notion of having a husband with an exciting and dangerous lifestyle had thrilled her at first; put her one up on her friends and their drab husbands with their dreary jobs and their nine-to-five outlook. At school she had always been the one to lead, the experimenter, tempting her friends into all sorts of risque schoolgirl enterprises. Jumpin' Jenny they called her. No, it would not do for Jennifer to marry a dentist or a lawyer.

But a special forces agent? That was a coup. That was life on the edge.

She had been swept off her feet by the handsome soldier at first meeting. Tall, muscular and brainy with it, he was everything you would expect from the job description. Chiselled Mount Rushmore features; lazy, droopy-lidded Robert Mitchum eyes; and a voice . . . well whose voice? Hmm. Bruce Willis, she decided after much consideration. Short-cropped sandy hair completed the man of action picture. He was by far the best-looking man in the nightclub, and Jennifer and her friend Rachel McGuire had been admiring and discussing him all evening.

'Go and ask him to dance,' said Rachel.

'No way.'

'Dare you. Go on.'

26

'No way.'

'Come on — whatever happened to the great Jumpin' Jenny?'

'She's not jumping into this.'

'All right, if you won't, then I will.'

'Go on then.'

'No way.'

'Dare you.'

'No way.'

They both fell about laughing. Then Jennifer drained her Vodka Collins and thudded her empty glass on to the bar. She rammed her handbag into Rachel's arms, smoothed her hair and shimmied across the floor.

'Hello, Soldier. Would you like to dance?'

She took his hand and he let her lead him on to the floor. He threw a helpless backward glace at his three mates, who, by now, were cheerfully egging him on.

'How did you know I was a soldier?' he asked as they danced.

'An educated guess, Jack. The four of you are too fit compared to other men of your age around here. A tight bonding between you, so you're in some kind of club. Then there's the military bearing.'

'Quite the little psychologist, aren't you?'

'Got an A-level.'

'And you worked it all out just from that

bit of observation?'

'Not exactly. There's a bloody great machine gun tattood on your mate's arm!'

He laughed, a booming, uninhibited laugh that cleared a space around them on the floor.

'But just a minute — how do you know my name's Jack?'

'Probably something to do with the fact that your mates are standing at the bar going: 'Nice one, Jack!''

'Oh. And I suppose you have a name too?'

'Jennifer. It's Jennifer.'

* * *

The first year of marriage was bliss. Mallund revelled in Jennifer's wicked sense of humour; and she in turn soaked in the aura of imminent danger that exuded from him. It was thrill by association, as if touching his body, holding him tightly in bed, clinging to him during their sex, caused her to draw out a bit of his world into her own, like a poultice. At first she didn't mind the long absences, the niggle of worry when he was away on operations. After all, he was indestructible. But, as the body bags started to come home, reality began to bite, and each tour of duty held nothing but a depressing sense of awe. Jennifer found little solace in the company of the other soldiers' wives. Like her, they came from humble beginnings, but Jennifer had a string of A-levels to her name and she found the conversation banal and unstimulating. The officers' wives might have proved more fulfilling company — but that was a no-go area. She once suggested to Mallund that he put in for a commission. After all, he was intelligent and had A-levels, admittedly only a couple of Bs and a C — but this was due more to lack of study and application rather than poor academic prowess.

'Me? A Rupert? Hell will freeze over first.' And that was the end of it.

Jennifer's mood slid further and further down the slippery slope towards utter depression, until a ray of sunshine appeared in the form of 8lb 3oz of bouncing baby called Alice. The baby kept her busy and lifted her spirits. She was at one with the world, and for a while it looked like the bleak life she had been living was turning out all right in the end.

Until that day in the African jungle.

4

Mallund could still hear the words that had greeted him as he stepped off the helicopter back at base ringing in his ears.

'Sergeant John Mallund? You are under arrest. Come with us.'

They took him to a room with a reinforced steel door and kept him locked up for two days. Normally on returning from a mission, he would have gone straight into debriefing to give his account while it was still fresh in his mind. But instead, he was being kept incommunicado. He was worried for his men, wondering if they too were locked up. This had to have something to do with the business at the village — but how could the news have got back to base in just over three days?

Each time a guard came to check on him or bring a meal, he questioned him.

'Am I being accused of something? What's the charge? What about my men?'

But the guards maintained a rigid silence.

'For Christ's sake, lads, tell me what the hell is going on!'

On the third day he was sent for and taken

to a hut where a major and two captains were seated at a trestle table. He was guided to a solitary folding wooden chair facing them.

'Well, what do you have to say for yourself?' asked the major.

'Say for myself, Boss?'

'Call me 'Sir', Sergeant. What the bloody hell did you think you were doing in that village?'

'Should I not have the right to legal representation . . . sir?'

'This is not a court martial. At least not yet. I repeat, what do you think you were playing at in that village?'

'What village? What country? I wasn't even there, was I?'

'Don't be impertinent!' snapped one of the captains.

'I would like to be told what I am being accused of if you don't mind, sir, and if this isn't a court martial, then what exactly is it?'

The three officers exchanged glances then nodded.

'This is merely an inquiry to establish the facts,' said the major. 'Within hours of your little escapade the phones were red hot between their government and Whitehall. They knew we had sent a Black Hawk into their territory. The only possible reason for that would be to recover spies — their terminology — and in no time at all they were raving about one man wiping out most of a platoon of their forces. That man was you, Sergeant, was it not?'

Mallund remained silent.

'There's no point in denying it, Mallund. As the rozzers would put it, we've got you bang to rights. But as I said, this is not a court martial. We just want to know what the fuck was in that head of yours when you disobeyed direct orders and ran amok among government troops with an assault rifle. Christ, man, the officer you shot was the son of their Culture Minister!'

'Some culture!' muttered Mallund.

'Don't be impertinent!' snapped the captain.

'We all get stressed out sometimes,' the major continued, 'so why don't you tell us in your own words what happened, eh?'

Mallund related the incident, leaving out none of the gory detail. He could tell by their faces that the three officers were sickened and trying not to show it.

'I felt I needed to do something,' he said. 'I could not stand by in the name of Her Majesty's Government and allow such barbarity to continue. In all conscience I had to act.'

'You're a soldier, Mallund; you're not

allowed a conscience; you're only allowed orders.' The major was looking him directly in the eye.

'I don't think you believe that, sir.' Mallund returned the steady stare.

'What I believe is neither here nor there.' The major glanced at the other two officers. 'I think we're finished here, gentlemen.'

★ ★ ★

There was no court martial, as predicted. How could there be? After all, he wasn't even in that village, was he? Not even in that jungle. Not even in that country. The shroud of deniability had unfolded over the entire mission. Nevertheless a price had to be paid. That price was Mallund's career. He had embarrassed Her Majesty's Government, a heinous crime. But, more importantly, he had disobeyed direct orders and put his men in danger. He was a loose cannon. A dishonourable discharge was also out of the question. It would attract too much attention. So he was gently eased out of the service under the catch-all umbrella of 'health reasons'.

Surprisingly, his commanding officer, Colonel Andrews, a tough disciplinarian of the old school with a ruddy face and a Colonel Blimp moustache, sought him out and shook him by the hand. 'Sorry to see you go, Mallund,' he said. 'Bloody waste if you ask me.'

★ ★ ★

'To tell you the truth,' Mallund told Porkhead Yates over a pint, 'I was on the point of quitting anyway. Thought of buying my way out. Instead they made it easy for me. The massacre in that village, it just freaked me out. I couldn't have lived with myself if I had done nothing. What was it a great man once said? 'The only thing necessary for the triumph of evil is for good men to do nothing' or something like that.'

'Edmund Burke,' said Porkhead, not for the first time surprising Mallund with his general knowledge.

'Yeah, whatever.'

'The rest of us felt like you did at that village. Sick to the stomach. We all wanted to rush in and blow those bastards away.'

'But you held it together. You followed orders — *my* orders — you were good soldiers. Me, I just lost it.'

'The lads had decided — to hell with it, we'd say we were all in it, that the government troops had rumbled us and attacked us and we fought back. But they knew from the ones who got away that there

34

was just one man shooting at them.'

'I know you would all have bent the truth if you could, but this was my call, Ben.'

'Bent the truth? We'd have lied through our bloody teeth.'

'Anyway, what's done is done.'

'So what now? What will you do?'

'Civvy Street beckons. Probably get a job in security. Ugh!'

'What a fucking waste.'

'Got to earn a crust, Ben.'

'So how's Jennifer taking it?'

'Pretty well. She's upset for me, but deep down I think she is secretly glad that I'm out of the service.'

'Hmm. *Schadenfreude*, it's called.'

'Is there no end to your fucking erudition?'

5

The drive home from Hereford had taken longer than it should have. Mallund knew his concentration had gone; his brain was still awash with memories and pictures, so he drove slowly. At last he pulled into the potholed tarmac driveway to his vicarage, got out of the car and pushed his green wheelie bin through the back gate. Not the romantic idea of a vicarage, this. No sweeping lawns for tea and fairy cakes; no distressed stone walls colonized by rampant ivy; no dark, studious rooms. This was inner-city ministry — a three-bedroom 1970s semi, built of brick with a blue-painted plywood facade, and with added-on double glazing. Mallund would have had it no other way. His SAS background was ideally suited to this tough neighbourhood and he had gained a grudging respect among the ruffians. They left him alone and, while he never expected to see them turning up for evensong in any of the three churches he serviced, he hoped that in some small way he affected their lives.

The first thing he did once he collected his thoughts was to call Porkhead and tell him to grab the DVD with the movie on it. Then he called police headquarters.

'DI Rowlands, please.'

'Who's calling?'

'Jack Mallund.'

'Mr Mallund, how can I help you?' The familiar high-pitched voice of Detective Inspector Chris Rowlands came on the line.

'There have been some developments. Can we meet up?'

★　★　★

Chris Rowlands had been the officer in charge of the investigation into Alice's disappearance. He already had her file on his desk when Mallund entered the room. He held the file up to Mallund as if to say: *You see, the file is still open. The case has not been closed.*

'New developments, you say?'

Mallund told him about the porn movie he had seen at the reunion party.

Rowlands sucked in his cheeks. 'We're going to need the source media — a DVD or whatever — for analysis.'

'That's in hand.'

'Good.' Rowlands leaned back in his chair and unconsciously stroked his light blue silk tie while he thought. Mallund took in his dapper dress — the new breed of graduate fast-track career officer on the way up. Sharp, narrow-lapel navy-blue suit hugging his well-toned health-club figure; one of those two-toned shirts, fine blue check with a white cutaway collar. Mallund had always thought of them as estate agents' shirts. Surely they weren't still in fashion? 'The thing is, Jack, I wouldn't build up my hopes too much if I were you. This is certainly good evidence. But how old? It could have been made ages ago.'

'But don't you see?' Mallund's eyes gleamed. 'It shows that somebody somewhere has got her. They are making money from her. She's an investment. An investment you'd want to keep alive.'

'A good point,' Rowlands said, nodding. Such a good point that it was obvious the detective had not even thought of it. 'Let's get the DVD and see what the guys in white coats can make of it.'

'Right away?' said Mallund.

'Yes, we'll get on to it right away. And Mr Mallund — let's have no repetition of last time, eh?'

★ ★ ★

No repetition of last time. It had been, to say the least, most unseemly — the sight of a man of the cloth being forcibly ejected from a police station. But Mallund had been at the end of his tether. After months of the investigation getting nowhere, he was down at the police headquarters almost every day, shouting the odds and arguing vehemently, urging them to get off their fat backsides and get out there and find his daughter. Finally, he had sat down on the floor of the police HQ and refused to budge.

'You can't do that, sir,' the desk sergeant had said. 'You're committing a . . .' What was he committing? A breach of the peace? Resisting arrest? Causing an obstruction? Yes, that was it. Staff and visitors alike were curiously dodging around the dog-collared cleric sitting cross-legged on the floor, some almost tripping over him. 'You're causing an obstruction, sir.'

Mallund had simply folded his arms in reply.

The sergeant had summoned two colleagues and entered into whispered conversation.

'But he's a vicar, we can't physically chuck him out.'

'Why not? He has no more rights than the ordinary citizen.'

'But what if the press got hold of it? Photos and all that. You know what that lot upstairs is like on bad publicity. Shit scared, that's what they are.'

'You're right.'

'You're the desk sergeant, George, it's your call — you'll have to make the decision.'

'You're right. My decision.' George had firmly taken charge and picked up the phone. 'I'll call the Inspector.'

Inspector Murphy had arrived wiping the remains of a Cornish pasty from his lips.

'What have we here, then?'

'This gentleman is refusing to leave the station, Inspector.'

'Is he now? We'll have to see about that, won't we?' Then, catching sight of Mallund's dog collar, 'Oh. What seems to be the trouble, sir?'

'His daughter is missing and he says we're not doing enough to find her.'

Liam Murphy did not get to be inspector by blunt, PC Plod-style policing alone. Rather, he fancied himself as a people person, more suited to the modern image of the force. Friendly and tactful; getting results by gentle coercion and applied psychology, that was the way to go. His favourite image of himself was as the guy with the megaphone in a hostage situation. This one needed delicate handling.

'Now then, sir, we're sorry about your daughter. But I can assure you we are doing everything in our power. Now why don't you just go home and have a nice cup of tea and leave it to us, eh?'

Mallund remained impassive.

'I promise we will keep you informed of any developments.'

No response.

'I know how you must be feeling, sir. I have two daughters of my own. Ten and six. Lizzie is a dab hand on the piano and Alicia has already got her swimming certificates. Would you like to see a photo?'

Mallund was staring resolutely ahead.

'No? No photo, then. All right, sir, take your time. Nobody's hurrying you. I'm here to help. By the way, I'm Liam' — holding out his hand to Mallund — 'and you are . . . ?'

No response.

'He's the Reverend Jack Mallund,' George, the desk sergeant, had supplied in a whisper.

'Well, Jack, this is a fine how-do-you-do, that's for sure. Come along now, then we can all have a nice cup of tea.'

A small knot of spectators had gathered, watching the inspector's crisis management prowess with vague interest. The officer had then felt compelled to play to the gallery.

'C'mon Jack, let's be 'aving you — 'aven't you got no 'ome to go to?' He had stolen a look at the spectators; the expected titter of amusement did not arrive. This was going nowhere, he had decided. Instead of being his golden hour of tactful negotiation, it had become a farce, and he was feeling a bit of a wally. He now needed to show his teeth.

'Now look here, Vicar, you can't just sit there all day. If you still refuse to leave, then I'm afraid we'll have to forcibly remove you from the premises. Now I'm going to count up to three, and if you do not move I shall have no option but to summon some constables to physically remove you. One, two, three . . . '

* * *

Two burly constables eventually arrived to 'escort him from the premises'. As they lifted him by the arms and led him out the door, Mallund instinctively weighed them up. Big and beefy as they were, he reckoned he could flatten them in a matter of seconds using a few simple manoeuvres. But such techniques were safely buried in his past. He would never need them again.

* * *

Mallund's demonstration at the police head-quarters had achieved nothing, apart from making him feel better. He had to concede that the police were doing their level best — but the investigation finished up a blind alley each time a new line of inquiry presented itself. It was as if Alice had taken one step outside her front door and walked into oblivion. Gradually, the investigation began to run out of steam, then virtually ground to a halt.

'We will keep the file open, Mr Mallund,' DI Rowlands had said, 'but we have no new leads. I know that this is hard for you to take, but we have to be realistic. As I said, the case is by no means closed, so all we can do is hope and pray.'

★ ★ ★

Hope and pray; prayer and hope. Two of Mallund's stock in trade. How often had he offered these comforts to distressed parishioners? Now it was a case of *physician heal thyself.* So he hoped and he prayed, clinging to the slightest vestige of hope. And where had it all led? Worst of all was the feeling of guilt. It would be so easy to blame Jennifer, after all she had been given custody of Alice. He could blame himself for not seeing the signs of Jennifer's breakdown, leaving Alice neglected and out of control. But how far do you go back in the blame game? Back to his behaviour that led to Jennifer walking out in the first place? Back to his discharge from the regiment? Back, again, to that day in the African jungle?

6

Mallund's first month in Civvy Street had turned out to be more difficult than he expected. The jobs market was at rock bottom. And there were not so many openings for a former Special Forces operative with alarmingly dangerous skill sets. Mallund had heard of all the lush positions ex-SAS men had landed as security consultants and bodyguards to Middle Eastern potentates, Russian oligarchs and the like. Lots of the guys had done it. But that was just the problem — *lots*. These jobs were all taken. The only thing going was run of the mill security, which boiled down to being a glorified night watchman. Again, the best of all these jobs had been filled by retired policemen.

So Mallund joined the ranks of the unemployed, enjoying days filled with daytime television and having rows with the wife.

He did get a job once.

Trust Eddie Security Ltd inhabited a unit in an industrial estate consisting of dozens of other similar anonymous units. It was well placed, because most of its clients were on the same estate — a conglomeration of garages, body shops, tyre depots, exhaust parlours, double glazing specialists, electrical supplies, discount stores and haulage depots.

It was owned by a bluff Yorkshireman called Eddie Johnson, whose main business was a huge and rather dodgy scrapyard, recently elevated to the title of Eddie Cares Recycling to lend it a modicum of social conscience. Johnson had all the social conscience of a psychopath. The dodgy dealings still went on despite the makeover. The two half-starved Alsatians who used to guard his scrapyard on the end of long chains had been cleaned up, fed, had a measure of domestication beaten into them, and now served as patrol dogs on leads with the uniformed security men. It had been a long, hard road of rejection that had led Mallund to the door of Trust Eddie Security.

'I don't take no nonsense,' was Johnson's welcoming gambit as Mallund entered the Portakabin for his interview. 'I've had you soldier boys before, nothing but trouble. Think you're a cut above the rest of us, well, we don't stand for that here. Nine quid an hour — that's better than the minimum wage, take it or leave it.'

You're all heart, thought Mallund. He took it.

46

The job was a doddle. Johnson's idea of security was definitely based on 'deterrent' — that is to say, put a couple of guys in official-looking uniforms, partner them with a pair of Alsatians, and get them to walk about at night. High visibility was the name of the game. Staff were trimmed down to the bone, so there was no time do proper security checks on premises apart from the most high profile businesses. Mallund was partnered with an overweight ex-cop who had been pensioned off the force because of a shoulder injury sustained while trying to shift a filing cabinet. It was the nearest Constable Fred Molson had got to physical danger in his entire career. The police lawyers tried to argue contributory negligence since he shouldn't have been trying to lift the cabinet in the first place, but Molson's own legal team put up a strong defence and they settled out of court. Molson was in his early fifties and world weary. He ate his way through the night shift with an endless supply of pies and cakes.

'Stick with me, mate, and you'll be all right,' he told Mallund on his first night. 'We have our own way of doing things here.'

They sauntered around the estate, the two dogs at their heels occasionally leaping forward and straining at the lead whenever they heard an unaccustomed noise. At the larger and more vulnerable properties who could afford top notch security systems they had to turn a key on a time lock to prove they had been there. The others they simply passed by.

'Shouldn't we be checking the other properties too? After all they're on the list,' asked Mallund.

'Naw, why bother? They don't pay as much as the big boys with the good security systems. They're just small potatoes.'

'But they're still paying for a service, and they're not getting it.'

'Ooh, get you — Mr Righteous! Look, why should we waste shoe leather on some dodgy garage that's been fleecing its customers anyway? So it's just a case of walking past. If you want to go and check every single door and lavatory window you're welcome. But the night isn't long enough for that. There's only two of us. Johnson doesn't care as long as he gets his money.'

'Still, I don't like it. It's fraudulent.'

'That's the way it is, pal.'

Mallund hated the job. He hated Molson and he hated Johnson. Molson was obviously Johnson's henchman, and both treated Mallund like dirt. When anything went wrong it was always contrived to be Mallund's fault.

Johnson would curse and swear while giving Mallund a dressing down, and Molson would stand smirking in the background. The constant humiliation was wearing Mallund down. For a while he could not bring himself to share his problem with Jennifer, feeling too ashamed. When he eventually did, she made sympathetic noises and urged him to tough it out.

'We need this job,' she said. 'God only knows it took so long to get it. You'll never get another one. Stick with it, things might get better.'

But they didn't get better. They got worse day by day, until Mallund was thoroughly miserable, wondering if he would ever be free of it all. He would probably have had a breakdown if it hadn't been for the mystery of Unit 73.

Unit 73 was one of the biggest and most expensive to rent on the industrial estate. It attracted Mallund's attention because they never went near it during their patrol.

'Why don't we ever check that one?' he asked Molson, as they passed the large corrugated-roofed building.

'We just don't bother. Forget it. It's not important.' There was something shifty in Molson's reply that struck a chord of suspicion in Mallund.

Each time he passed the unit his eyes were drawn to it. There was never any activity around it, yet there was always a glimmer of light escaping from it all night long. One night as he and Molson were checking a nearby unit, a black Mercedes drew up outside Unit 73. Two men got out of the car.

'Wait here,' said Molson, and headed off in the direction of the men.

'Need any help?' asked Mallund.

'Just wait.'

Mallund watched as Molson approached the two men and started talking to them. After a while one of them handed an envelope to Molson. The two men entered the unit and Molson slouched back to Mallund.

'What was that about?' Mallund asked idly.

'Just a bit of business. *My* business.'

They walked on in silence.

It did not take long for Mallund's curiosity about Unit 73 to be satisfied. At the end of his second week in the job, Mavis, Johnson's bimbo with the title of office manager, called him in.

'Molson's been taken ill. You'll be on your own for the next two nights.'

'Don't we have a replacement?'

'We're not made of money, you know. You'll have to manage by yourself.'

Mallund shrugged and went to collect the

dogs. As he did his rounds he kept thinking of Unit 73. Something not right was going on there. It was something secret. Secrets bothered him.

When he arrived at Unit 73 he walked around it. Only he was not looking for signs of entry by criminals; he was looking for a way in for himself. When he found it, he made a note of what would be needed.

The next night he arrived with a set of screwdrivers with various heads, long and short-nosed pliers, and a grip-wrench. The security on the building was surprisingly low level and easily overcome. There were no company signs or names proclaiming what business went on there. Anyone looking at it would think it was empty. Maybe that was what they were meant to think. The entry point he had earmarked was a panel where piping for the air conditioning exited the building. With that removed there was just enough room for a man to squeeze through, he reckoned. It took just twenty minutes to remove the panel. Another twelve to worm his way through the gap, twisting and turning every which way. Inside, he blinked as a blinding glare assaulted his eyes. Then he smelt an overpowering familiar odour.

'Bloody hell!' he breathed, as he took in a sea of green foliage covering the entire space inside. 'They're growing weed.'

The cannabis plants were everywhere, blanketing the floor and stacked in tiers up the walls. Powerful lights turned the interior of the unit into day, nurturing the plants with artificial sunlight. So this was the racket Molson was turning a blind eye to in exchange for his envelope full of cash. It was a full-blown dream factory. He crawled back through the gap in the wall and carefully screwed the panel back in place, dusted himself down and continued his patrol, thinking hard.

He told Jennifer what he had seen.

'I need to get out of that place,' he said.

'But it's not any business of yours what they get up to, is it?' she said.

'I can't stand by and say nothing. If they get raided we could all go down. The very fact that I know about it could make me an accessory.'

'And what about the job? We're already deep in debt and I can't see any way out of it. It's driving me to despair. You need that job and that's the bottom line. Just turn a blind eye and get on with it.'

Reluctantly, he returned to work the following evening, and for a week suffered agonies of uncertainty over what to do. Jennifer was right, they could not live without his wages, meagre as they were. In the end the decision was taken out of his hands.

★ ★ ★

Johnson was apoplectic as Mallund entered the office.

'You didn't feed the dogs when you finished last night,' he bawled. 'You stupid bugger, they've been starved.'

'Molson said he was going to do it,'

'Is that right?' Johnson looked at Molson.

'No way,' said Molson, shifting his feet uneasily.

'But you definitely said you would feed the dogs. I was going to, but you said leave it and you would do it.'

'No I didn't. You're making that up to save your own skin.'

'Molson, you're a liar. A bare-faced liar.'

'Anyway it's his word against mine.' Molson folded his arms.

'And we know whose word he's going to take, don't we?' Mallund was fighting to control his temper. 'Oh, sod it! You're welcome to each other. I quit as of this minute.'

'You're duty bound to give us notice, soldier boy,' said Johnson.

'So sue me.'

'What about your uniform?'

'I'll post it to you. Right now, I'm walking out that door.'

On the way home Mallund felt as if a great weight had been taken off his shoulders. Just one more chore had to be done. He stopped by a payphone and dialled a number.

'I'd like to talk to someone on the Drug Squad.'

'What name is it please?'

'Never mind that. I have some information for you.'

★ ★ ★

'You what?' Jennifer stared at him in disbelief.

'I quit.'

'Now isn't that just fine and dandy. Here we are struggling for every penny and you go and throw away the only job you ever got. What's got into you, Jack?'

'I just couldn't take any more from those two. The cannabis factory was the clincher. Those two bastards have got a big shock coming to them.'

'You need to learn to be more tolerant, Jack. Not everybody plays by your rules. You're too hard on yourself.'

'What am I supposed to do? Sink down to their level? No thanks. Not so long as I still have an ounce of pride and dignity.' He tried to make himself feel good about that, but it was not happening. His pride and dignity were at a lower level than he imagined. And sinking fast.

★   ★   ★

Once again, Mallund was unemployed. Interview after interview brought no result. Either it was obvious they wanted somebody younger, but didn't so much as say so, or they wanted previous experience in security, or they didn't want to employ ex-servicemen who might be unstable and have short fuses, or the pay and conditions were rubbish. On top of all that, he had no references from Johnson.

'Have you thought of taking some other kind of work?' they asked him at the Job Centre.

'I don't know anything else.'

'Hmm. We get a lot of ex-soldiers who have difficulty adjusting to civilian life.'

'I don't have difficulty adjusting. I just can't find a job to start adjusting to.'

'We have a few jobs on the books you might want to consider.'

'Like?'

'There's a vacancy in telephone marketing,

low basic pay but commission top up.'

'Telephone marketing? You mean cold calling? Next, please.'

'A large night club is looking for security staff. That might suit your experience.'

'For security staff read bouncer. No thanks, got caught with that one before.'

'Mr Mallund, looking at your file, it seems that you are determined not to take up any job we put your way.'

'That's because they're a load of bloody crap.'

'There's no need to take that tone.'

And so he earned a black mark at the Job Centre. As the months passed he became more and more irritable. Hardly a day passed without a blazing row with Jennifer. He tried to keep up his physical exercise regime, but imperceptibly it was falling off and he was losing his shape. He had taken to lying on the sofa in front of the TV for most of the day, going running twice a week instead of every day. The runs shorter and shorter. Unable to sleep, he would get out of bed and switch on the television in the early hours. Even he had to agree that it has come to a pretty pass when you're half-watching the signed version of *Hill Street Blues* at four in the morning. One afternoon Jennifer was vacuuming around him as he lay on the sofa, one leg dangling on to the floor.

'For God's sake, you might have the decency to lift your bloody leg while I'm trying to work around you, you lazy sod!'

Mallund shrugged, got up and went to the fridge for another can of lager and returned to the sofa.

'Are you going to look for work today? Of course not, how silly of me.' Mallund could read the signs. Jennifer was spoiling for a fight.

'No point,' he said.

'No point, no point. Is there any point to anything anymore? Is there any point to you? Is there any point to *us*? I just don't know you anymore, Jack. You're not the man I married.'

'I'm going out for a run,' he said.

'That's right, anything to avoid the issue. Go for your run then. Run, run away, run from every problem. You're a coward, Jack Mallund — and that's a sad thing to have to say about a man who took on a gang of murderers because his conscience told him to. But that man is no more, because he changed when he lost the thing he loved more than anything else — the SAbloodyS!'

Running along the canal towpath, Mallund was only too well aware of how his fitness level had slumped. It was hard work even to maintain a jogging pace on sections he used to take at a sprint. All too aware also of how his life had slumped, somehow he lacked the will to do anything about it. Occasionally — very occasionally — he would rally and make a determined effort to find work, but when none was forthcoming he slipped back into moody depression. He could see his marriage crumbling before his eyes, but again was helpless to stop it. He didn't know how. They still shared rare golden moments, often filled with laughter, but short-lived. They enjoyed good sex whenever it happened. But that 'whenever' was becoming less and less frequent, and when the euphoria faded, thoughts of the bleak day that would follow crowded in to blot out the memory. Life was so much less demanding there on the sofa with his lager for company. And soon he had a new friend joining him. A friend called Johnnie Walker.

7

The doorbell rang as Mallund was settling down to watch the six o'clock news in the front room of his vicarage. He rose and went to answer it.

The broad beaming face of Porkhead Yates filled the doorway.

'Ben! What a nice surprise. But you should have rung to tell me you were coming. I could have been out.'

'Never underestimate the element of surprise. It's in the manual.'

'Oh, dear. Does this mean I'm the enemy then?'

'Not at all, not at all. I'd have brought a bottle, only I know you've given up, and I wasn't sure about drinking on holy ground.' He waved his arm, taking in the lounge of the small semi.

'Hardly the conventional idea of a vicarage, but it's cosy enough for me. And it's OK to drink. In fact I've got a bottle of fine malt whisky with your name on it. I've been keeping it for just such an occasion as this.'

Mallund disappeared into the kitchen and returned with a bottle of Tomintoul. He poured Porkhead a generous measure. 'Hope you like it.'

Porkhead took a sip and smacked his lips. 'Aah! Nectar!'

'It's sixteen years old, according to the label.'

'Reminds me of the time when Frank Sinatra, aged fifty, announced he was going to marry the young Mia Farrow. Dean Martin is supposed to have told him: 'Frank, I've got Scotch older than her!''

'Same old Porkhead. A mine of useless information. I was given this bottle by a vicar friend who is a bit of a connoisseur. Instead of taking his parishioners on outings to religious sites he takes them on visits to distilleries for whisky tastings. No word of a lie.'

'I hear you used to be a bit of a connoisseur yourself, Jack.'

'Not exactly a connoisseur, I'd have drunk it through a shitty nappy. But those days are all behind me now, Praise the Lord.'

'OK, Jack. No more pissing around. This business of your daughter. Where are you up to?'

Mallund sighed. 'Same old stalemate. The police have got nowhere. They traced the DVD to Dubai, one of countless thousands being sold door to door by Chinese peddlers.

They reckon it was probably at one point downloaded from the Internet, so it's impossible to trace. I can see what's going to happen: the investigation will be put on ice again. Ben, I'm convinced Alice is alive. And I'm going to find her. Even if I have to go it alone. I'll hunt these people down. As God is my witness.'

'Which brings me to the real purpose of my visit.' Porkhead moved to the edge of his seat, took another swig of his whisky. 'Me and the lads have been talking. And we've decided we can help. There's a lot of highly trained talent there, with multiple skills. You'll be up against some nasty people, but we're the boys who can teach them what nasty is. We'll get the old four-man patrol together — you, me, Cleggie and Slippery Sam, and go hunting — '

'No, Ben, no, no, no!' Mallund was thumping his hand on the table beside him. 'You lot would end up blowing up half the city! I'm no longer Sergeant Jack Mallund, I'm the *Reverend* Jack Mallund. I have taken certain vows that commit me to a way of life that forbids killing and the sort of violence we used to practise. I have searched my conscience and I think I have found a way forward — '

'Would that be the same conscience that got you into trouble in the African jungle?'

'Maybe it is, Ben, and it will probably get me into trouble again. But that goes with the territory. We don't have to go maiming and · killing. That brings us down to their level. That's why I have to do this alone and do it my way without causing harm to anybody.'

'You mean you're just going to knock on the door of these animals and say, 'Hi, guys, let's have a nice cup of tea and talk this over . . . by the way, I would be grateful if you could let me have my daughter back?' Brother, you are going to get creamed. This is likely to be a heavy mob you are going up against, probably Eastern European — Lithuanian, Albanian, Russian. They don't play by any rules and they take no prisoners. Life is cheap and they'd slit your throat as much as look at you if you go snooping on their turf. Jack, that's why you need to fight like with like.'

'You mean like you, Cleggie and Slippery Sam? No, I need to do this on my own.'

'At least take this. Just in case. A last resort, you might say.' Porkhead handed Mallund a package wrapped in a black bin liner which he had brought in a Harrods carrier bag. Mallund started to unwrap it, discarding layers of newspaper padding until he came to an oiled cotton bag. He weighed it in his hand. Mallund did not need to be told that the item inside weighed precisely 875 grams. He had toted that weight a thousand times during his career.

'I hope this isn't what I think it is,' he said, with a disapproving glance at Porkhead. He extracted it from the oiled bag and laid it flat on the palm of his hand. A black 9 mm Browning Hi Power semi-automatic pistol, the favoured tool of generations of SAS men. It was first introduced in the 1930s and was modified over the years, but still retained its original basic design giving it an unequalled reputation for reliability in the field. For close quarter combat such as hostage and hijack situations, they preferred the lighter, more compact SIG-Sauer P228. The hairy Browning was difficult to handle in confined spaces. On top of that, its hefty punch was likely to send the bullet clean through the target's body and into a hostage or innocent bystander.

'How did you manage to come by this piece of kit?' Mallund checked the magazine was safely out of the gun, then made sure there was no round lurking in the chamber before testing the mechanism.

Porkhead tapped the side of his nose. 'We all managed to smuggle a few souvenirs back home from major operations abroad. You probably did yourself.'

Mallund was forced to admit that he had brought a Kalashnikov AK 47 back from a tour in Iraq. He had quickly got rid of it following the arrests of some of his comrades for illegal possession.

'I can't accept this, Ben. It's highly illegal, and anyway I've already told you — no killing. I'll do it my way. And that's final.'

'Tell me something, Jack. Does your Church approve of suicide?'

'Of course not.'

'Then why are you so hell-bent on committing it?'

'I can still look after myself, make no mistake about that. It's just that I can't allow myself to do harm to others.'

'Be realistic, Jack. That's the way the world is. Violence is the only language that violence understands. We of all people should know that. We've seen it at its worst, time and time again. You can't fight it armed with nothing but a good heart and a Bible.'

'I can try.'

Porkhead rose and shook his friend firmly by the hand. 'Anyway, the offer is there if you need it.'

'Thanks, mate. I really appreciate it. But apart from anything else I don't want you and the lads putting your necks on the line. This is Civvy Street. And it's Civvy Street law. They do things differently here.'

'What are mates for? Take care of yourself, Jack.'

'God be with you, Ben.'

'And with you. Something tells me you're going to need Him.'

It was ten minutes after Porkhead left that Mallund realized he had left the Browning on the table.

$$\star \quad \star \quad \star$$

Mallund had indeed been battling with his conscience. More than anything in life he wanted Alice back, and in his wildest moments he felt prepared to do anything to get her. Anything? Even break his vows? It was tempting. He had skills and techniques that would go a long way towards achieving his goal if he chose to use them — but the price to pay was too heavy. He juggled the pros and cons, looking for a balance. *Thou Shalt Not Kill.* The commandment was indelibly branded in his brain. Was killing the only way to deal with killers? The more he thought about it the more he realized Porkhead was right. A good heart and a Bible were not sufficient weapons for this mission. But could his SAS skills be used in a way that did not conflict with his vows? It would mean walking a tightrope, but it might just be possible. *Be adaptable*, that was one of the first things they taught you. Use what you've got. Even the simplest thing can be a life-saver. One of many lessons. And lesson number one:

TAKE THE FIGHT TO THE ENEMY

8

There was just one snag with Mallund's plan to track down the people holding his daughter: he hadn't the remotest idea where to start.

Where did these shady people hang out? If they were such a big organization as he had been led to believe, then there would be many layers to their command structure. And at the top, Mr Big himself. That would be his target, he decided. Aim for the head. But first, how to get there? He was agonizing over the seeming impossibility of the task as he arrived for his weekly session at Buddies.

Buddies was a drop-in community centre for the detritus of society: drug addicts, homeless, alcoholics, abused youngsters — in fact anyone with a problem was welcomed with open arms. It was run by volunteers with the aid of a pittance from the local council. The church provided the accommodation in a draughty prefab building with a basic kitchen that dispensed free tea and sandwiches and cakes and biscuits, depending on what volunteers had brought. The atmosphere was relaxed and unstructured. Visitors could talk over their problems with each other or with the volunteers, or simply chill out by themselves. Most just came in to get out of the rain.

Mallund listened patiently and gave advice and comfort to the lost and confused souls who unburdened themselves to him. He regarded this as a top priority of his ministry, but found himself almost powerless in the face of the human tragedies being played out daily on the streets. Still, every little bit helps, and Mallund took great joy in the few successes he had chalked up in saving youngsters from a life of misery. He had recognized his past self in their predicament.

As he entered the room he found it bustling and noisy with more bodies than usual. Of course, he noted, it was raining outside. The usual volunteers were being kept busy, but there was a new face among them: a red-haired woman in her thirties was handing out mugs of tea and chatting with the others. One of the volunteers, Andrea, pointed him out to her. She smiled and pushed her way through the mass of bodies towards him.

'Hello, you must be the Reverend Mallund,' she said, extending her hand.

'I guess the clue's in the dog collar,' he said, taking her hand.

'I'm Ros Forster. I thought maybe you

could use a bit of extra volunteer help.'

'Never say no to that. Let's have a cuppa and a chat.'

They perched on a couple of bar stools. The tea was strong and dark. He winced as he watched her pile three heaped teaspoons of sugar into her cup. She saw him staring.

'Sweet tooth,' she said, stirring noisily.

'Sorry about the cracked mugs,' he said. 'We exist on cast-offs.'

'Cast-offs for the cast-offs of society, eh?'

'That was rather profound for this time of the morning.'

'Was it? It just came out.'

Mallund took an instant liking to this newcomer. Slim and tall; yet instead of the angular features you would expect with someone of her build, she had a round and open face. What his dad would have called 'bonny'. She had one of those frizzy hairstyles that Mallund disliked intensely, yet he could forgive that if only she would smile at him again with that generous mouth and perfect teeth. A smile that instantly found its way to those mocking pale-green eyes.

'Well, Ros Forster, what makes you want to muck in with our little band of do-gooders?'

'Just want to do some good, like any do-gooder.' She shrugged. 'I thought maybe you could use some professional help.'

'Professional?'

'Yes, I'm a social worker by trade.'

'That's great. We could certainly use your expertise.'

'I've got a lot of free time, now that I'm single again so to speak. Thought I might as well put it to good use.'

Divorced? Widowed? Split up from the boyfriend? Mallund chose not to pursue the point.

'Just split from my partner. Six long years. Found out he was two-timing me with the receptionist at his office.' She blew on her tea and took a sip.

'I'm sorry,' said Mallund.

'Don't be. Good riddance, if you ask me.' She tossed her head, and that frizzy hairstyle coiled and sprang like a nest of vipers.

'So what branch of the social services are you in? Are you a field worker or a desk jockey?'

'Very much in the front line. I'm particularly interested in grooming and trafficking.'

'Really?'

'I specialize in missing girls.'

Mallund nearly fell off his stool.

9

Looking back on it, Mallund had to admit that he and he alone was responsible for the break-up of his marriage. First there had been the blazing rows, then came the separation, then the divorce. Mallund did not contest it, for he knew what a monster he had been to live with since he was expelled from the regiment. They'd had sessions with marriage counsellors. They left the interviews on a high with good intentions, but it came to nothing in the end. He had seen a psychiatrist, who wasn't much use, just playing around with terms like Post-traumatic Stress Disorder. But Mallund knew it was more than that. Something much deeper. He could handle stress — had a lifetime of conquering it; what he could not handle was a deep-rooted fear of being useless. It gnawed away at his soul, devouring his pride and self esteem. So, reclining on the sofa all day drinking lager and — more and more often — whisky, was the easy option. The more he drank, the more the gap between him and Jennifer widened. Life was becoming just one screaming match after another.

He had no answer when she told him she had seen a lawyer and started divorce proceedings. He shrugged. Maybe it was for the best. Jennifer was given custody of Alice and Mallund was awarded visiting rights. For a while he played the part and spent Saturday afternoons in McDonald's with Alice, along with all the other divorced fathers. You could tell them by the way they indulged their kids' every whim. Never a raised voice — just a pained smile as they strained to make as good an impression as possible on the youngsters, as if they were being interviewed by their own offspring. Soon, he began to miss the odd visit, ringing up with a lame excuse. And, as his downward slide increased its momentum, the visits ceased altogether. He moved into a bed-sit in a crumbling Victorian terraced house in a run-down area. It was ideal for his purposes, which had become mainly sleeping and drinking. People left him alone, he came and went as he pleased, and there were still some pubs in the area he wasn't barred from, although he could count them on the fingers of one hand. The landlord never bothered him so long as the rent was paid by the bank on standing order. The pay-off he received from the regiment had been invested and he and Jennifer agreed to let it scroll up, to be touched only in dire emergency. When they separated it was divided between them, with Jennifer getting the major share. Mallund used it to top up his benefits, and almost his entire budget was devoted to paying the rent and booze. Eating was something of a movable feast; sometimes he did, sometimes he didn't. He lost so much weight his clothes were hanging off him, but it didn't cross his mind to buy new ones no matter how worn or soiled they became.

★ ★ ★

Mallund was experiencing a familiar sensation that had visited him all too often since his split from Jennifer and his nose dive into rough living. He was crossing that ill-defined threshold between sleep and waking, when things are just too solid to be dreams, yet too flighty to be reality. But the real world is just a flicker of the eyelid away. Ah, that first flicker, the re-entry into a world where time only runs forward and perspectives are true; where reality is made up of benchmarks . . . like what bed/sofa/floor have I been sleeping on? What building? What town?

I don't want to go out there, pleads the unconscious mind.

Got to face up to it sometime, old boy, says the conscious.

Mallund opened his eyes, and the real world came storming through his brain in a rampage of pain.

'Sheee . . . it!' he croaked and tried to roll over on to his side, but thought better of it. His head was a jangle of tormented raw nerve ends. His throat was a parched Sahara being rubbed down with sandpaper. His stomach a cement mixture full of sludge and slop. His legs were . . . too distant to be recalled just yet.

Doctors call it *veisalgia*. But to Jack Mallund it was better known as a hangover. The daddy of all hangovers.

He closed his eyes and wished for sleep, but it would not come. He opened his eyes and searched out the rest of the clues. His raincoat, still wet and crumpled over the arm of a chair. He was still wearing his shirt. One solitary shoe and sock marooned in the middle of the floor. His other senses slowly came to his aid. Touch . . . an encroaching dampness down his right side; a chill, hard object nestling under the armpit. Put together in the erratic computer that passed for his brain this morning, this added up to the realization that he had fallen asleep embracing an open bottle of fizzy lemonade. With the smug sense of precaution that only drunks can manage, he had opened it the night before to combat the parched throat that he fully expected upon waking; but had dropped off before he could drink it. His throat was still painfully dry and the bottle was empty, its contents seeped deep into the mattress.

Into play came his sense of taste, followed by smell, and together they turned his body over like clumsy gumshoes raking through a dustbin. The clues were easily enough found . . . the revolting stench that bounced back from the cupped palm of his hand when he breathed into it; the acid burn that blazed a trail from his mouth right down his windpipe to his stomach, where it bounced around for a bit before re-tracing its route. It all added up to one thing: a curry. A very hot curry.

Would he never learn that spicy food and alcohol just do not mix? For a start, he reasoned, spices mean the East. The East means Muslims and other like religions who eschew alcohol; who see evil in the holy matrimony of port and Stilton, of *boeuf* and Bourguignon. It's not in their culture. So never the twain should meet, spices and alcohol.

This theory holds especially true when the alcohol has lured the diner into such a state of bravado that he insists — as Jack Mallund had done the night before in the Eastern Delights Tandoori — 'Bring me the hottest you've got, Sonny Jim!'

He belched, and the acid raced back up his throat. *Mohammed's Revenge, that's what they ought to call it,* he thought to himself as he drifted back into merciful sleep.

It was just after twelve noon when he awoke. His eyes were focusing better now, his brain less of a turmoil. Anytime now he could consider easing one foot out from the corner of the duvet and on to the floor, a promising start to another day. But could he get the day right? Getting days right was not one of his strong points at the moment. In fact the last couple — or was it three? — had been a bit of a blur. It happened every now and again. Or, to be honest, not so much now and again as again and again. It began with a cancerous self pity that gave way to remorse that in turn became anger, and like a snowball waxed bigger and bigger with each revolution, picking up guilt and frustration on the way as it rolled towards one inevitable destination . . .

A bar. Any bar. A whisky glass. Johnnie Walker. Make it a double. And a beer chaser. Another. And another. Forget the beer chasers, they're too slow. Into conversation with a stranger at the bar, all hail-fellow-and-well-met. Fun and repartee flowing, for Jack Mallund could tell a good yarn. But soon that old Mr Hyde would creep out from the fog created by the Scotch, and soon the bonhomie was gone, and a cutting edge came into the voice, and the laughter around the bar gave way to embarrassment, then to anger and outrage.

Usually, it ended in violence. A punch-up if he was physically up to it, or a rough chucking out into the street if he wasn't. Had there been a punch-up last night too? He searched for evidence, running his tongue across his teeth one by one. They were all there, nothing loose. He reconnoitred the other front-line parts of his body that would sustain most casualties in a brawl. Knuckles first: no grazes. Nose, cheekbones, groin and shins: no aches or pains to be found, so he had got off light. Except for that bloody headache and the afterburn of that appalling curry.

He dragged himself out of bed and to the bathroom, where he splashed cold water over his head. He saw himself in the mirror over the sink and stood hunched and staring at the face before him. Unshaven, hair wet and straggly over his brow. He suddenly realized he was crying. Tears were running down his cheeks. His throat was tight and he could make no sound; no sobbing. He watched the tears in silence as they mixed with the droplets of water on his face and formed little rivulets.

'Jack Mallund, Jack Mallund,' he said to the face, 'how in God's name have you come to this?'

* * *

A persistent banging at the bed-sit door woke him the following morning.

'Mr Mallund, open the door please,' a voice shouted over a lull in the banging.

The voice seemed half-familiar. The banging resumed.

Mallund dragged himself to the door and opened it. The face confronting him also seemed half-familiar.

'It's me, Mr Mallund, Bert Walters,' said the face. Mallund screwed up his eyes in an attempt at recognition.

'I'm your landlord, remember?'

'Oh, yeah . . . the landlord. Well, what can I do for you?'

'What can you do for me? Didn't you get my letters? Didn't you get the court papers?' The landlord's eyes took in the untidy pile of unopened mail on the floor. 'Obviously not,' he said, and sighed.

'Oh, them . . . never got a chance to open them.' Mallund yawned and scratched his chest through his vest.

'You people . . . I dunno! Anyway, the top and bottom of it is you're being evicted, my son, as in *put out*, as in *given the bum's rush*. I have a court order, and these gentlemen are bailiffs who will help you to remove your belongings.' Two heavyset bruisers stood behind the landlord nodding their heads.

'You don't mean right now, do you? Surely I'm due some notice.'

'Notice? You had all the notice in the world. It's lying there unopened on the floor, as far as I can see.'

'But why?' Mallund's head was clearing now.

'Non-payment of rent.'

'But the bank pays that automatically.'

'Not for the past seven months. Funny geezers, banks. Before they pay your bills they like you to have at least a few bob in your account.'

'But there's lots of money in the account.'

'When was the last time you read a statement?' The landlord nodded to the pile of mail on the floor.

The three men stood and watched as Mallund gathered up his belongings — not a major task, since his entire possessions fitted easily into two suitcases which he man-handled down three flights of stairs and out on to the street, into the chill of mid-November. He took stock of the situation. He had managed to scrape together £87.62. If the money in the bank had run out, then that was all he had in the world. He went in search of cheap accommodation, something that would give him the minimum of a roof above his head. But first he needed a drink. He bought a can of Special Brew from Bargain Booze and drank it in a bus shelter. Now he felt ready to proceed. Down an alley stuffed with wheelie bins and skips, he found a flophouse that suited his pocket.

'Seven quid a night, no breakfast,' said the surly owner. 'No smoking, no women, and I don't want to see you here between the hours of nine in the morning and eight at night. Money up front.'

Mallund handed him the money and dragged his two suitcases up to his room. There was no window, just a ten-inch-deep slit of glass that ran the length of the outside wall at ceiling height. Mallund noted that it did not open. 'Bloody death trap this if there's a fire,' he muttered. He flopped down on the bed and sent the springs a-jangling; he could sense every bump and lump in the faded striped mattress. It was stained with God only knows what, and a complex range of odours was reeking from it. The entire room, from the peeling flowery wallpaper to the worn linoleum floor with its two threadbare rugs, held a faint smell of urine. A yellowing pedestal sink with two dripping taps filled one corner; above it a mirror with most of the silver backing worn away, leaving haphazard areas of black, so that only a patchwork of his face stared back at him. He was glad he couldn't see the full picture. This pitiful room was likely to be his home for as long as the money lasted, and he despaired.

Yet it was a palace compared to what lay ahead for Jack Mallund.

10

Mallund's hopes rose after his meeting with Ros Forster at Buddies. *She specializes in missing girls.* It couldn't be any better. Here was the starting point he lacked, handed to him on a plate. He needed to pick her brains.

'Ros, you're an angel sent from heaven,' he said.

'Such compliments! And I hardly even know you, sir.'

'And I sure could use your help.'

'My help?'

'It's my daughter. She's missing. She's only sixteen.'

'How long?'

'Ten months.'

'Phew! A long time.'

'I know what you're going to say. The police said the same . . . after all this time, blah, blah, blah. But I know she is alive. I know it!'

'I'm sorry, Reverend, but — '

'Jack.'

'Jack. I'm sorry Jack, but ten months is an awfully long time. From experience, if this was a run-of-the-mill missing teenager, she would have been back long before now. Either she has a very strong motive for staying away, or we have to suspect something more sinister. If you take my meaning.'

'You don't beat around the bush, do you?'

'I've learned the hard way to be realistic, Jack.'

'The difference here is that I now have evidence she could be alive. I've seen her in a pornographic movie.'

'A porno . . . Listen, Jack, this is getting heavy. We could be dealing with the organized sex trade. It's big and powerful and stops at nothing. What do the police say?'

'The file is still open.'

'Now where have I heard that before? So they've got nowhere, and now they've run out of time and resources to devote to it.'

'So I'm going to find Alice myself.'

'Be careful what you wish for, Jack. She may no longer be the Alice you knew. You can't do this alone. It's a minefield out there. We've only scratched the surface of it, but one thing has become clear: the nearer you get to it the more dangerous it becomes.'

'So will you help me?'

Ros lifted her almost empty coffee cup to her lips using both hands, and tilted her head back so that her pale-green eyes were peeping over the brim as she spoke.

'Of course I will.'

★ ★ ★

They opted for a room at the church for their meetings, rather than the vicarage. That way they wouldn't attract gossip. Ros wanted a full account of Alice's disappearance.

'I blame myself for that.' Mallund's voice was low and calm. 'The way I behaved after I was forced to leave the regiment would have driven anybody out — '

'Whoa . . . whoa there! The regiment? I thought you were starting at the beginning?'

'Sorry. I used to be in the SAS.'

'Wow! And now you're a vicar. Do tell me.'

'It really all began in Central Africa.'

He told her of the African village, his discharge from the SAS, his futile job-hunting, his divorce from Jennifer, his drinking, his descent on to Skid Row.

'I had just over eighty-seven quid to my name and the future was looking very bleak,' he recalled.

★ ★ ★

The £87.62 that stood between Mallund and the streets was soon gone, spent on drink and rent in that order, and he was forced to quit the flophouse. The realization dawned on him that he had absolutely nowhere to go. He briefly flirted with the idea of throwing himself on the mercy of Jennifer, who still had the house, but a mixture of pride and fear of the reception he would get steered him away.

Darkness came down quickly and by five o'clock a frosty chill was in the air. Mallund wandered the streets aimlessly, watching the traffic go by. Buses, cars, taxis, full of people ending their working day. People going home to warm flats and houses. Going home to hot meals and perhaps a night in with the telly. Lugging his two suitcases, he passed door-ways filled with homeless people bedded in for the night, so tightly zipped up in their anoraks you couldn't see their faces. Only the eyes and the outstretched hand revealed the life inside the bundle of clothing. Mallund had always been one to take pity on these shabby inhabitants of doorways and stair-wells, and would never pass one by without handing over whatever change happened to be in his pocket. Who could say what human tragedies had driven them to this? So he always had a smile and a word of encouragement as he parted with the coins and continued on his way feeling cleansed and lucky. But now, as he wandered aimlessly past these pitiful human beings, a shocking truth dawned on him: he, Jack Mallund, was now one of them.

★ ★ ★

The doorway was wide and welcoming. Mallund reconnoitred it as he would a potential base observation post for an SAS mission. Flanks were protected from the wind and intruders by large Doric pillars on either side; a huge studded wooden door covered his rear; a commanding view of the area forward. And all of it situated up a flight of steps that gave him command of the high ground. With a sigh, he unpacked warm clothes and put them on in layers: a second pair of trousers, a second sweater, extra socks. He was glad he had kept his old SAS cold weather gear which he slipped on top of the rest. Propping the two suitcases on either side of him for extra protection from the wind, he lay awake for three hours before dropping into a deep sleep.

Something was shaking him from his sleep. He felt his body rocking as if at sea. He awoke to find a large boot pushing at his right leg. And a voice.

'Come on, fella. Wakey-wakey. You can't

stay here. Up you get.'

'But I've only just got here.' Mallund's head was fuzzy and his eyes weren't focusing yet.

'Tough. This is the entrance to County Hall, you ought to know that.' The policeman's voice was harsh and impatient. 'This is out of bounds to you lot. How many times do we have to tell you? You've got two minutes to move on. Don't let me catch you round here again.'

'I didn't know,' said Mallund. 'It's my first night. I'd got nowhere else to go.'

'Not my problem, matey. Just stay off my patch.' The officer walked away, then stopped and turned. His voice softened slightly. 'New to the game are you? You'll find more of your lot down on Bedford Street. They've got a brazier made from an oil drum going. Bloody fire hazard if you ask me. And there's a late night soup kitchen in the park. Now bugger off and don't let me see your face again.'

★   ★   ★

Mallund was dying for a drink as he headed for Bedford Street, but it was three in the morning and there was nowhere to buy alcohol. Maybe one of his fellow travellers at Bedford Street would sell him a bottle, or lend him one until the morning. Bedford Street ran through a rundown area of wasteland awaiting redevelopment. Some buildings were boarded up, others empty shells, while some had already been flattened. On the flattened areas three distinct colonies had sprung up, each with an oil drum brazier blazing away. Around it sat and stood groups of shabby men and a few haggard women. Some were shouting and arguing among themselves. In other areas brawls had broken out and there was a lot of pushing and shoving. One man broke out from the crowd and ran away with others shouting curses at him. Mallund approached a brazier and held out his arms to warm them. The hostile stares from the others warned him that he was not welcome here. He nodded a greeting to his immediate neighbours around the fire, and was rewarded with the same hostility. Many of them were eyeing up his two suitcases. Mallund quickly worked it out. *These are not the homeless. These are drunks and vaga-bonds. This is Skid Row!* He cast his mind back to what that cop had said . . . *you'll find more of your lot down on Bedford Street.* It was that 'your lot' that disturbed him. Had the cop taken him not for a homeless person, but for a wino? Had he been relegated to the ranks of the meths-drinking underclass?

Perhaps it was his appearance: the unkempt greasy hair, the four day growth that certainly didn't look like designer stubble; maybe he was beginning to smell. He couldn't remember the last time he had bathed or showered, or washed his clothes for that matter. Anyway, sod it! He didn't know and he didn't care. All he knew was that he needed another drink, and morning was still a long way off.

11

He desperately needed somewhere safe to bed down for the night until he could get that merciful drink as soon as the shops opened. He found a corner in one of the derelict buildings and settled down for a few hours of fitful sleep. He awoke chilled to the bone and rubbed his arms and legs to get his circulation going. Sitting up, he looked around to see what his billet looked like in the daylight streaming through the glassless windows. The building was a shell. The floors of the four storeys above him had collapsed and he gazed up into a vast space, like inside a cathedral. A scuffling noise came from a nearby corner of the building. Rats? He began to search for a weapon and found a piece of wood with a nail protruding through it. The noise was coming from what he had dismissed as a pile of rags when he arrived the previous evening. It now seemed to be coming alive, bulging and twisting. Mallund raised his weapon. Just then the pile of rags parted and a head popped out.

'Jesus, man. Don't hit me. I didn't do anything!' said the head. Two arms appeared from under the rags and crossed themselves protectively over the scalp.

'I thought you were rats,' said Mallund, lowering his weapon. 'Don't worry, I won't hurt you.'

'Jesus, you scared the shit out of me, man. That bloody great club of yours. I thought I was done for. You just never know around here. Got to watch your back all the time. Don't suppose I can bum a score off you? No? Thought so. A beer then?'

'I could use a beer myself.' Mallund dragged the back of his hand across his dry lips. 'Where's the nearest place?'

'I'll show you. There's a Pakistani off-licence that opens early. It's not far. By the way, I'm Spency, and this is my little palace.' He gestured round the ruins.

'You can call me Jack.' Slowly, a plan was forming in Mallund's mind. 'How about I buy you a beer, Spency?'

'Epic!' Then, with a note of suspicion, 'Why whould you do that?'

'You're going to have to earn it.'

'I don't do funny stuff, mister. No fear. You can find yourself another boy.'

'Nothing like that, Spency. I just want you to be my guide. I'm new on the streets, and I need someone to keep me right, show me the strokes. Know what I mean?'

'Yeah, man. I can do that.' Mallund detected a hint of pride in Spency's voice.

'Right then, let's find this bloody booze shop. I'm gagging.'

'Let me help you with the cases,' said Spency, taking one of them.

They headed off across the wasteland, each striding forcefully, eager to get to the booze, Spency trailing behind. It was fitting that Mallund had first mistaken Spency for a nest of rats, because the first description that came to mind on meeting him was 'rat-like'. Thin and undernourished; straggly black hair; eye sockets hollowed out by drugs and booze.

On some missions for the SAS Mallund had been provided with a stash of gold sovereigns and American dollars. They were meant for emergency use to buy his way out of trouble if he got stranded behind enemy lines. Bribes for locals and the inevitable corrupt officials. He smiled as he considered his present situation. *Same thing, only this time the tariff is a can of Special Brew.*

They arrived at the small supermarket which was already busy with shabby customers buying beer and spirits. They hauled the suitcases through the door, and Mallund went in search of Special Brew while Spency browsed among the rows of booze. There was no Special Brew on the shelves.

'I'll get some from round the back,' said the proprietor. Two minutes later he returned carrying a large carton of the strong beer and began laying out the cans on the shelf. Mallund picked up two and took them to the till. He paid and, while taking his change looked around for Spency whom he had left at the drinks section. A panic grabbed him.

'Did you see another guy with a suitcase?' he asked the checkout girl.

'He left,' she said, and turned to the next customer.

Mallund dashed out into the street, looked right and left. Spency was gone. So was his suitcase.

Jack Mallund of the SAS had been trained to survive on practically nothing in the most hostile of environments. He could find food and water in the deserts of Arabia. He could melt snow and fish through the ice in the Arctic Circle. He could purify water to drink in swampland, using just the rays of the sun. He could cook insects to eat in the steaming tropical jungle.

But there was one thing they had omitted to teach him: how to survive in the Urban Jungle.

* * *

Mallund cursed himself for his stupidity in letting Spency out of his sight. He hurried back to the building where he had slept, but there was no sign of Spency. He spent the day wandering aimlessly, having taken stock of his finances. Just £18.54 left. He studied the beggars in the streets, peering into their tins to estimate how much they were earning. They repulsed him with a snarl and a string of curses. Of course, he would never have to resort to begging in the streets, but it was handy to know. He needed to get an income. You can't sign on the dole without an address. And anyway, he wasn't too popular there. So what else was there? These were the thoughts he fell asleep with on his second night in Spency's 'little palace'.

He scoured the area for Spency, but each time he asked 'I'm looking for a geezer called Spency,' he was met with the same hostility he had encountered that first night round the oil drum brazier. 'Never heard of him,' was the usual grudging answer. *They look after their own*, Mallund had decided after hours of fruitless searching.

★ ★ ★

Three days later as he returned to the derelict building he now regarded as home, Mallund spotted a shadowy figure sneaking out the doorway. Darkness was closing in and it was difficult to make out the shape at first, but he was almost certain it was Spency. He sprinted across the waste ground. The figure saw him coming and ran, Mallund in hot pursuit, his longer legs easily outpacing the fugitive. As he shortened the distance between them, Mallund could plainly see that it was Spency. No more than six feet between them now, when Spency suddenly dodged to his right into an open doorway, causing Mallund to overshoot.

'Damn!' Mallund skidded to a halt, backtracked and barged through the doorway. It was a derelict warehouse, and he glimpsed Spency disappearing through a window at the far end. The lad was remarkably nimble considering his neglected and abused body. By the time Mallund reached the window and peered through it, Spency had disappeared into a maze of side streets. His local knowledge would give him a huge advantage over Mallund. Besides, night was closing in and there was no point in continuing the chase.

'I'll catch you again, you little bugger!' Mallund yelled into the darkening streets.

12

Mallund and Ros Forster sat drinking tea in the room at the back of the church which they had designated as their 'campaign headquarters' in the search for Alice. For three weeks the 'campaign' had been running round in circles getting nowhere.

'The trouble is, no one will talk; they're too scared,' said Ros. 'The people we're dealing with exact terrible retribution on anyone who grasses on them. Beatings, maiming, even killing. One prostitute I spoke to was splashed with acid and the whole of one side of her face was disfigured. Her 'crime'? — she sent a note to her brother appealing for help, but it was intercepted. When she asked the pimps how she was supposed to ply her trade after the acid attack they shrugged and said, 'Grow your hair long and the punters won't know the difference in the dark'. Within a week of talking to me she was found dead, an apparent suicide. The grip these people have on the streets with sex and drugs is unbelievable. But this is only the end of the food chain. Their influence spreads down through major organized crime — gambling, protection rackets, pornography, people trafficking, you name it. If it's dirty they've got their fingers in it directly or indirectly, either running their own show or taking a cut from somebody else's. And at the top there are a handful of fat cats taking all the cream.'

Mallund was shaking his head in disbelief. 'But what about the police? Surely they know who these guys are? Why not just round them up and chuck them in gaol?'

'Not so simple, Jack, they cover themselves well. They are cloaked in respectability. I've worked with a lot of police officers who are frustrated as hell about not being able to get to them. They never get their hands dirty, and duck and dive when anyone tries to go after them.'

Mallund made a mental note: *Let the enemy come to you.*

'There must be somebody with a grudge who would talk to us,' he said. 'Even just to point us in the right direction, set us on the road to finding Alice.'

'I'll do my best, Jack, but don't get your hopes too high. There are some girls who confide in me — but that's just it, a confidence. They trust me and know I won't use any information I get from them. If it got traced back to them . . . well, who knows what?'

There was a timid knock at the door.

'Come in,' said Mallund.

The door opened about ten inches and a worried face poked through the gap. It wore heavy-rimmed tortoiseshell glasses and a three-day stubble on the chin.

'Come on in, Robin,' said Mallund.

'I hope I'm not disturbing you,' said a lanky youth stepping apologetically into the room and pausing after the second step.

'Not at all, come on in, Robin.'

The youth took another step. He was carrying the base unit of an elderly desktop computer. 'I've fixed the motherboard, Jack, it's running perfectly now.'

'That was quick. The shop told me it would take about two weeks, and said I would probably need a new computer in the end.'

'Fixed it in about five minutes,' said the youth, with a shy smile that somehow seemed to be saying 'sorry'.

'Well done you!' said Mallund. 'Ros — meet Robin Makepeace Thackeray, our resident computer whiz-kid. In fact we call him the IT Department. He fixes any problems we have with the equipment. He's a great asset to the church and Buddies. And, what's more, he doesn't charge a penny.'

'Pleased to meet you, Robin,' said Ros, smiling brightly.

Robin smiled back weakly.

'I'll be going now,' he said, backing towards the door. 'Just thought I'd let you know . . . the motherboard . . . fixed . . . '

'That's great, Robin, catch you later,' said Mallund.

Robin tugged the door closed as he left.

'Strange fellow,' said Ros nodding towards the closed door.

'An interesting story,' said Mallund. 'Apparently he was a high-flying programmer, worked on several hugely successful games — you know, zapping aliens and all that — until he went off the rails. He became obsessed with trying to write some perfect algorithm. It drove him half mad. Something to do with prime numbers — it's all too mind-boggling for we mere mortals — but anyway the search took over his life. He wasn't eating or sleeping and eventually had a complete breakdown. He was in therapy for a couple of years, but was never completely cured. For a while the very sight of a keyboard or monitor would cause him to break out into a cold sweat and tremors. When he walked into Buddies he was a pathetic sight. He had lost all his confidence and was as timid as a church mouse. But he is slowly coming round. We got him to solve problems with our electronic equipment, anything from the church PA to the TV at Buddies. Now, he is fit enough to teach basic computer use to our senior citizens, and to do minor repairs to the equipment. But the very thought of doing anything more complicated scares the pants off him. It's a crying shame to see such enormous talent locked up and going to waste. Still, we're getting there. Slowly, slowly catchee monkey as they say.'

Ros got up to pour more tea. 'It's amazing the characters who get washed up on the shoreline of society,' she said. 'And we're always there picking them up, like beach-combers. But back to the point, Jack, we must face some hard facts about Alice. Are you ready for some tough love?'

'Fire away,' said Mallund.

'I'm afraid it's an odds-on certainty that Alice has been groomed. I know you were not closely involved in her daily life, but I'm going to run by you some of the tell-tale signs of grooming. Stop me if Jennifer ever mentioned any of them to you. OK?'

'OK.'

'Did Alice ever become excessively secre-tive?'

'Sorry, I wouldn't know.'

'Did she come home with presents — clothes, cosmetics, DVDs, mobile phones, anything that you couldn't account for?'

'Again, sorry . . . '

'Did she no longer talk about her friends or bring them home?'

Mallund shrugged.

'Did she stay out late at night?'

'I think Jenny said something about that.'

'Did she spend a lot of time in online chat rooms and did she leave the public room to go 'private' at times?'

'Sorry.'

'Was she secretive or protective about what she did when she was online?'

'I never saw her with her computer.'

'Did she display any changes in behaviour or personality, or inappropriate sexual knowledge or behaviour for her age?'

'Sorry, Ros. I'm not much help, am I? It's my fault. I should have pushed harder to take responsibility for Alice when I saw Jenny going off the rails. But Jenny had sole custody and the law on her side.'

'I hate to say it, Jack, but between you — a mother losing control and an absentee father — you both set Alice up as a perfect target for groomers.'

13

Leanne was thin and nervy. She sat chain smoking, attacking her cigarette in short, anxious drags. She had the face and body of an anorexic, but this was not because of an eating disorder: it was pure and simple bodily neglect aided by drugs and alcohol. She glanced suspiciously at Mallund seated opposite her with Ros Forster at a table outside a dingy pub.

'You said you'd come alone,' she said.

'I know, Leanne,' said Ros, 'but Jack here is a vicar. We can trust him. Anything said here stays between us.'

'Still, I dunno . . . ' Leanne took another swift and deep drag at her cigarette, holding it in for about ten seconds then exhaling it through pouted lips. There were only two other customers, yet her eyes kept darting around and she spoke in a low voice. She might have been attractive a few years back, Mallund reckoned. But the high cheekbones that had once lent a cool air of sophistication were now just skeletal protuberances. Lips, once no doubt well-sculptured and eminently kissable, had shrivelled to an off-putting meanness. The shoulder-length hair was lank and badly bleached. Mallund could only guess at the original colour. And the eyes. The eyes were just dead. They now appeared to Mallund like twin black mirrors.

'You know me, Leanne.' Ros lowered her voice. 'You know I'm on your side. I'd die before doing or saying anything that might get you into trouble, you know that.'

'He don't look much like a vicar,' said Leanne.

'I know he doesn't. That's because he's special.' Ros threw a quick glance at Mallund. 'Very special.'

'What does he want to know?'

'Jack has lost his daughter. She was just like you. We think she might have been groomed and used like you were. It was nearly a year ago.'

'Way before my time. Anyway, a year . . . they'd have finished with her long ago.'

'What do you mean by 'finished'?'

'Just that.' Leanne shrugged. 'No longer of use to them.'

'And what then?'

'Who knows? All depends. If they just dump them they might find their way home, but most can't face that, they're too ashamed. They can't go to the police, they're too terrified. Those who give any trouble just disappear.'

'You mean they're killed?'

'I've not known that to happen personally. But there's talk.' Leanne drew deeply on her fifth cigarette and shivered.

'Leanne, I'd like you to look at this photo.' Ros produced a large colour print of a smiling Alice. 'Have you seen her before?'

'I told you it was before my time. After all that time there's not much point . . . '

'Just look. Please.'

Leanne sighed and took the photograph, gave it a cursory glance and said, 'No, never seen her before.'

'Please look more carefully.'

'Never seen her, that's for sure, not one of us. Sorry,' Leanne said after a long study of the happy, innocent face. She handed the photo back to Ros.

'Well, thanks anyway, Leanne. It was just a shot in the dark.' Ros put the picture back in her bag and rose to go.

'Just a minute.' Leanne stretched out her hand. 'Let's see it again.' Ros handed the photo back to her. 'She's very pretty, isn't she?'

'Yes, she is!' It was the first time Mallund had spoken.

'Now that's different. The pretty ones, they got the Rolls-Royce treatment. Kept aside for greater things. The rest of us were kept locally by the people who groomed us, but if you were a looker you didn't spend long here. You were kept separate and then disappeared within a week or so.'

'Where to?' Mallund could not conceal his impatience.

'Could be anywhere. Even abroad. I heard the Middle East mentioned a lot. We were all too much out of our skulls on drugs and booze to care. There was talk of lavish parties in country houses here, where the pretty girls were used as 'hostesses'. Wild, wild parties for millionaires, where anything goes. Some very depraved stuff. Very private and very secret. Top people. Even government people. Top cops too. But you didn't know what to believe. All of us wanted to get on to the party scene, get away from the squalid places they put us in. But as soon as you even asked about the parties all you got was a smack on the mouth and told to shut up and never mention them again to anyone. And you did as you were told. Look, I've got to go now or I'm in trouble, big time. Time to get to work.' She rose to go.

'Just a minute please, Leanne. We need names. Can you point us to any of these people? Just one name will do. Please.' Mallund could not control himself.

'What is this?' Leanne stared furiously at Ros.

'Sorry, Leanne, he doesn't know the score. I'll keep my promise. I promise — '

'I'm outa here!' Leanne picked up her cigarettes and headed for the door as if the hounds of hell were after her.

'Did you have to do that?' Ros was as furious as Leanne had been. 'I warned you to keep quiet. It was a very delicate situation and you jumped right in with your size tens. She'll now go back to her masters wondering if there's a beating waiting for her.'

'You mean she's still being held by these people?'

'Of course she is, I thought you knew that.'

'But she spoke of it all in the past tense, as if it was all in her past. I thought she was out of it and that's why she felt free to talk.'

'That's just a defence mechanism. They tend to talk like it's all over and they're expecting a bright new future any day now. Some have become so beaten down they accept this life as kind of normal. Leanne is one of them; that's why she's allowed to come and go. She's become institutionalized and has nowhere else to go.'

'And I blew it. Again.'

'Don't blame yourself too much, Jack. I

should have briefed you properly, but there just wasn't time.'

'So where do we go from here?'

'There's not much point in dealing with the trash working the girls at this level. We need to move up the chain. Up to the fat cats and their parties. But how we are going to do that, I just do not know.'

Take the fight to the enemy.

'I have an idea, Ros. We need to ruffle some feathers.'

'What makes me think this is going to be a bad idea that's going to get us into big trouble?'

'It goes like this.' Mallund was outlining his plan to Ros. 'I need to get the attention of the big guys, start hitting their business where it hurts, and to do that I need to start at the bottom and work up. If I can find a way into where these girls are being kept and free some of them — only a handful would do — it should shake things up. A sort of calling card to let them know somebody is after them.'

'Jack, you can't seriously be thinking of breaking into their premises. Even if you managed to get in, how would you get the girls out?'

'That's in the fine detail.'

'Fine detail? It looks like pretty major detail

to me. It's a cock-eyed plan. Why, you don't even know where these places are, to start with. It's doomed from the very outset.'

'Don't worry, I've got it all worked out.'

'That's what I'm afraid of.'

'But I'm going to need your help.'

'Oh my God!'

★   ★   ★

Mallund had guessed that the dingy pub where he had met Leanne would be one of her regular haunts. It would be off her turf, and a place where she felt safe. He staked it out for two days, watching from his car parked across the way, and on the third day she turned up. When she left the pub he followed her through a maze of back streets, to a red-painted door in a warehouse. She used a key to get in and immediately closed the door behind her. Mallund waited. Twenty minutes later a well-used Ford Mondeo pulled up and parked outside. It bore a taxi sign and a phone number in large letters across the door. The driver, a middle-aged bearded Asian, got out and went to the door. He stood looking up and down the empty street, then knocked on the door. It opened and he went inside. Another twenty minutes later he emerged, got into his taxi and drove off. Soon, another taxi pulled up and the Asian driver entered the building only to come back out half an hour later. This was repeated throughout the afternoon and evening. Mallund recalled that in his reading of one of the high profile trials involving Asian groomers, taxi drivers were prominent among the 'clients'. From time to time young girls also came and went. So too did some Asian youths. A few men of Middle-Eastern appearance also turned up, as did some whom Mallund put down as Eastern European. A group of three Asian youths knocked at the door. When it opened there was some kind of discussion. They were apparently being refused entry. A large Asian man in Western dress stepped out on to the street and confronted the youths who were waving their arms and remonstrating with him. Eventually they dug into their pockets and produced wads of cash and offered it to the man, who shook his head. They produced more money which he counted up, nodded and opened the door to let them through. He looked up and down the street before closing the door behind him.

'You're the man I want, my friend,' Mallund muttered under his breath.

14

The factory warehouse where the girls were kept was on seven storeys. As he reconnoitred the building, Mallund realized it would be impossible to get in by the front door, even in the early hours of the morning when the girls and any minder would be asleep. Each floor had large rectangular windows which were curtained all except for the top four. By night the lower four floors were lit, but the fifth, six and seventh were always dark, obviously unused. Half of the fourth floor was also unlit.

He decided that would be his route in. It was a madcap scheme. Mallund had decided to rescue the girls. Not all of them — that would be impossible. He knew that for a start some of them might not even want to leave, terrified to anger their masters. But if he got a handful out it would suit his purpose, which was to hurl a spanner into the works and get the attention of the criminals. He had spotted an old iron fire escape on a neighbouring derelict building of the same height which was just about serviceable. There was a fourteen-foot gap between the two buildings.

The day before he had hidden an aluminium ladder round the back under some builders' rubble. It would serve as a bridge. Dressed in black jeans, a black sweater and wearing a black balaclava, it seemed just like old times as he hauled himself up the groaning, rusting metal of the fire escape. Parts of it had rusted away completely, other bits were missing, and the spring-loaded folding stages had seized up, so it was hard going. *It's like trying to climb the Eiffel Tower*, thought Mallund. His heavily loaded Bergen tugged at his back, threatening to pull him off the structure, but he held fast, gripping each rail tightly hand over hand. The ladder, taped to the back of his Bergen, created an additional hazard as it repeatedly snagged in the metal framework. He kept having to let go of one of his handholds to steady the ladder and stop it from clanging against the fire escape. Once on the roof, he undid the ladder and carried it over to the gap between the two buildings. He had judged the gap perfectly. The ladder stretched neatly between the buildings. He now had a bridge. With his Bergen feeling like a dead weight on his back, he tested the end of the ladder with his toe to make sure it was safe enough and not likely to slip. He put his right foot on to the first rung, took a deep breath, then another step. *Don't look down!*

Eyes firmly fixed ahead, arms outstretched for balance, he gingerly picked his way across the ladder and heaved a sigh of relief as he felt his foot land on the concrete of the roof. Then he went to work. He unpacked a maze of ropes, pulleys and clamps from his pack and swiftly set to work assembling them. 'Thank you, SAS,' he breathed, grateful for the abseiling training. He anchored the ropes to a chimney stack and hauled on them testing for security. The chimney stack was not in the best condition, but it was more than rigid enough for the task. He lowered the rest over the edge and then eased himself over, making last minute adjustments to make sure he was comfortable, for this would be a long operation.

Mallund pushed himself away from the wall with his feet and swung out, at the same time releasing rope to enable him to drop. He arrested the descent when he was approximately at the height he wanted at the third floor. He finely adjusted his position to bring him level with the large window. It was leaded in a square pattern and very old. The leading would help dampen the sound when he smashed it, but not sufficiently. He reached back into a side pocket on his Bergen, pulled out a roll of gaffer tape and set to work criss-crossing the window with it.

When he was satisfied it would not shatter, he manoeuvred his feet to the top lintel and pushed himself out into space. As he swung back in towards the window his outstretched boots made contact with the glass and the entire frame came away and went flying into the room, landing with a dull thud. Mallund followed it into the room and set about reconnoitring his position with the aid of a powerful flashlight. There was a half-glazed door at the opposite end of the room leading out on to a corridor that Mallund guessed would run the full length of the building. He calculated the girls' accommodation would begin three or four rooms to the right along the corridor. He opened the door and crept into the corridor. There was a faint glimmer of light ahead, so he switched off his flashlight, pausing for half a minute for his eyes to adjust to the dark before continuing. He found a door barring his way. It was locked. He examined the lock, a fairly basic type. 'Easy peasy', he muttered under his breath, and from his pocket took a pair of thin steel rods hooked at the ends. Three minutes fiddling with it and the lock clicked open. *Thanks again, SAS.* Lock picking was part of his training. He gently eased the door open and found himself in a continuation of the corridor. By the faint glow of a security light he could see that the rooms similar to the one into which he had come crashing had been fitted with solid doors rather than the half-glazed ones he had passed. The rooms were now in fact bedrooms. Some of the doors were open and he could dimly make out a girl sleeping in each. There was no sign of a minder or guard. As he had guessed, they were on the ground floor, secure behind the strong front door, never for a second imagining that an intruder could enter from the sky. Mallund decided to concentrate on the rooms where the door was open. Having to open a door would create another obstacle and might spook the girls into raising the alarm before he could get to them and explain he had come to help them escape.

Now or never. He edged into the first room. The girl was about fifteen or sixteen. He shook her gently awake and put his hand over her mouth.

'Don't scream,' he whispered. 'I'm here to help you get away from here. Do you want to escape?'

The girl's eyes, at first wide open in terror, softened slightly and she blinked and nodded her head.

Mallund took his hand from her mouth and put his finger to his lips. He eased the girl

114

up to a sitting position.

'Get dressed as fast as you can,' he whispered. 'Go down the corridor to the fourth room and go inside and wait. Take this flashlight and leave it on. There will be other girls joining you.'

Mallund moved to the next room with an open door where a fair-haired teenager was sleeping. He woke her and gave her the same instructions.

The third room contained an Asian girl. When he woke her she struggled fiercely and bit his hand when he put it over her mouth. He had to be rough with her to keep her quiet while he explained.

'Do you want me to help you get out of here?'

She shook her head violently. 'No, no. They will find me and kill me.'

'But we will protect you.'

'No one can protect me.'

Mallund could not afford to waste any more time.

'All right,' he said. 'But you saw and heard nothing. Understand?'

The girl nodded and he moved on to the next room.

He soon had his quota of four girls. Two had refused to go with him. They were assembled in the room through which he had entered. He rearranged his abseiling equipment and lowered his Bergen to the ground. Then he put a simple safety harness on the first girl. 'Don't be afraid,' he said. 'You will be clamped to me so you can't fall. Just hold on to me and you'll be all right. When you get to the ground go to the end of the alley. There is a blue van waiting with a woman at the wheel. She will take you to a safe place.'

With the terrified girl clinging to him, Mallund launched himself out into space. The girl gave a little yelp as they fell earthwards. At the last minute Mallund arrested the descent and they were safely on the ground. He undid the girl's harness. 'Go quickly now. Don't forget. A blue van at the end of the alley.'

Mallund then began his ascent back up the wall of the building. It was a slow and tiring process, even though he was using ascenders on both hands and feet for speed. He brought down a second girl, then inched his way back up the wall again. When the last girl was on the ground he led her to the van and they piled into the back.

'Go!' he commanded.

Ros Forster gunned the engine and the van shot forward, causing its passengers to collide with each other, bumping heads.

'Why do I feel like I'm in the middle of a

Hollywood movie?' said Ros, as she sped through the empty streets.

'Just keep driving,' Mallund grunted from the back of the van.

They had gone about four miles when Ros pulled up without warning. 'OK, Jack, you need to get out,' she said. 'This is as far as you go.'

'Whaaat?'

'The place I'm taking them to is a shelter for victims of domestic violence. No men are allowed in, or even told of its location. It's a closely guarded secret. Sorry, Jack, that's the way it is. They will be safe until they decide what their next move will be.'

'Terrific! And what am I supposed to do, walking through the streets in the middle of the night dressed like a cartoon cat burglar? All I need now is a bag with 'swag' written on it!' He pulled off his black Balaclava.

Ros laughed. 'Don't worry, Jack, I'll pick you up here in five minutes.'

★ ★ ★

The night after the rescue of the girls, Mallund was back at the warehouse. He had arrived at ten o'clock at night and parked a hundred yards away on the opposite side of the road where he could command a good view of the red door. There were the usual comings and goings, and Mallund ate a cold jumbo sausage roll washed down with lukewarm coffee in a takeaway carton as he kept watch. Just after midnight the Asian man whom he had seen taking the money from the youths came out, turned to his left and walked past Mallund on the opposite side of the street. Mallund slid down in his seat and ducked his head below the dashboard until the man had passed. He quietly slid out of the car and followed him at a good distance through the side streets until he saw him enter a small terraced house. The lights were on but went off an hour later. So this had to be where the man lived. On the way back to his car, Mallund checked out alleyways and dark corners. Somewhere suitable for an ambush.

There could be no guarantee that the man would leave and go home at the same time the following night, but Mallund was prepared for a long siege if necessary. However, most people are creatures of habit. He was in luck. At just after midnight the man came out of the warehouse and turned left. This time Mallund had parked well up the road, giving him time to get out of the car and have a head start on the man. He found the alleyway he had selected the night before, checked all around and waited. As he heard the man's footsteps approaching, he tensed. The man's shape appeared passing the entrance. Mallund sprang forward and grabbed him, jammed his gloved hand over his mouth and dragged him back into the alley. He put a painful arm lock on him.

'Keep quiet and I won't hurt you. Understand?' Mallund gave a warning twist on the arm and the man shuddered and nodded vigorously.

'I just want you to take a message to your bosses. Tell them there will be more of what happened the other night. Tell them I'm coming after them, right up the ladder, no matter how high they are. I want my daughter back. Got that?'

The man nodded.

'Repeat it!' Mallund tightened the arm lock and the man gasped as he repeated the message. 'Now go. And don't look back.'

The man walked a few paces then broke into a frenzied run.

15

The Revd Jack Mallund kept a soft spot in his heart for the dispossessed. He spent a disproportionate amount of his pastoral care on the homeless, hardly surprising, since he had once been one of them. He understood their needs, sympathized with their problems, provided encouragement, guidance, and solutions. He got things done. He often wondered how he would have fared on the streets if there had been someone like himself around to help. Instead, Jack Mallund's introduction to life at the tail end of society had been a baptism of fire. As he walked to the soup kitchen he worked at in the park, the Revd Jack Mallund could not help but picture the other Jack Mallund in his threadbare clothes shambling to the same soup kitchen many years previously as a customer. A beaten man jiggling a few coins in his pocket . . .

Enough just for a few cans of Special Brew, but it was better than nothing. It had not been a very successful day at 'the office' as some of his fellow street beggars referred to their pitch. But tomorrow would be better — the streets were always busier on a

Saturday. At least he thought it would be Saturday. Ever since he had taken to the streets the days of the week had blended into each other and had lost their meaning. He couldn't even remember what day it was when he finally swallowed his pride and settled down on the cold pavement outside a travel agency, gazing up at pedestrians as they hurried by. How tall they looked from down here! Down low, looking up at the world. As low as a man could get. He had collected a mere 74p before the police moved him on. He did not protest, but quietly gathered up his things and shambled off. Forty minutes later he found a new pitch outside a bingo hall. Maybe, he reasoned, some superstitious punters would tip him a small part of their winnings as a token for future luck. But he soon learned that there are more losers than winners. He ended his first day with £7.24 and a Nigerian 25 kobo coin. He kept the foreign coin because it added weight to the hoard in his pocket and made the jingling sound more reassuringly substantial.

Most nights he slept wherever he could. He had learned early on to avoid the homeless shelters. Well intentioned as they were, they were shunned by most of the genuinely homeless. For a start they were usually full, but on top of that there were unpleasant side effects.

'You don't want to go there, mate,' advised Gordon, a fellow street sleeper. 'Not unless you fancy a dose of scabies with your night's lodging. A good night's sleep? That's a laugh. It's the last thing you'll get. If you're not kept awake by the bedbugs then the guys in the other beds will do the job. Half of them aren't right in the head. There's shouting and screaming going on all night long. Arguments and fights. Most of them have chest trouble, so the coughing is like a bloody steam engine wheezing away in the next bed. Once you're in you're in. You can't come and go as you please. It's like being banged up. And they keep strict hours which just don't suit the way we live. There are some shelters which manage to avoid a lot of this, but then you're back to square one — the good ones are all full. If you want my advice, pal, take your chances on the street.'

So Mallund crashed down anywhere that would offer a bit of shelter from the rain, some warmth and security. If he had anything that he might, with a stretch of the imagination, call 'home' then it was Spency's 'palace' to which he would return from time to time, drawn to it like a homing pigeon. His luck on the streets was no better. At first he would just sit there in his adopted doorway waiting for passers-by to toss him a coin or two. He could not even bear to look up at them, hiding his face with a turned-up collar and a pulled down cap. He could not bring himself to utter the words: 'Spare some change for the homeless, sir?' As a result, he was the most inexpert of beggars, and this was reflected in his takings. He was on the brink of starvation. Worse still, there was hardly enough for a daily dose of Special Brew.

There's a theory that if you give enough monkeys a typewriter and enough time, they will eventually produce the complete works of Shakespeare. A sister theory states that if you stand on a street corner for long enough, every resident of the city will eventually pass by you. Mallund learned the proof of this in a painful way.

*   *   *

It was the bright, blinding orange of the scarf that first caught his eye. A familiar shade of orange, approaching at the same height as Mallund as he sat bundled in his doorway. There was only one scarf of that particular shade in the whole wide world that Mallund had ever come across. It was around the neck of a large teddy bear, battered and maimed by years of love. A teddy bear called Joey. And it was approaching fast, propelled along in a navy-blue pushchair with a squeaky wheel. Mallund broke into a sweat of trepidation as he filled in the rest of the picture.

Cradling the teddy in her arms was a little girl with long Goldilocks hair.

Alice!

Pushing the chair was her mother.

Jennifer!

Mallund shrunk into his coat and pulled his cap over his eyes as his daughter and ex-wife approached. He squinted out through a narrow gap as Jennifer halted, rummaged in her purse, and tossed some coppers into his blanket. She looked down briefly but could not see his face.

'There you go,' she said lightly, smiled and walked on.

Mallund listened as the pushchair rolled on its way with its squeaky wheel, and wondered briefly if the new man in Jennifer's life was handy at fixing such things. Then came the voice of his daughter:

'Why is the silly man sitting on the ground, Mummy?'

That night Mallund went back to Spency's palace and drank his stash of nine cans of Special Brew one after the other.

And wept.

16

Mallund's money had all gone, and he would have starved but for the soup kitchen in the park. It was there that he finally caught up with Spency. The lad spotted him first, dropped his bowl of soup and chunk of bread and legged it. This time he did not have the advantage of the backstreets, and Mallund quickly caught up and pinned him against a tree.

'Hi, Jack. You owe me a beer!' Spency's attempt at flippancy barely disguised the fact that he was resigned to taking a good battering, and he was holding his arms in front of his face for protection.

'I owe you . . . ? You cheeky little shit! Where's my suitcase?'

'Oh, man, you ought to know that's long gone by now.'

'I should wring your scrawny neck, you cheating little scumbag.' Mallund had not had a drink for three days and was feeling murderous as he held the lad by the throat.

Spency's nimble brain slipped into survival mode and he spotted a slim chance of saving himself.

'You don't want to do that Jack,' he said, 'I was only doing my job.'

'What do you mean doing your job? You've never done a day's work in your life.'

'Don't you remember, Jack, you were going to buy me a beer, and in exchange I would teach you about surviving on the streets?'

'So what?'

'Well, that business with your suitcase, can we regard it as lesson number one?'

Mallund didn't know whether to laugh or throttle the squirming little rat. But when he thought about it, he had learned a salutary lesson with the loss of his suitcase — trust nobody.

He released Spency's throat. 'OK, you little shit. You're on. But any more monkey business and they'll be scraping you off the walls of your palace. In fact, that's where we'll sleep tonight, so I can keep an eye on you.'

As they settled down for the night, Spency said, 'By the way, Jack, how much did you take on the street today?'

'Just over six quid.'

'Shit, man, that's Mickey Mouse money. I'll come with you in the morning. We can do a lot better.'

★ ★ ★

At eleven o'clock the following morning, Spency watched as Mallund set up his pitch on a fairly busy street in the main shopping area, laying out his roll of foam rubber to protect his bones from cold and wet.

'This place just won't do.' Spency was shaking his head like a frustrated schoolmaster.

'What's wrong with it?' asked Mallund. 'It looks busy enough.'

'Well, we entrepreneurs have a saying: Location, location, location.'

'So? Who do you think we are? Marks and bloody Spencer? All I'm doing is setting up a pitch to cadge a few bob.'

'But just look where you are. You're in front of a big shop, right?'

'Right.'

'And did you check out the name of the shop?'

Mallund stepped back onto the roadway so he could see the shop sign:

CASH GENERATOR

'That's right — you've set yourself up in front of a pawn shop! The people going in and out of here are either skint and flogging off the family TV, or they're after a cheap second-hand bargain, in which case they're skint too.'

'See your point,' said Mallund, contrite.

Spency found a better pitch outside British Home Stores. 'Good cross-section of clientele, so the demographic is good, and a lively footprint in and out of the store. This'll do us.'

Location, footprint, demographic, thought Mallund. *Now he thinks he's bloody Lord Sugar.*

'So let's see you go to work, Jack.'

Mallund settled down and pulled his coat collar up and pulled his cap down over his eyes as usual.

'Jack, Jack, Jack. This won't do. Who are you? The Invisible Man? 'Cos that's all the punters will see. Or not see, as the case may be. A pair of hostile eyes peeping out at them. You've got to give a performance, Jack. Smile at them, make them feel good. C'mon, give me a performance, you know you can do it!'

Christ, now he thinks he's Steven fucking Spielberg.

Mallund summoned up what he thought was a smile, but to the outside world appeared as a malevolent grimace.

'Shit, man, you're supposed to be welcoming, not scaring the living daylights out of them. Smile, Jack. Like this . . . ' Spency's attempt at a smile turned out to be no better than Mallund's. 'See what I mean?'

128

'I wouldn't like to meet you on a dark night with a face like that,' said Mallund.

'Well, maybe we both need a bit of practice, Jack.'

When was the last time I smiled? Mallund couldn't remember. *Maybe if I'd smiled more I wouldn't be where I am today.*

'Anyway, Jack, practise, practise, practise. Even if you just show your face and make eye contact it will help. Eye contact unsettles the punters. They feel bad about passing you by without tossing some change. You've created a kind of bond. If you can't smile, then just nod a greeting at them. They like to be acknowledged too, you know. And don't forget to thank them. That's important for repeat business.'

Mallund had an idea. 'Why don't we try the shopping malls, there's plenty of people spending money there?'

'No go, Jack. These places have their own security staff. They'll move you on before you even have time to unpack. Mind you, they can often be ideal for a good night's kip. They have these huge areas planted out with trees and shrubs, and exhibition sites where you can easily hide out of sight of the guards. Spent many a warm, dry, comfortable night there myself in the past. Luxury!'

Spency sniffed the air with relish, and

smiled like a contented Bisto kid. 'Here's a good tip,' he said. 'See that bakery over there? That's prime real estate for the likes of us. For some reason the smell of fresh baking does something to people's senses. It makes them mellow, like a good hit of — ' Spency stopped in mid-sentence, remembering a feeling; shivering and rubbing his arm, his eyes went wild. Mallund had spotted the needle marks on Spency's arms at their first meeting, and noticed the edgy, jerky movements of the addict on the brink. It explained Spency's long absences, when he was presumably away getting clean.

'A hit of what, Spency?'

'Nothing. See that bakery? We're moving.'

They set up outside the bakery and, true to Spency's word, business was brisk. Mallund ended the day with £13.43.

'See? We've more than doubled your take by doing practically nothing,' said Spency back at the palace. 'Tomorrow we start in earnest. But first, a word about your appearance.'

'My appearance?'

'When was the last time you shaved, Jack?'

'Dunno. Couple of days or so, I guess.'

'More like a couple of weeks. That ain't designer stubble on your face: it looks more like a dead rat. And your hair. If you can't afford to get it cut, which you can't, then trim it yourself. It doesn't have to be neat, just less like the Wild Man of Borneo. Better still, I can trim it for you ... no, don't look so alarmed, I've done it for quite a few of the guys and they've been very happy with the job.'

'Hardly the most discerning of clientele, though, are they?'

'Beggars can't be choosers.'

Mallund tried in vain to remember the last time he had looked in a mirror. It was lost in the mists of time and booze.

'Appearance counts for a lot in this game,' said Spency. 'It's the difference between looking like a genuine guy fallen on hard times and a bum on Skid Row. Even carrying a magazine when asking for cash gives the impression that you're not just after boozing money.'

Mallund had indeed noticed that Spency kept himself fairly well presented, considering his lifestyle and his drug habit. Yet he was always on edge, looking around, twitching like a rabbit about to take flight.

'I don't notice you working the streets much, Spency,' he said.

'Only when I need to. I have other ways of earning a crust.'

'Like what?'

'That's for me to know. Anyway, tomorrow we start early, catch the commuters.'

'Back to the bakery?'

'No, it pays to keep on the move, unless you've found a really good spec with plenty of regulars. Tomorrow it's the railway station.'

17

Early next morning Mallund, sporting Spency's rough haircut, washed and shaved in one of the better public conveniences. Spency insisted on bringing a travel bag.

'Why, where are we going?'

'We're not going anywhere. It's a prop.'

They set up outside the main station entrance as the first commuters came bustling through. Mallund was quick to learn that this location was a double-edged sword. For sure, there were masses of people, but most of them were in a hurry, late for their train. Nevertheless many were happy to toss a few coins as they went.

'It'll be more relaxed after the rush hour,' said Spency. 'Then there's a lull with a steady trickle of punters. The evening rush hour is best, they're not in such a hurry. And if they've had a decent day at work they might be feeling generous. In the meantime, you're going to need a sign.'

'A sign?'

'Well, if you won't talk to them you have to communicate in some other way. A sign is very effective. But not just any old sign. I'll scoot off and find some cardboard and something to write with. In the meantime, try not to scare the punters, try to be pleasant.'

Spency returned half an hour later with a square of cardboard and a black marker pen, and sat down cross-legged on the ground beside Mallund.

'Now,' he said. 'What's the story?'

'Story?'

'We need a story. It's no use just sitting with a sign saying 'Please give me some money'. We need human interest.'

Now he thinks he's Rupert Murdoch, thought Mallund.

'So we need a story, Jack. Let's see . . . what about 'Please help. I'm stranded. I need sixty pence towards a ticket back home to Leeds'. Short and specific. It needs to be a specific amount or they'll ignore it. And by stating sixty pence you are often likely to get a pound. It's good marketing.'

Richard Branson now.

Mallund was feeling uncomfortable. 'But it's a lie!' he said. 'I've never even been to Leeds.'

'Jack, at our level of existence, all life is a lie. So we're allowed a bit of leeway. There's an old Japanese saying: *It is a beggar's pride that he is not a thief.*'

'Hang on a minute — you nicked my suitcase, remember?'

'A momentary lapse, for which I have paid the penalty. So, Jack, it's important to look the part. If you're supposed to be playing the stranded traveller, look like one. Be neat and tidy. Have a travel bag as a prop. Now, let's see what we can do, eh?'

* * *

'Thirty-six pounds and eleven pence!' Mallund could not believe the day's total as he added it up on the pavement. He thrust it into a side pocket of his coat.

'No, no, Jack.' Spency was tut-tutting. 'Remember, keep it out of sight. And not all in the same place. Spread it around your body. Keep some in a sock. Remember the life we lead, the areas we inhabit. We're easy targets for muggers, junkies who will beat the shit out of you for a couple of bob. If they hear you've been spending big at the booze shop they'll be on you like flies on a fresh turd. Just watch your back.'

That night they celebrated at the palace with takeaway chips, sausage and gravy, washed down with copious Special Brew.

After half-a-dozen cans, Mallund was mellow enough to voice a question that had puzzled him since his first meeting with Spency.

'Tell me, Spency, how did you fall into this way of life in the first place?'

'Why, what's it to you?' There was a defensive edge to Spency's voice.

'Nothing. Just curious, that's all. You don't look the part, you don't act the part, you don't even talk like you belong here. Just curious.'

'Well, keep your fucking curiosity to yourself.'

'OK. OK. Subject closed.' Mallund offered him a fresh can of Special Brew. 'By the way, I've been thinking: why do we always work the streets down town? There must be some rich pickings in the posh suburbs. Maybe we should go up market, as they say.'

'Not a chance, Jack. Stay away from those areas. The rich folk are less likely to give you a penny and more likely to call the filth. Same goes for the trendy streets with their swish bars, clubs and restaurants. If the cops don't move you on, the bouncers will. And you're likely to get a kicking from the pissed-up customers just for the fun of it. No, down town is the place to be, with the honest to goodness lower middle class. I know you're the sort of guy who knows how to take care of himself, Jack, but you need to be careful. The homeless and the bums are under constant attack from gangs. The teenagers are the worst. They'll rob you and then kick you half to death just for the thrill. So you need to learn how to pick a good safe spot to bed down at night.'

'We're pretty safe here,' said Mallund, looking around.

'The palace won't be here forever, Jack. Sooner, rather than later, it will be sealed up, the signs will go up and the wrecking balls and bulldozers will move in, and Presto! — a new block of luxury apartments is born. So you need to learn how to pick a good billet.'

'What makes me think you're about to tell me how to do it?' said Mallund.

'In the morning, in the morning, Jack.'

18

They slept well, aided by their Special Brew, and were up and about early.

'We're going for a walk around the manor,' said Spency. 'First stop, the university.'

'The university? What the hell for?'

'It's the one place where you can blend in with people who are as scruffy as yourself. They call them students. In the summer it's great for a quiet, undisturbed kip on the grassy areas where the students sit, talking and studying. Nobody bothers you. I do it all the time. And you don't look too old when you're scrubbed up, Jack. You could pass as a mature student. I've even used the showers in the sports centre. At night there are lots of dark, open spaces where you can bed down in safety. Just keep an eye open for nosy security patrolmen. Not that they're very effective. They're so used to high jinx from the resident students that nothing surprises them and they're likely to turn a blind eye.'

After his guided tour of the campus, Spency took Mallund down town and pointed out several choice bedding down sites. He paused at an alley full of skips and bins brimming with foul smelling rubbish.

'Surely not here?' Mallund screwed up his nose.

'Why not? It's secure, and the pong keeps the riff-raff away. You'll not be disturbed. But watch out for the collection trucks or you could get squashed in your sleep. It pays to know their collection times. Talking of pongs, you're not going to like this one, Jack. Public toilets. They're good for a short emergency nap when you're dead on your feet. Disabled toilets have all you need: facilities for washing, a lockable door and plenty of space to crash out. But don't spend too long, or you'll attract attention. If you've got a few bob, a day rover ticket on the city buses is a good investment. Again, take short naps and change buses regularly. You've probably already noticed, Jack, that your rest has become made up of cat naps. The contented, good night's sleep of the Ovaltine ads is a thing of the past for us.'

Mallund was feeling an encroaching mood of despair as, one by one, they visited the stairwells of multi-storey car-parks, the backyards of the larger chain stores — rich in cardboard for insulation in the winter — and a dozen other unwelcoming billets.

As they scouted out one of the seedier areas of the city favoured by hookers and addicts, Spency was in full flow again. 'This is where it all happens, Jack. You'd shit yourself if you knew what goes down here. I know the people who own this district, like I mean really *own*. Own the streets, own the people. There was one guy — '

Spency froze in mid sentence. His face went white and he jumped behind Mallund's back, trying to hide. 'Shit, they've seen me!' Spency disappeared up an alleyway before Mallund could find words. Further down the street he saw two heavy bruisers, one black, one white, break into a run towards him. They raced into the alley after Spency. Mallund hung around for a few minutes and was just about to move on when the two men re-emerged from the alley.

'This geezer was with him,' said the black one.

'Let's have a little chat with him,' said the other, grabbing Mallund and pushing him into the alley.

'Where's the little shit hang out?' The black one had Mallund by the throat with one hand. With the other he fished inside his expensive black leather jacket and pulled something out of the pocket. Mallund immediately recognized the cold chill of gunmetal pressing under his chin.

'Where's he at?' The gun barrel jabbed into

the soft flesh just above Mallund's Adam's apple. He broke into a cold sweat.

'Where's who?'

'Don't fuck with us, man. You know who. That little turd Spency, that's who.'

'Spency? Oh, is that his name?'

The barrel pressed further into Mallund's throat.

'My oh my, we've got a joker here, Mal.'

'Don't like jokes, me. Just blow the bastard's tiny brains out,' said Mal, the white one.

'And make a mess of that cool designer jacket he's wearing? What is it — Armani?' The black one was fingering the lapel of Mallund's threadbare black coat.

'More like Salvation Army reject, Don,' said Mal.

The gun barrel moved to Mallund's forehead.

'I'll ask you one more time,' said Don.

'I tell you I don't know the guy.' Mallund's head was aching from the pressure of the cold metal. 'The little toe-rag just came up and tried to bum a cigarette off me. Off me, of all people. I ask you . . . '

'C'mon, Don, forget it, this geezer's just a bum. He knows nothing.'

'He's lying. He knows Spency, that's for sure.'

'Now how do you know that?'

'Spency doesn't smoke. I think Mr D will want to talk to this piece of shit.'

They marched Mallund to a black Mercedes parked three streets away on double yellow lines. There was no penalty ticket on the windscreen. They bundled him into the back seat. Don slipped in beside him while Mal took the wheel.

'Where are we going?' asked Mallund.

'Shut your face,' said Don. He produced a scarf and tied it around Mallund's head to act as a blindfold.

★ ★ ★

The busy streets gave way to dual carriageway as they left the suburbs behind and sped through rolling countryside. They left the main road after five miles and turned down a narrow lane. The house at the end of the lane was partly obscured by trees. They drew up in the gravel forecourt and Don removed the blindfold. Mallund blinked rapidly in the sunlight, and his eyes focused on a stone-built manor house, L-shaped on three storeys. A British racing green Bentley, a dark-blue Aston Martin and a black Range Rover were already parked outside.

'Some posh friends you have, Don,' said Mallund.

'Shut your face and get out,' said Don.

They led him through double oak entrance doors and into a black-and-white tiled hall which they crossed to a highly polished mahogany door.

'Wait here,' said Don. He knocked softly on the door.

'Come!' said a voice from within.

They entered an airy room furnished as a study. A wall of leather-bound books to the left; to the right a wall of delicate tapestries; ahead, a wall of glass looking out on an ornamental garden and the softly undulating hills beyond. Behind a large ornate desk sat a balding man in his early sixties, heavily suntanned with an orange glow. He liked the good things in life, if his well-developed paunch was anything to go by. *Bet this place has its own gym which he hardly ever uses,* thought Mallund. The man raised his eyes from the desk as they entered, looked Mallund up and down and grimaced.

'Christ almighty, Don. What on earth have you brought me?' He wrinkled his nose in distaste. 'I hope you hosed him down first.' There was the residue of what Mallund guessed was an Irish brogue in the voice.

'We think he knows where Spency is, sir.'

'Does he now?' The man's eyes turned again to Mallund. 'So where is he then?'

Mallund decided that playing the dumb tramp was his best bet.

'Begging your pardon, sir,' he began, and immediately felt a trifle silly, 'I don't know nothing about that fella. I tried to tell these two fellas here I don't even know his name. He just came up to me in the street. Never seen him before in my life.'

'He says Spency tried to cadge a fag off him, but I know Spency doesn't smoke,' said Don, beaming. 'I used my initiative, sir.'

'So you brought him here? To my home? I'm afraid initiative isn't your strongest suit, Don. Let me ask him myself.' He turned to Mallund. 'Don't be afraid, it's just that we need to contact your friend, do you see?'

'He's not my friend.'

'But if he did happen to be your friend, we owe him some money, and we need to see him.'

'He's not my friend, sir. I don't know nothing about him. I keep to myself.'

'Shall we ask him nicely, sir?' Mallund didn't like the way Don said the word *nicely*.

'Don't you ever think beyond your knuckles, Don?' The man was shaking his head. 'Always look for the course of least resistance. Let me show you my way.' He reached into a desk drawer and withdrew a wad of £50 notes with a bank wrapper round it. He flourished it at Mallund. 'You see, it's important that we get this money to your friend, who isn't your friend, but if he happened to be your friend then there would be something in it for you.' He peeled off one of the notes. 'Say, fifty quid?'

Don and Mal were rolling their eyes at the ceiling.

'I sure could use all that cash, sir.' Mallund was licking his lips as if in anticipation of an ocean of Special Brew. 'And I sure do wish he was my friend. But I just don't know who the hell he is. Jesus Christ! Fifty quid!' He was looking longingly at the banknote dangling from the man's hand.

The man spread his hands, leaned back in his leather swivel chair and looked at Don and Mal. 'You see, both of you, this guy would sell his soul for a drink. He's just a bum. Take him back where you found him. And don't hurt him. We're trying to keep a low profile here. The less unnecessary violence, the fewer ripples we cause the better. Understand? Now don't bring me any more trash. Just get me that toe-rag Spency before he does any more damage.'

The three of them had just reached the door when the man's voice stopped them.

'Just a minute. Come back. No, not you two — him.'

Mallund shuffled back to the desk. The man stood up and pulled a £10 note from his wallet. 'Here, for your trouble.' He held it out at arm's length to Mallund.

'Thank you, sir,' said Mallund, bowing.

They drove back to town in silence, Mallund again blindfolded. The car pulled up at the very spot where they had found him. Don extended his hand, palm up.

'Give,' he said.

'Give what?' Mallund was puzzled.

'That tenner the boss gave you. Give.'

'But he said it was for me, for my trouble.'

'Well, now I want it for *my* trouble. Give.'

Mallund sighed and handed over the crumpled banknote.

'Out!' said Don, giving Mallund a rough punch in the ribs to facilitate his exit from the car. 'Don't let me see your ugly face again.'

Mallund watched as the Mercedes drove off and disappeared into the narrow streets.

Talking of ugly faces, just wait till I get my hands on Spency, he vowed. What's he mixed up in? And what's he got me involved in now?

19

The sonorous tones of the bishop's voice echoed around the stone walls of the church, the congregation silent as the lone man stood facing him.

'Do you trust that you are inwardly moved by the Holy Ghost to take upon you this office and ministration, to serve God for the promoting of His glory, and the edifying of His people?'

'I trust so,' answered the man.

'Do you think that you are truly called to the will of our Lord Jesus Christ, and according to the canons of this Church and the ministry of the same?'

'I think so.'

'Will you reverently obey your ordinary and other chief ministers of the Church, and them to whom the charge and government over you is committed, following with a glad mind and will their godly admonitions?'

'I will endeavour myself, the Lord being my helper,' said the man, now kneeling humbly before the bishop.

The bishop laid his hands on the man's head.

'Take thou authority to execute the office of deacon in the Church of God committed unto thee; in the Name of the Father, and of the Son, and of the Holy Ghost. Amen.'

'Amen,' said Jack Mallund, rising from his knees.

As parishioners, friends and relatives gathered round to congratulate him, he could still hardly believe it. He had just taken the first major step to becoming a vicar.

He shook hands and took hugs with a smile on his face, but his mind was elsewhere. Later, in the quiet of the church, he said a silent prayer and reflected on the events that had brought him to this watershed in his life . . .

★   ★   ★

It began on a dank November evening as Mallund was just settling down for the night in a corner of the stairwell in a multi-storey car-park. He heard laughter and screaming from a patch of waste ground outside. Just the usual Friday night disturbance, he thought. None of his business. Lads out of their minds on happy hour drinks and happy pills. Paralytic girls with their skirts halfway up their backs, screaming, cursing and peeing in the street. Just another Friday night.

But there was something different about this screaming. The more he listened the more he realized these were screams of terror. And the laughter sounded hysterically evil. He crept out from under his bundle and poked his head round the corner of the car-park wall. In the dim light he could make out about half-a-dozen teenagers kicking what looked like a bundle of rags. It took several seconds before Mallund recognized the squirming bundle as Roger, one of the oldest dossers in the neighbourhood. He was screaming in pain and trying to shield his head with his arms as they were kicking the life out of his fragile body. Two of the teenagers were girls, egging the boys on.

'Give it to the old bastard!' screamed one of the girls.

'Kick his head in! Let me get a shot of it!' said the other. Mallund could see that she was recording the whole episode on a tablet, calling out instructions like a film director. In the background he could just make out a tall, elderly man in a black overcoat who was pleading with the gang to stop.

'Piss off, Granddad, unless you want to be next,' said an orange-haired youth.

'Don't do this! Think of the consequences. Please, I beg you. Stop this now. For God's sake, you could kill the man!'

'For God's sake, you could kill the man . . . for God's sake, you could kill the man . . . ' the youth mimicked him in a whining voice. 'What do you think the general idea is, you stupid old fart? Now piss off before we start on you.' He strode over to the man and pushed him to the ground. He gave him a hefty kick in the ribs. 'Now beat it, it's none of your business.'

That's right, mate, get well out of it. None of your business. It's look after number one around here. Mallund continued to watch while the beating of Roger continued and the elderly man lay breathless on the ground. Mallund spotted a dog collar and realized the man was a vicar.

'Burn the bastard!' screeched the girl holding her tablet up for filming.

'Who's got the lighter fuel?' said the other girl.

'Got it here,' said one of the boys.

'Please, in the name of God, no!' pleaded the vicar, raising himself on one elbow.

None of your business, Vicar, get out while you can. This was the Jack Mallund of today talking.

A giggling youth dowsed Roger in lighter fuel, while another held a lighter aloft, tantalizing the cowering tramp.

At that moment it was time for another

Jack Mallund to speak; not the Jack Mallund of today, but the Jack Mallund of more than a decade previously, in a jungle village, watching a man about to be burned alive.

'That's enough!' yelled Mallund, and he sprinted towards the clearing.

In one movement, he snatched the lighter from the youth's hand. At the same instant there was a loud cracking sound of breaking bone as the youth let out a scream of pain.

The ringleader pulled a knife from under his hooded jacket and waved it at Mallund. 'Well, lookee here, it's the Caped Crusader!' he sneered.

'Stick it to him, Gerry!' yelled one of the girls.

'Yeah, go for it!' screamed the other.

Gerry moved slowly forward, passing the knife from hand to hand. It gave Mallund time to weigh him up. Young and fit, six foot and a bit, but over-heavy with it. Which hand would he use for the knife? Gerry drew the back of his right hand under his nose, a nervous reaction. That's it. He favours his right. The youth continued passing the knife from his right to his left as he advanced.

Mallund was seriously out of shape, his muscle gone flabby. His reactions would be slowed by disuse and drink. But had his unarmed combat skills deserted him too? He was about to find out.

Gerry lunged at him. Mallund instinctively sidestepped to the left, away from the knife. He grabbed the youth's free arm and twisted, letting the attacker's own momentum do the rest of the job. There was a loud crunch as the lad's shoulder dislocated and he dropped the knife and fell to the ground writhing in agony. One of the girls picked up the knife and jabbed at Mallund's thigh. He felt a searing pain, but managed to kick out, catching her full in the face. She fell to the ground nursing a broken nose. Just then he felt a stranglehold on his neck. The other girl had jumped on his back and was trying to strangle him to the ground. She was heavy. He relaxed his neck muscles, making it harder for the strangling to continue. This also enabled him to grab her little finger and yank it back to break it. She howled as Mallund continued bending her finger and, as she relaxed her grip, he drove his right elbow backwards into her stomach, at the same time stamping backwards on her foot. No sooner had he freed himself from the girl than he caught another attacker sliding into his peripheral vision. This youth was brandishing a baseball bat in his right hand. Mallund's training was now on auto pilot. *Don't back away. Move inside the arc of the* *swinging bat. Step in and to the right so that the strike comes down on your left and misses. Block it with your left arm as well. Continue the movement round his arm, trapping it against your body. The weapon is now harmless. Now for the attack. His head is now slightly forward and vulnerable. Twist round and drive the heel of your right palm up into his chin. Follow this with a knee into his exposed groin . . . .*The lad's shattered teeth hit the ground before he did. He, Gerry and the two girls were lying on the ground in agony. Another youth was about to step into the fray, but thought better of it. He rushed past the prostrate clergyman cursing all the way. 'I'm outa here! It's like a fucking Jackie Chan movie in there!'

Mallund went to the aid of Roger, who was curled up in a ball on the ground, whimpering. When Mallund tried to lift him to his feet he curled himself even tighter.

'It's all right, mate. They've gone. I'm a friend.' Gently, he raised Roger to a standing position, but the old man was too badly injured and collapsed to the ground again.

The elderly vicar had picked himself up off the ground and came over to help. 'We need to get him to a hospital,' he said. 'I'll go and find somebody to call an ambulance and the police.'

Mallund sat with Roger cradled in his arms until the vicar returned.

'They're on their way.' The vicar squinted at Mallund in the half light. 'You'd better get to the hospital too — just look at you.'

★ ★ ★

The knife had gashed a slice of Mallund's left leg above the knee. It needed ten stitches.

'That cut in your leg was too close to an artery for comfort. You are very lucky to be alive,' said the nurse. 'But Doctor says you're to be allowed home.'

Home! That's a laugh, thought Mallund.

The vicar had been checked out for a bump on the head sustained when he was knocked to the ground, and was waiting for a parishioner to pick him up from hospital.

'If you like we'll drop you back to town,' he told Mallund, as they stood at the hospital exit shortly after giving statements to the police.

'Thanks,' said Mallund.

'You know, that was a very brave thing you did tonight. You could've been killed.'

Mallund shrugged.

'So where will you sleep tonight?'

'Dunno yet.'

'Right. It's settled. You're coming with me

154

to the vicarage. You can stay there the night. In fact, you can stay as long as you like. I have a spare room.'

'Thanks, but I'll be all right on my own. I don't want to be a burden to you.'

'God lays burdens on us to test us. It's not the burden that matters, it's what you make of it that counts.'

Mallund winced inwardly at this morsel of homespun wisdom, but let it go. Life was a lot more complicated than that, he knew only too well. He needed to leave, get away from this man offering him kindness he did not deserve; kindness he would eventually end up throwing back in his benefactor's face. But how long had it been since he slept in a soft, dry, warm, comfortable bed?

'Thank you,' he said. 'But only for tonight.'

20

The following morning, Mallund woke in agony. Every limb, every muscle in his body was screaming as if locked in a vice that was getting tighter by the minute. That soft, dry, warm, comfortable bed had turned into a bed of nails for him. So acclimatized had he become to sleeping on cold, hard surfaces that his body had rebelled against the softness. The well-worn duck feather pillow had seduced him into an unaccustomed posture that left him with a stiff neck and a raging headache. He had no idea of the time, but could see a slit of daylight at the join in the curtains.

There was a soft knock at the bedroom door. The vicar entered with a mug of tea which he placed on the bedside table. 'Thought you might need this,' he said.

'Thanks,' Mallund grunted as he tried to move.

'Sleep well?'

'I'm not really used to beds.'

'So how long have you been on the streets?'

'Longer than I care to remember.'

'You don't seem to me to be the usual type

to be roughing it.'

'What do you mean 'the usual'? Is there a type?'

'No, no — it's just that you seem to have a lot more about you. How did you end up like this?'

'It's a long story.'

'I've got plenty of time. And listening is my job.'

'Maybe some other time. I'd best be on my way.'

'Not before breakfast you won't.'

It had been a long time since Mallund had eaten such a breakfast. What the hotels call Full English. Two fried eggs, lashings of bacon, two fat sausages, beans, mushrooms and toast with marmalade. He pushed the empty plate aside and leaned back on his chair in the large kitchen of the draughty Victorian vicarage.

'Phew! That was delicious. I can't remember when I last had a meal like that.'

The vicar was looking at him steadily through his rimless glasses. Mallund studied him in return. A tad over six feet, slim and aesthetic looking, with battleship grey hair and a hooked nose. Eyes that had seen a lot of grief in their day. Mostly other people's grief, Mallund reckoned.

'You know, Vicar,' he said, 'I've just realized

I don't even know your name.'

'The Revd Edward Fallon. But less of the vicar stuff. Everybody just calls me Eddie.'

'I'm Jack Mallund.'

'Pleased to meet you, Jack Mallund. Listen, how would you feel about having a breakfast like that every day?'

'Every day?'

'Yes, you could stay here. As long as you like.'

'Thanks, but as I said before I don't want to impose on you.'

'It won't be charity. You could earn your keep. I could use someone to help with the chores that get in the way of my ministry. A bit of gardening, help with the house, help running the drop-in centre. Since my wife Mavis died two years ago there are lots of community services that have been neglected — '

'Me? The vicar's wife?' Mallund smiled at the image of himself arranging the church flowers and baking Victoria sponge cake for the garden fête.

'No, of course not,' Eddie smiled back. 'Things like driving elderly people to appointments. I think you are a strong, no-nonsense leader. You'd be invaluable at the youth club. All unpaid, of course, but you'd have a bed and meals. What do you say, Jack?'

Mallund was sorely tempted. Could this be his salvation? His re-entry into the world he had lost? Tempting, yes, but he was only too well aware of the power of the dark side tugging him back.

'I'm sorry Eddie, but you don't know me. I'd only screw up. I always do. For a start, I have a drink problem.'

'We can address that.'

'Easier said than done.'

'You don't have a drink problem, Jack, only a problem that leads you to drink.'

'I'd only end up disappointing you, throwing your kindness back in your face.'

'My shoulders are broad enough to handle that, Jack.'

'I've been too long on the streets. It's become my way of life. I'm comfortable with it.'

'No you're not, you're simply inured to it, just like a lifer gets comfortable with prison. You need to get out of it, Jack. It's a crying shame to see a man like you go to waste. You could do so much with your life.'

'Whatever's left of it.'

'There's a lot left of it. You're still in your prime. All you have to do is change direction. Turn one simple corner to change it all.'

'Again, easier said than done.'

Eddie stood up from the breakfast table.

Mallund got up and helped him clear the dishes.

'I'm sorry, Jack.' Eddie put a hand on Mallund's shoulder. 'I'm afraid I've been preaching at you. Goes with the territory. End of sermon. But please, just remember what I said.'

'I will,' said Mallund. 'And thanks for the bed and grub. Now I really have to be off. Important business appointments and all that.'

The vicar did not smile at Mallund's flippancy.

As he walked down the overgrown path from the vicarage to the wrought-iron gate, Mallund did not look back. If he had, he would have seen the look of abject sorrow on the elderly man's face.

21

Life on the streets was becoming more difficult by the week. The economy was in free fall. The recession was biting hard, with pay cuts and redundancies, swingeing government cutbacks in social services, interest rates not worth talking about, massive bail-outs for troubled banks, businesses going to the wall, long established insurance and pension providers going belly up, the Footsie at an all time low, the Hang Seng struggling and the Dow Jones squirming ... and down at pavement level, a shortage of pennies for the likes of Jack Mallund and his fellow denizens at the rump end of the economy. The last in line, they were suffering as Joe Public and Mrs Public began seriously counting the pennies, cutting household bills, sacrificing holidays, and sacrificing the reassuring warming of their conscience that caused them to toss a handful of coins to somebody sitting in a doorway. Those coins were now being tossed into jam jars in the kitchen and bedroom as mini-savings projects for specific items. The slump in his micro economy came home to roost one day when Mallund turned up for business at one of his best pavement sites only to find that it had been turned into a charity shop for Help the Aged. Takings were diminishing by the day, but he was glad he had a secret stock of Special Brew buried at the palace. Along with the recession came the symptoms of a sick economy — an increase in crime, and an increase in self interest, and they were particularly virulent in the world inhabited by Jack Mallund. One evening he returned to find all his meagre belongings had been stolen. He needed a drink. Frantically, he ripped up the loose floor board concealing the void in which he had secreted his booze. Empty. Twelve cans of Special Brew. Gone.

Still on his knees, he bent over and wept as a strangled cry of anguish burst free from his throat.

* * *

The following morning he made a decision. He tried to spruce himself up a bit — difficult without the aid of his missing washing materials — and set out on foot for the other side of town. He hung around outside for ten minutes, hesitating, putting it off. Then he strode up to the solid oak door with its stained-glass panels and knocked. The door opened.

'Jack! Come on in, come on in,' said the Revd Edward Fallon.

★ ★ ★

Mallund spent a happy couple of years at the vicarage. There was plenty to do, and he got a buzz out of helping people in the parish. He was popular in the youth club, leading it with a good sense of fun tempered with a firm hand when necessary. He was a big hit in a drag act at the senior citizens' Christmas party, dressed as a char-lady with a fag in his mouth and brandishing a broom. However, he never took part in the church services.

'I take it you do not care much for the act of worship?' said Eddie one morning.

'Not my scene I'm afraid, Eddie.'

'Hmm. Pity.'

Nevertheless, Mallund was impressed with the comfort the parishioners derived from their church visits. Maybe there was something in it after all. He began to drop in, standing at the back of the church, listening to Eddie's uplifting and often light-hearted sermons. The look of peace and devotion on the faces of the congregation strangely attracted him, so that he felt the internal rage that had dogged him for so many years beginning to subside a little. Soon, he was sitting among them. With Eddie's help, and the ministrations of Alcoholics Anonymous, he had managed to control his drinking. He had weaned himself off Special Brew and on to an occasional glass of wine with dinner. Now, he was celebrating his first anniversary completely 'dry'.

'I think, Jack, that you are beginning to appreciate the act of worship,' Eddie said one Sunday, as they watched the last of the congregation happily make their way homewards.

'A little. I find it relaxing.'

'Relaxing? Is that all?'

'Well, maybe a bit more. Kind of . . . comforting.'

'You're a stubborn man, Jack Mallund. But I think you will come to the bosom of the Lord eventually.'

'Don't hold your breath.'

★   ★   ★

Many evenings were spent just talking, Mallund and Eddie together in the thought-provoking ecclesiastical gloom of the old vicarage. Electric lighting had done its bit towards relieving the severe tone of the place, and the one surviving coal fire blazing in the snug room favoured by Eddie made for comfortable late-night talks. More often than not the conversation drifted to God and belief. Eddie made a good case. Mallund found himself not only sitting in on the services, but taking an active part. After a while he was acting as a sidesman. Eddie was so easy to talk to, and Mallund opened up to him, even telling him about the incident in the African jungle.

'I just opened up on them like a madman,' he told Eddie, slowly shaking his head from side to side as he relived the massacre in his mind. 'I just lost it. Simple as that. I just lost it.'

Eddie fixed him with his unrelenting gaze. 'No, Jack, you didn't lose it. On the contrary, I think you *found* it.'

'How so?'

'You saw an injustice and you righted it. In your own way, with the only means at your disposal. You listened to your heart, not your head. You obeyed your conscience, not your masters. You found your conscience, Jack, and it was facing a major crisis. I think you came out of it well, all things considered.'

'Dunno about that,' said Mallund. 'Just look at me now.'

'I *am* looking at you, and I see a man who

should be able to hold his head high, but chooses not to. You have humanity, a rare and precious attribute in this human race. Everybody talks about the moral compass these days. Especially the politicians. I'm not sure what a moral compass is supposed to be, or where you're supposed to get one, but if they mean it guides your conscience in the right direction, then I'm all for it. You've found your conscience, Jack, now all it needs is a sense of direction.' The old man paused, nodded to himself, and laid his hand on Mallund's. 'Jack, what I'm going to say to you now might come as a shock, but it is something I have thought over very carefully: I think you have a vocation. You should think about taking Holy Orders.'

'Me? A priest?' Mallund burst into laughter.

'I'm serious. I've watched you with people and you would make an excellent pastor. You have all the right attributes. You might not believe it, but you are exactly the sort of person the Church needs these days.'

'Me? I'm a trained killer.' Mallund held out his hands palms upwards. 'I have killed. My hands have blood on them.'

'Exactly. You have seen the worst in men, but you have also seen the best. In short, when you preach you will know what you're talking about. What an amazing life experience you would be able to bring to the ministry. Just think what comfort you could bring to the needy, the dispossessed, the uncertain, the sick, the depressed, those who see no point in living. You'd be an inspiration.'

'Don't make me sound like a saint, Eddie. I'm anything but.'

'You don't qualify, Jack. The Church prefers its saints to be dead.'

'I've got as much chance of becoming a priest as I have of ending up as prime minister.'

'Don't sell yourself short. I firmly believe that I will live to see you in a dog collar.'

'That'll be a cold, cold day in hell, Eddie.'

★   ★   ★

Eddie piled on the pressure at every opportunity, cajoling, taunting, even browbeating him into submission.

'But I'm a divorced man,' Mallund had protested. 'A single man. Vicars have to be married, don't they? They need a wife to complete the package.'

'Not necessarily. Look at me.'

'Yes, but you're a widower. That's different.'

'There are many single vicars.'

'Well, I've never met one.'

'Yes you have, Jack.'

'Like who?'

'Like Jane Wallace over at St Thomas's.'

'Yeah, but . . . well, I never thought of her as single.'

'What did you expect? Like she had a hubby tucked away in a cupboard? I'll bet you'll find most female vicars are single.'

'I very much doubt that.'

'The Vicar of Dibley was a woman.'

'C'mon, Eddie, I'm talking reality here.'

'So am I.'

And so their discussions, arguments and debates rolled on, with Eddie winning by a knockout almost every time, until Mallund began to hope that maybe there was something in this after all. He couldn't quite place the tipping point at which he agreed; such was the subtlety of Eddie's unremitting campaign, but it was in June. Or July. Or maybe August. Anyway, after a rigorous round of interviews, intense self-examination and appeals, he found himself enrolled at a theological college in the south of England. Three hard years of study culminated in a soul-searching examination by the bishop. He was now ready.

22

Mallund settled easily into his pastoral role and was a popular and pro-active vicar. There had been a few concerned voices raised about his past, but they were quickly overcome. In the end, all agreed that he had been an excellent choice. He felt an inner peace and contentment the likes of which he had thought he would never know again.

Until . . .

The phone rang.

'Jack Mallund here.'

'Is that the Reverend Jack Mallund?'

'The very same.'

'Mr Mallund, this is Detective Sergeant Gordon at West Side police station. I don't want to alarm you, but we'd like you to come down to the station.'

'The station? Now?'

'It's a matter concerning your daughter.'

'Alice?' Is she — '

'She's all right as far as we know. It's just that your wife is here and has reported Alice missing overnight. Mrs Mallund is a bit under the weather, so we thought it better to contact you.'

'Under the weather? — You mean she's drunk.'

'I'm afraid so, sir.'

'I'll be right there.'

★ ★ ★

As he drove the three miles to the police station, Mallund turned over in his mind the events that had led to this situation. Jennifer had been looking rather rough when he first re-established contact with her shortly after his ordination. She was smoking heavily and, he suspected, drinking. She had quit the family home which had been sold and the proceeds squandered by a succession of boyfriends. She now lived in a council house on a run down estate which had not quite yet earned the status of 'sink', but was within an ace of doing so. On his first visit, he could see a sad reflection of his old self, the down and out no-hoper, in her attitude.

'Well, look at you, the preacher man,' she said, with a cynical curl to her lip.

'Hello, Jenny, how are you?' He had deliberately not worn his dog collar.

'How am I? Look around you.' She waved her arm around the unkempt room with its second-hand furniture and stained and threadbare carpet. Through the open door to

170

the kitchen he could see a pile of unwashed dishes overflowing from the sink and piled on the draining-board. *Whatever had happened to the once house-proud Jennifer?*

'And Alice?'

'An awful handful, that girl, I don't know what to do with her.' Jennifer moved to the hallway and shouted up the stairs, 'Alice, get down here, your dad's here!'

'Which dad?' The question stabbed at Mallund's heart.

'Your real dad.'

'I haven't got a real dad.'

'Yes you have, and he's here. So get yourself down.'

Footsteps came echoing down the uncarpeted wooden stairs. A slim, blonde girl of fourteen emerged carrying a bag.

'Say hello to your father, Alice.'

'What?'

'Take those damned things out of your ears.' Alice grudgingly removed her earphones.

'Hello . . . Father.' The girl stared at him sullenly.

'Is that all you have to say?' Jennifer was taking rapid drags at her cigarette.

'I don't know him. Where has he been all my life?'

'That's a long story, Alice,' said Mallund.

171

'Maybe we can spend some time together and I'll tell you all about it.'

'Suit yourself. I'm in a hurry, meeting the guys down town.' She headed for the door.

'When will you be home?' Jennifer called after her, lamely.

'Whenever.' Alice banged the door behind her.

'Can't you control her a bit more?' asked Mallund, still looking at the closed door.

'You're a fine one to talk.'

Mallund had no answer to that.

'Look, if it's money, I have a small stipend from the Church. If it's any good . . . '

'It's not about money, Jack.'

'What is it about, then?'

'I don't know. It's about this life.' She waved her arm around the room once more. 'I'm so tired, Jack, I just can't bring myself to do anything. I just sit here and . . . sit here. Would you like a drink? I've got some gin.'

'No, thanks, I don't any more.'

'Well, bully for you! I'm going to have one.' She got up and fetched a bottle from the kitchen, poured a hefty slug into a soiled glass. 'No tonic, I'm afraid. Here goes . . . ' She gulped it neat.

'Listen, Jenny. You can unburden yourself on me. Let me try to help. I'm a priest.'

'Ha!'

'I know it sounds strange after all we have been through together, but since God has guided me I'm a different man to the one you knew.'

'No, you're not. You've got a change of uniform, that's all. Underneath you're still the same old Jack Mallund, trying to do the right thing at the expense of those around you. Parading your naked soul for all to see. To hell with your family and your friends just so long as you can clear that precious conscience of yours. Well, you're in the right job for it now.'

'That was below the belt, Jenny.'

'Tough. It was meant to hurt.'

* * *

Mallund came screeching into the police station car-park which was full except for one space evidently reserved for some top brass. He half-parked, half-abandoned, his battered Kia in that space, jumped out of the car and barged through the front door. A startled desk sergeant looked up from his charge sheets and put a hand up to stop Mallund, as if he was directing traffic.

'Now then, sir, slow down. What's the hurry?'

'Detective Gordon — where can I find him?'

'Is he expecting you, sir?'

'Yes, dammit, just tell me where he is.'

'Your name?'

'Mallund. The Reverend Jack Mallund.'

'Mallund . . . Mallund . . . Mallund.' The sergeant consulted a list on a clipboard. 'No Mallund here, as far as I can see. How would you be spelling that, sir?'

'Look, he just called me and told me to get here. It's urgent. My daughter's missing and my ex-wife's here and is very upset.'

'Oh, *that* lady, sir.' The sergeant could not conceal his knowing smile. 'Second floor. You can't miss them.'

Mallund sprinted up the stairs and into the large open-plan space. Jennifer was sitting on a steel and plastic chair in front of a grey steel desk behind which a slim young man with closely cropped fair hair was earnestly trying to explain something to her. Frustration was written all over his face.

'I say again, madam, we are doing everything we can, but it is early days yet. She could be staying with a friend and didn't think to tell you. We need to explore the most likely explanations first. In the UK we get some three hundred and sixty thousand missing person reports a year. Only about two hundred thousand of them turn out to be confirmed missing person cases.'

'*Only!*' Jennifer's hackles were up, Mallund could tell. 'And what if my daughter is one of the two hundred thousand?' She saw Mallund approach and waved him over with an unsteady sweep of her arm. 'Jack! Thank God! Can you try to get through to this knucklehead that they need to get out and look for Alice? Get up a search party. She's been gone since teatime on Saturday and I'm at my wits' end. She's never done anything like this before. And this lame excuse for a detective is doing nothing. Nothing!' She reached forward and was on the point of slipping off her chair when Mallund grabbed her by the shoulders to steady her.

'Just calm down, Jenny, we'll get this sorted.'

'Calm down! Calm down! That's your solution to everything, isn't it? Can't you see? My daughter — *your* daughter — is in great danger. Anything could have happened to her. Oh my God, when I think . . . '

The detective gave a helpless shrug.

'You're Gordon, right?' said Mallund.

'DS Alan Gordon. I've been trying to explain to your wife — '

'Ex-wife.' Jennifer said bitterly.

'I've been trying to explain to your ex-wife that we have not been idle. There is a well-tried procedure in place and we have to work by eliminating every possibility. It will take some time, but be assured we are doing everything we can. It would be helpful if you could give us a list of friends and acquaintances whom Alice might have stayed with overnight. We've already checked the hospitals and there's nothing to worry about there. Same with the police stations.'

'The police stations? Why on earth — ?'

'She might have been arrested. It's a check I always like to make just in case. We'd look pretty stupid if we launched a dragnet for somebody we already had in custody. It's happened before. So, if you could give us the names of her friends it would help enormously.'

'Sorry.' Mallund scratched his chin. 'I don't know of any. I'm afraid we haven't been too close.'

'Well perhaps when the lady is feeling better you could get her to provide them. Can you make sure she gets home safely?'

'Certainly,' said Mallund, putting his arm round his ex-wife's shoulders, his face close enough to hers to register the long-forgotten scent of her favourite perfume, Poison, now mingled with the juniper aroma of gin. 'Come on, Jenny, let's get you home.'

Jennifer's aggression had subsided slightly but she still had a stubborn set to her mouth. 'I'm not moving till something gets done.' She wriggled and shook Mallund's arm from around her shoulders.

'It's better if you go home and let the officer get on with his inquiries. The longer you detain him the less time he has to find Alice, surely you can see that.'

Gordon was nodding agreement.

'He'll let us know the very second they learn something.'

The simple logic found its way through to Jennifer's troubled mind and unsteadily she got to her feet. Mallund led her out of the room and helped her down the stairs and into the car. On the drive home she sat in sullen silence, staring straight ahead.

'Come in if you want,' she said, as she struggled with the key in the lock. Mallund took the key and opened the door, led her to a sofa and sat her down. The place was in the same unkempt state as when he had last seen it.

'I'll make some coffee,' he said, and headed into the kitchen. He washed two mugs and made her coffee extra strong.

He sat opposite her on an upright dining chair. There were tears in her eyes.

'It's all my fault, Jack. My fault. All my fault.'

'You can't blame yourself, Jenny. We're both responsible for the way things have turned out. You've had a lot to cope with.'

'But I've been a bad mother. She's left home because of me, I'm sure of it. I should have cared less about myself and more about Alice. I should have kept a tighter rein on her. But I was too busy wallowing in my own misery to look after her. If she comes back home I'll change, that's a promise.'

'Not *if*,' said Mallund, '*when* she comes back home. You're blowing this up out of all proportion. Lots of teenagers go off the rails. As the detective said, she's probably stayed overnight with a friend. She'll likely come sheepishly walking through that door later today.'

But Alice never came through that door again, sheepishly or otherwise. And, as the police investigation wound down and despair began to eat away at the hearts of Mallund and Jennifer, the presumption that Alice was likely dead grew stronger by the day.

Then one Sunday just after evensong, Mallund's doorbell rang. He opened the door to find DS Gordon on the doorstep.

'I'm afraid I have some bad news for you, Mr Mallund.'

'It's Alice. You've found her? She's dead, is that it?'

'No, sir, I'm afraid it's about your ex-wife this time . . . '

★ ★ ★

Mallund could only guess at what horrors Jennifer must have suffered, grief and misery piling pressure upon pressure. God alone knew how he himself had been driven to the edge of reason by the nagging uncertainty, the hope that soared up only to be shot down again and again. And all the time wondering: *if only I'd been a better father could this nightmare have been prevented?*

Yes, who can say what depths of despair Jennifer had sunk to that pushed her into taking her own life. A bleak, lonely death, swallowing pill after pill in her bare bedroom. A slow death, one that keeps you waiting. Plenty of time to watch its progress, even from a state of semi-consciousness. No turning back now even if you wanted to.

Yes, Jennifer must have battled against some terrible demons for her to have surrendered so willingly.

23

Four days after he had freed the girls from the warehouse, Mallund was doling out food at the soup kitchen. After a while, he found, he didn't even notice the faces of the recipients; just kept doling a ladle of soup and handing it over without looking closely. He knew it was unforgivable; he should take a keen interest in every one of them, but the trouble with a repetitive job is that it dulls the senses.

'There you go, my friend.' A ladle of soup and a grunt in response.

'Hello, there you go.' A ladle of soup and a grunt in response.

'Hi there, some soup for you.' A ladle of soup and a cursory, 'Ta, mate.'

'Some soup? There you go. Enjoy.'

Then one night one of them spoke.

'Hello, Jack. Don't suppose there's any chance of a can of Special Brew to go with this?'

'Not in a — ' Mallund stopped short. He looked up. The face had changed little in the intervening years; still the same weasely, bedraggled look, just a bit more so. But the voice was deeper and less panicky.

'Spency!'

'Well, Jack, never thought I'd ever see you on the other side of the counter.'

'Never thought I'd ever see you at all, Spency. Where have you been? It's been what . . . three years?'

'Four . . . more, probably. Sorry I never said goodbye. Had to leave in a hurry.'

'Yeah, and you dropped me right in it with those two bruisers who were chasing you. So where have you been? What have you been up to?'

'Oh, around. Around. Getting myself straight . . . you know.' An involuntary twitch of the shoulder and right eye betrayed the fact that his rehab had not been entirely successful.

'For four years? C'mon, you must have done other things.'

'Business to attend to . . . you know.' Spency shrugged.

'Listen, I'll be finished here in half an hour. Do you know where Buddies is?' Spency nodded. 'I'll meet you there in half an hour. A lot has happened here while you've been away.'

'I can see that,' Spency said, pointing at Mallund's dog collar.

They sat talking over beakers of coffee at

Buddies. Mallund told Spency how his life had changed, and was in turn surprised by how subdued Spency was. He had matured somehow, lost the cheeky don't-give-a-damn persona that Mallund had both liked and hated in turn. He seemed sadder and more controlled. Yet he still would not talk about what exactly he had been up to for four years. Mallund was fascinated by the twilight world Spency inhabited.

'You know what you are, Spency? You're an enigma. You disappear and reappear like Gandalf in *The Lord of the Rings*.'

'The what?'

'*The Lord of the Rings*. It's a movie.'

'When did I ever go to see a movie?'

Mallund had to concede the point. Cinema-going was not exactly part of Spency's lifestyle.

'Anyway, Jack, enough about me. Look at you, eh? What gives with the God-bothering bit?'

'It just kind of happened. No one was more surprised than I was. I met Edward and one thing lead to another. Spency, it's the best thing that ever happened to me.'

'Yeah, I heard you were a bit of a hero.'

'Hero?'

'Saving old Roger from those toe-rags.'

'Oh, that.'

182

'You never told me you were in the SAS.'

'You never asked. Anyway, it's not the sort of thing you talk about.'

'I heard about your daughter. Tough, eh?'

'It's tough. You seem to know a lot of what's going on for someone who's invisible most of the time.'

'Yeah, I keep my eyes and ears open . . . This business about your daughter. Don't do anything stupid. These are real heavy people; believe me, I know.'

'Why should I do anything stupid? I'm sure these people have my daughter and I want her back. Simple as that. I'm going after them. And I'll stop at nothing to get her back.'

'You mean like that stunt you pulled the other night?'

'Stunt?'

'You know what I mean. A certain warehouse. Four disappearing girls?'

'How the hell do know about that? And, more important, how do you know it was me?'

'Like I said, I keep my eyes and ears open.'

'Listen, Spency, I know you're mixed up in something bigger than street level. I don't know what it is and I don't even want to know. All I want to know is — will you help me?'

'To commit suicide? Anyway, what makes you think I can help you? I'm just your friendly local junkie.'

Mallund leaned forward on his seat. 'I need a name. Remember the last time we saw each other? It was in the street. You spotted those two heavies and you took off like a bat out of hell. You were scared shitless.'

'Don and Mal,' said Spency, nodding his head. 'Two very nasty pieces of work.'

'Well, they were very interested in finding you. I told them I didn't even know your name. They roughed me up, blindfolded me and took me to this huge mansion in the country. There was this guy behind a big desk, looking like the lord of the manor, and he was very, very interested in finding you. Even tried to bribe me with fifty quid. But I played dumb — so you owe me one, Spency.'

'And you didn't get this guy's name?'

'No, but when Don and Mal were talking among themselves they said something about taking me to 'Mr D', if that means anything.'

'Donlan! Jesus, Jack, you met *Donlan* and lived to tell the tale?'

'So where does this Donlan character fit in?'

'Fit in? Hell, Jack, he is *numero uno*. Mr Big. If this was the Mafia he'd be *Il capo di tutti capi* — the Godfather. Patrick Edward

Donlan. Born Kilkenny, Ireland. Thought to have amassed a small fortune in the 1970s running drugs to fund the Provisional IRA in Belfast. Turned it into a big fortune on the mainland. Now he's international. Into everything: drugs, arms-running, prostitution, porn, people-trafficking, money-laundering — you name it. In bed with the Russian Mafia too. And he has a bamboozling maze of legitimate businesses to hide behind. As far as anybody knows he is a respectable business-man and financier with contacts in high places. He's untouchable, Jack. Please don't tell me this is the man you're going after.'

'Sounds like my man, Spency.'

'Heaven help you then.'

'I've got some contacts there too.' Mallund gave a wry smile.

'What about your SAS buddies? Surely they could help.'

'Too rough and tumble. This needs to be handled cleverly and low-key. They'd go in with all guns blazing and before we knew it we'd all be in gaol. In fact, I'm expecting one of them in half an hour. Porkhead Yates. He was my right-hand man in the regiment. He'll be having another crack at persuading me to let them help. It happens every now and again. The thing is, Spency, I have taken vows which I cannot break. *Thou shalt not kill.* I

185

am bound to act by that commandment. The Lord knows how much killing I did in the past. But no more. No more.'

'Then you don't stand a chance in that jungle, Jack. Killing means nothing to them. They'd think nothing of popping off a vicar if you got in their way. But Donlan, shit! You actually got to him, man! I've been trying to get to him for years. Fucking years!'

'You're after him too?' Mallund was puzzled. 'Why on earth would you want to get to him?'

'I have my own reasons. It's personal.' Spency was silent for a few moments, as if trying to make a major decision. He leaned forward. 'Listen, Jack, I have an idea. If you're determined to continue with this crazy suicide trip, what if we pool our resources? I have a lot of contacts and information that could be useful to you. I've found out a lot about Donlan's business dealings. Sometimes I know in advance when he has a major caper going. He might be immune from the law, but there are some people who would like to see the back of him. Rivals. Rivals who are grateful for any titbit of info about his dealings. I've been walking a tightrope playing one against the other. That's why I have to disappear sharpish from time to time. I can feed you information about his operations. Big stuff. Stuff that will make your caper at the warehouse the other night look like a walk in the park. What do you say, Jack? If it's Donlan you're after, you can count me in.'

Mallund thought for a good five minutes. Then he spat on his hand and offered it to Spency. They shook. A done deal. 'Spency, I think this could be the beginning of a beautiful friendship.'

From the corner of his eye Mallund spotted the mobile bulk of Porkhead Yates taking up the doorway. 'Here's Porkhead now. Only don't you call him Porkhead whatever you do.'

'I'll get off-side.' Spency rose to go.

'No, don't get up. I'd like you to meet him.'

Mallund greeted Porkhead with a hug and a slap on the back.

'Spency, say hello to Ben Yates, my best mate. Ben, this is Spency, a friend.'

Porkhead and Spency eyed each other with mutual suspicion. After ten minutes of small talk, at which none of the three was any good, Mallund pulled his chair back and crossed his legs.

'OK. Relax, both of you,' he said. 'We can talk in front of Spency, Ben. He knows what I'm doing.'

'You shouldn't be telling anybody about

that, Jack. Need to know basis. Every person who knows about it is a security risk.' Porkhead was still glowering at Spency, measuring him up and down with his eyes.

'In fact, Ben, Spency and I have decided to pool resources. He has inside intelligence that will be invaluable.'

Porkhead was shaking his head in disbelief. 'So apart from you, me and this character, and Uncle Tom Cobley and all, who else knows about it?'

'Only Ros Forster.'

'Where does she fit in?'

'She's a social worker.'

'A fucking social worker? This pantomime gets better by the minute. Have you taken leave of your senses, Jack? I seriously think you're losing your marbles. You turn down professional help from your mates and instead put your life in the hands of a couple of dreamers. Get real, Jack, this is the big, bad world. Your team is about as effective as a wooden popgun on the Gaza Strip.'

'That's unfair, Ben,' said Mallund. 'Spency has some real good stuff. He's got the dirt on the people I'm after. And Ros has already proved herself. She knows the grooming and trafficking of girls. But for her I would never have been able to identify the target on a mission I accomplished the other night. She even drove the getaway vehicle.'

'Still, I don't like it, Jack. Not one bit.' Porkhead rose to his feet. 'I can see I'm not going to get anywhere here, so I'll say goodnight. Think it over, Jack, and when you come to your senses, just remember the offer is still open.' He made his way to the door in high dudgeon. Spency stood up to follow him.

'I'll have a word with him, Jack. Try to calm him down.'

'No, that could do more harm than good, the mood he's in.'

But Spency was already halfway to the door. Mallund shrugged. 'Best of luck, then,' he muttered. Through the window he could see Spency catch up with Porkhead, who kept on walking, ignoring Spency. Then he stopped and the two men stood talking for a few minutes. Porkhead nodded a few times, then walked on.

'I think I calmed him down a bit,' said Spency when he returned. 'Don't like to see you and your best mate falling out over me.'

'Oh, we'd never fall out,' said Mallund.

24

'So we've had one successful operation,' said Mallund, as he met with Ros and Spency in their church hall HQ. 'Getting those girls out of the warehouse was a fluke. I took a lot of chances with very little intelligence. Luckily, it paid off. But we can't always trust to luck. We need quality intelligence if we are to guarantee a high percentage chance of success. And above all to make sure we don't get caught. That's where you come in, Spency. You say you have a contact inside Donlan's organization. We need details of his operations in advance — dates, times, locations. Get to work on it. You, too, Ros: you know these girls on the streets. They're sure to hear things. Every scrap of information, no matter how insignificant, counts. Remember, the aim is to harass and worry Donlan. Hit and run. Hit his profits. Hit his reputation among his bosses further up the line. Embarrass him with failures in front of his competitors. High-profile attacks that will get in the media — that's what he fears most. I want him to want to deal with me. I want the enemy to come to *me*. I know it's a tall order, and it's dangerous, and it doesn't have a snowball in hell's chance of success, so if either of you wants out now, that's OK. Just say the word.' Mallund looked at each in turn.

'I'm in,' said Spency, no hesitation.

'I'm probably going to regret this, but count me in, too,' said Ros.

'Right. So where do we go from here?'

'There's something big coming off soon,' said Spency. 'Don't know what, when or where, but according to my source Donlan's been really hyped up over it. Can't stop smiling, which is just not like him. It's going to be a feather in his cap if he pulls it off. He's playing it real cool. Not even his most trusted colleagues have been told anything yet.'

Mallund had been taking notes, and held up his hand. 'Any idea when he might tell them, Spency?'

'A job as important as this?' Spency sucked in his cheeks. 'He'll likely brief them at the monthly meeting, which takes place religiously on the first Wednesday in the month at his home. I've spied on the parade of Rolls-Royces, Bentleys and Ferraris arriving at his pad. They have the meeting at precisely nine o'clock in the morning, then have lunch.'

'I'd love to be a fly on the wall at that meeting,' said Mallund.

'Forget about that, Jack. There's no way you could get near him. The house is dripping with security systems, and if you get past them there's a couple of bloody great Rottweilers to deal with.'

'So there's no way we could plant a bug in the room?'

Spency shook his head, eyes closed. Final, no more to be said.

Ros had been taking notes, and looked up from her writing pad. 'Talking of bugs — maybe we could hack his phone? You know, like those guys at the *News of the World*?'

Spency shrugged. 'Not my field. Wouldn't know where to start.'

Mallund sighed. 'Me neither. Anyway, I thought they had now made that too difficult with encryption devices.'

They sat in an awkward silence.

'What we need is an expert in IT who can get round the encryption,' Ros said at last.

'Brilliant, Ros!' said Spency. 'Absolutely fucking brilliant. And how do you propose to find one? Put an advert in *Spy News* saying 'Expert hacker wanted to break into mobster's phone'? This is a highly illegal business.'

'It was just a thought,' said Ros, glaring at

him. 'At least I came up with *something*, which is more than you did.'

Spency spread his hands, appealing to Mallund for support.

But Mallund waved him down. 'No, Spency, she might have something here . . . I think I have an idea . . . '

'Oh dear,' said Ros.

★ ★ ★

'Ah, there you are, Robin.' Mallund edged his way through the half shut door to the large broom cupboard at Buddies that served as a tinkering room for Robin Makepeace Thackeray. 'Time for a chat? We've never really had a good talk, have we? Always too busy to catch up with each other.'

Robin was soldering a terminal on to an ancient computer monitor that took up half his bench with its bulbous glass screen and cumbersome casing.

'Don't see much of these around these days,' said Mallund, nodding towards the monitor. 'It's super-slim plasma and all that now.'

'Yes, it's a real museum piece,' said Robin, blowing on his soldering iron. 'But I like that. Can't be doing with the modern stuff. This came in as one of the charity cases. It's knackered, but I can easily get it working again. Might be of use to the senior citizens.'

'Robin, what say we take a break and have a coffee?'

'Coffee?' Robin was bemused.

'Yes, coffee — a strong dark-brown powder you pour water into and drink.'

'I meant . . . why?'

'No 'why' — just thought, you know, we ought to get to know each other better.'

'Why?'

'No particular reason, it's just one of the social things people do.'

'Oh.'

'Like, talk a bit. Chew the fat.'

'Fat?'

'Robin, you really should get out a bit, mix with people.'

'I'm not very good at that . . . people.'

'Now's a good time to start. C'mon, let's have that coffee.' Mallund took Robin by the elbow and led him to the counter. He ordered the coffees and found a quiet corner. There were few people in Buddies, it being mid-morning, so Mallund knew they could talk in private.

'You know, Robin, something I've always been meaning to ask you. How did you get your middle name, 'Makepeace'?'

'That was my dad. His favourite novelist

was William Makepeace Thackeray. He wanted to call me William, too, but Mum put her foot down and insisted on Robin. I think I would have liked William better.'

'That explains it. And how are you enjoying your time here at Buddies?'

'It's good.'

'You've been a great help with the computers. I for one wouldn't know where to start.'

'It's kid's stuff, really.'

'But you used to do some big-time stuff, I hear. You were a bit of a whiz kid. Is that right?'

'I don't do that anymore.'

'Why's that?'

'In case.'

'In case what, Robin?'

'Nothing.'

'In case what, Robin?'

'In case I get sick.'

Mallund already knew of the bizarre affliction that had struck Robin four years earlier and driven him to the edge of madness. He had spoken at great length to Dr Jacob Wright, the psychiatrist who had put Robin on the slow road to recovery. Doctor Wright was an intense man with worried eyebrows and a voice laden with doom. A Scotsman, from somewhere in the Western

Isles that Mallund had never heard of, he now had consulting rooms in Harley Street. He was expensive, with a list of private clients that read like a *Who's Who* of celebrity. A list that any tabloid hack would give his eye teeth for. But he took Robin on as a *pro bono* case because he was deeply interested in the lad's symptoms. Mallund had contacted Dr Wright after Robin wandered into Buddies out of the blue one day looking lost and fragile.

'Basically, you might call it an extraordinary case of Obsessive-Compulsive Disorder,' the doctor had told Mallund. 'Robin became so obsessed with chasing a goal he had of perfecting some esoteric computer algorithm that it literally took over his life. He wasn't eating or sleeping. Chasing this goal was the only thing that mattered to him. It was something to do with prime numbers, but it has left him with a deep-seated fear of them. 'Arithmophobia' is its Sunday name. So much as the mere sight of a long string of numbers can cause him to break out in a sweat and trembling. He is disturbed by anything hi-tech — remarkable since he once had a high-flying job in IT. We've done all we can, and he's made good progress towards full recovery. All he needs now is understanding and gentle handling. Just an environment where he can take things easily. Give him simple tasks to do, and avoid anything hi-tech for the moment. He'll eventually come around.'

Now, sitting opposite Robin, Mallund was studying him closely. He had come a long way from the twitching wreck who had walked through the door of Buddies. Still nervy and unsure of himself, he had nevertheless gained a degree of confidence and was comfortable with low-level programming. *How far can I push him?* wondered Mallund. *Go in too heavy-handed and I could set him back to zero.* He decided he needed to gain the lad's confidence above all. And to do that he needed to be up front and honest.

'Robin, can you keep a secret?'

'A secret?'

'What I'm going to tell you now must go no further.'

'I don't know . . . '

'Robin, this is a matter of life and death and I would like you to hear me through. OK?'

'OK.'

Mallund told him the complete story of Alice, leaving out nothing, right up to the need to hack into Donlan's phone and emails.

'So I need your help, Robin. Simple as that.'

'But it's against the law.' Robin shifted uneasily in his seat.

'So's stealing girls and using them as sex slaves.'

'I'm sorry, Jack, but I don't do high level stuff anymore. It's bad for me. All those numbers . . . ' Robin shivered.

'Robin, the biggest number you'll have to deal with is a phone number. I promise I'll keep a close eye on you. Even the slightest sign of you getting 'sick' and we quit. That's my promise. And I always keep my promises.'

'All right, I'll try. What do I have to do?'

'Robin, you're a star!'

★ ★ ★

There were times when the events in the African jungle all those years ago came back to haunt Mallund. He did his best to blank them out of his mind, but they came bursting through his defences like a torrent through a breached dam. It was at times like this, sitting in his armchair in the front room of his vicarage, the evening light drawing fresh patterns on the flowery wallpaper, thinking about things, just things, that his mind was drawn back to the horrific scenes in that remote village. He still felt justified in blindly gunning down the marauding government troops. It was his first crisis of conscience and he would stand over it till the day he died. He now bore no grudge against the regiment for his dismissal; time had healed that wound and, on the whole, his life had turned out all the better for it. He was glad his three mates had not been tainted by his rash actions and had served out their time. Did they miss him? He often wondered if they did: he missed them. They had been together through thick and thin, the four of them, the ideal four-man patrol.

The four-man patrol. It was conceived in 1940 by a young commando lieutenant, David Stirling, serving in North Africa, and has proved to this day the most efficient small reconnaissance unit. Stirling was wedded to the idea of a small, efficient team operating behind enemy lines. He managed to convince his superiors, and his plan went up the ranks, finally reaching the desk of General Auchinleck, Commander-in-Chief of the Middle East. And so the SAS was born. Stirling launched the four-man patrol, arguing that four is small enough to avoid detection, yet large enough to carry sufficient supplies and to provide a formidable firepower when needed. It is the smallest tenable patrol unit possible since it allows for a wounded member to be carried by two others whilst being covered by the fourth. Each is assigned an arc of fire to cover, providing all-round protection for the entire patrol. The last man — 'Tailend Charlie' — is usually armed with a small belt-fed machine gun to put down a hail of covering fire if the patrol is bumped from the rear. Each man is a specialist in one of a set of skills, ranging from signals, sniping, medical, explosives and demolition, guiding aircraft to targets, languages. They are knitted together like a spider's web, interchangeable, each with a good knowledge of the other's specialty, so that if one goes down another takes over his role in addition to his own.

Altogether a lean, mean, efficient fighting machine.

Mallund dismissed all thoughts of the village from his mind as the last rays of the sun dipped below the horizon and darkness usurped his living room. Lying in bed later, he took stock of the situation.

So what have we got?

A peace-loving vicar vowed not to kill.

An on/off junkie.

A woman social worker.

A computer nerd afraid of his own shadow.

Welcome to my four-man patrol.

Lord help us!

25

'First of all, we need Donlan's mobile phone number,' said Robin; casually, as if it were the easiest thing in the world.

'Don't look at me,' said Spency, folding his arms.

'I'm sorry, but without it I can't do anything.' Robin glanced at Mallund, seated opposite him.

Mallund turned to Spency. 'What about your special contact? Any chance he could get it?'

'No way, man,' said Spency. 'He's good, but he's not *that* good. I'd be pushing too far even by just asking him to get the number.'

'So we're stymied.' Mallund could feel his confidence swiftly draining away. 'Just see what you can do, Spency. It's vital that we get that number.'

★　★　★

Spency swept into the room with a smug smile creasing his face. Mallund, Robin and Ros sat watching in silence.

'Who's the genius of the month?' he

announced, waving a tiny piece of paper over his head. 'Who's the cat that got the cream?' He waved the paper under Robin's nose. 'Who's Mr Mission Impossible?' He waltzed round and round the room with the piece of paper held out in his outstretched hands.

'OK, Spency, we believe you,' sighed Mallund. 'What's on the piece of paper then?'

'Only . . . ' — Spency went down on one knee and pompously offered the paper to Mallund — 'only the personal mobile phone number of one Patrick Edward Donlan, gangster of this parish.'

'I don't believe it!' Mallund was on his feet. 'Spency, you're a genius! How on earth did you manage it?'

'Don't ask, Jack. Don't ask. Just let's say I'm now mortgaged up to the hilt with favours for the rest of my life.'

Mallund glanced at the paper. 'Over to you now,' he said, passing it to Robin.

Robin unravelled the paper and read the number. Mallund watched him closely for any signs of trauma or unease. Nothing. Quite calm. Good. If anything, Mallund reckoned, the lad was actually enjoying all this intrigue, and his voice was more assertive as he spoke. 'I've got everything in place, the software and all, but I still need to get Donlan to call or send a text message to my control phone.'

'Why all this rigmarole?' said Spency. 'Lots of guys have hacked phones in the past without all this palaver. Why can't you, Mr Whiz Kid?'

Robin spoke slowly, as if explaining to a child. 'There's so many new encryption defences nowadays and Donlan's sure to have a very sophisticated handset with up-to-the-minute protection. Besides, I want to do things other than just hack his calls.'

'Like what?'

'Well, you mentioned this big important meeting he has every month? If he has his phone switched on at the meeting I can get it to activate its loudspeaker. No one at the meeting will hear it, but we will.'

'Amazing!' said Ros. 'Just like having our own bug planted in the room.'

'Exactly. I can also get it to send us his SMS messages and emails.'

'Brilliant!' said Spency.

'And so long as his mobile is switched on we can track his movements with it, find out where he is day or night.'

'Just like MI5 on the telly,' said Ros. 'This gets better and better.'

'Robin, you are a star!' said Mallund, clapping him on the back. Robin smiled wanly, the first time Mallund had seen him smile.

26

The day of Donlan's meeting arrived. Robin was bent over the mobile phone that would be used for the hacking.

'I've managed to install my spyware in Donlan's phone,' he said. 'Normally we would have had to trick him into either calling my phone, sending me a text message or downloading a booby-trapped website in order to activate it. However, we couldn't find a way of tricking him without making him suspicious. But with Spency's help I've managed to get in through Donlan's Bluetooth — that's the short range wireless connection that works within a few metres of the phone — to activate the spyware.'

'Sounds very, very complicated,' said Mallund.

'It is, believe me it is. I can't think of anybody else who could have done it.' Robin allowed himself a modest smile.

'Yes, but does it work?' said Spency.

'We'll know in a minute,' said Robin.

Robin entered a message:

This is your master.

'I thought I'd give it a human touch for

your benefit,' said Robin.

I am ready to serve, came the reply from Donlan's phone.

'So we're up and running,' said Robin. 'Donlan's phone is now under our command. We can do anything he can do — make calls, send and read texts, read voicemails . . . anything. It all runs on a hidden programme inside his phone which leaves no traces. He won't even know we have been there. We can now turn on the loudspeaker on his phone. He won't be able to hear it, but we will. Listen.' He tapped at the keypad.

Monitor now 1

The voice that boomed over the speaker on Robin's phone was loud and angry:

' . . . I don't give a shit what McCallum wants. It's what *I* want that matters. Get back to him and tell him we do it my way or not at all. I'm not having that nutter putting the whole operation at risk.'

'It's him! That's Donlan, no mistake.' Even after many years Mallund had no difficulty recognizing the voice.

They listened in on the meeting which consisted of day-to-day business, facts and figures, revenues which were mind-blowing in their size. Nothing of much use to Mallund and his crew until, right at the end . . .

'Right then.' Donlan's voice again. 'About

the shipment. Where are we up to?'

'It arrives on Tuesday.' An unidentified voice. 'The boat's called the *Black Swan*. She'll be anchored off the coast near Torquay for three days. Then we unload her at night.'

'Three days?' Donlan sounded worried. 'That's pushing it a bit, Mike. The longer she sits there the greater the risk she'll be discovered. And Torquay? Christ! You couldn't have picked a busier place! I don't like it.'

'We need three days to make sure it's safe to land the merchandise.' The other voice was firm and confident. It was the voice of Mike Handley, Donlan's second in command. 'We need to check there's been no breaches of security, no police activity. Make sure the distribution is up and running. We chose the location because it's busy with boats. After all, where's the best place to hide a tree? — in a forest, of course. *Black Swan* will look like just one pleasure yacht among dozens. As you say, we can't take chances with this one.'

'This is the biggest single shipment we've ever made.' Donlan's voice still had a worried edge to it. 'I was against it from the start. Much better to make two or three smaller shipments. Hedge your bets. But I got overruled by those bastards across the pond. We stand to lose millions if the shipment gets rumbled. Not to mention incurring the wrath of the Colombians. Just make sure the boat's secure. If this goes wrong heads will roll. And be assured mine will not be among them. Anything else? Right, lunch, everyone.'

Mallund had been taking notes of the conversation. He looked up from his notepad and said, 'That's the one. We go for the drugs shipment.'

27

At first it manifested itself as a vague feeling of unease. A sense that all was not well. You couldn't get a grip on it, but it is there, gnawing away at the back of your brain. Call it instinct. Call it paranoia. Call it what you will, but Mallund had a gut feeling that he was being followed as he wound his way through the streets around Torquay, sussing out the lie of the land for his mission. He tried all the techniques involving doubling back and round and round but none revealed a shadow.

You're getting twitchy, Mallund, he told himself. *Concentrate on the mission.*

From his chosen observation point on a rocky outcrop, Mallund surveyed the *Black Swan* through his night vision binoculars. He had spent two days watching the vessel. About fifty-feet long, quite old, thirty to forty years, steel hull, twin diesel engines, probably quite stunning in her day; but in close up through his lenses quite rough round the edges, betraying her age, which even her fresh coat of white and blue paint could not disguise. She would likely have been a rich man's plaything once. A large comfortable salon, a state room and a small cabin aft, a four-bunk crew's quarters in the bow. The salon would likely convert to additional sleeping quarters. She would certainly have seen some jolly times. Now, she was reduced to hauling Class A drugs around the world.

More importantly, Mallund's interest was focused on the two men aboard who were guarding the vessel, looking for chinks in their armour, any lapses in security. He quickly established that they were nothing more than jobbing criminals. No discipline. Lazy and careless. Sooner or later he would find a fatal flaw. He did not have to wait long. On the very first night, one of them lowered himself into one of the two tenders, yanked the outboard motor into life and headed shorewards. He drove the tender up on to the beach, secured it, and walked straight into the nearest pub. He returned two hours later, unsteady on his feet, almost fell into the tender, and set an erratic course for the *Black Swan*. His mate secured the tender and helped him aboard. Both were laughing heartily. The following night it was the second man's turn for this bit of unofficial shore leave. He spent nearly four hours in the pub.

'Good,' Mallund muttered to himself. 'Only one to deal with.'

The harbour was reasonably well lit, and the *Black Swan*'s own lights cast a wide pool of light around her where she was anchored some 500 metres out in the bay. Any boat approaching her would be seen from a comfortable distance. So, once more, Mallund had to enlist the aid of his SAS training. He found a dark corner behind a screen of rocks and unpacked his Bergen. He struggled into his black wetsuit, re-checked his air tank level, ensured all connections were sound, and slipped on his wetted face mask, then launched himself into the dark water. He had already established which way the currents were running by noting the position of the yachts relative to their anchor chains, a tip he picked up during scuba training, so he calculated to surface just aft of the *Black Swan*. He had seen the one remaining guard sitting smoking a cigarette on the bow. He was able to cover about 150 metres on the surface without fear of being seen, then submerged to a depth of three metres. With his flippers, he was able to cover the remaining distance rapidly, and soon his head broke the surface almost within an arm's length of the stern. He hooked his left arm around the anchor chain to stabilize himself while he undid the low-charge plastic limpet mine clipped to his belt. The mine had cost him dearly in favours. He had not asked where his contacts had procured it from — better not to know. He had been assured it contained just enough shaped charge to blow a neat hole in the hull. He set it for fifteen minutes — enough time, he reckoned, for the guard and himself to get safely free of the vessel before the explosion. He submerged and groped his way along the underside of the hull until he located a spot beneath the engine compartment, then fixed the mine to the steel hull with its magnetic contact. He swam back to the stern and hoisted himself aboard. He could see the guard sitting on the bow, beside him a radio playing a dismal Morrissey number. Mallund had spent hours agonizing over how to get the guard off the boat. *Thou shalt not kill* — the commandment ever present in his planning — was as always the limiting factor. So it would come down to a physical tussle which, hopefully Mallund would win. He had weighed the man up through his powerful field-glasses. Big, but out of shape. He would be slower than Mallund, and not as skilled. Mallund's chances were good, but a physical struggle was always unpredictable; too many buggeration factors waiting to gum up the works.

Perhaps there was an easier way. Mallund strode boldly up to the guard.

'Good evening, mate,' he said. 'Just thought I'd let you know I've planted a bomb on this boat. You've got sixty seconds to get off. Goodbye.'

Any normal bully-boy criminal coward would have jumped at the chance to save his skin. But not this one. He stood up and glared at Mallund.

'Fuck you!' he said.

Damn, thought Mallund. *Trust me to get the conversationalist.*

'Fuck you!' repeated the man, squaring up to Mallund.

Mallund's little ploy had failed, mainly owing to the guard's lack of intelligence and imagination. As a result, Mallund had now lost the element of surprise, and now the odds were tilting in favour of his opponent.

Especially since the man had a knife in his hand and was advancing with steady, menacing steps.

In his former life, Mallund could easily have taken the man down by going on the attack. He was trained to kill with his bare hands, but Mallund did not have the luxury of using these techniques. He needed to be on the defensive — a huge handicap since the essential mindset in unarmed combat is that you must be one hundred per cent confident you are going to win. The SAS five second knockout, a combination of split second seamless moves involving blocking, attacks to the eyes and groin using the palm of the hand, elbow and knee, would quickly disable the guard and leave him alive. But first there was the matter of the knife, with which his attacker was now readying to strike. Mallund had a mere second to determine from the man's body movements whether he intended to strike from above, into the chest, or from below, into the abdomen. This is the tricky bit. Knife attacks are usually erratic and unpredictable. *Yes, he's going for the chest, right-handed*, Mallund concluded. He stepped forward into the advancing man's space, eyes firmly trained on the hand with the knife, raised and ready to strike. At the same time he formed his hands into a V-shaped cup with both thumbs open and overlapping, making a cradle that would fit the attacker's wrist as it came down for the kill. He used the cradle to block the blow and tightly grabbed the wrist, twisting his own body sharply to the right. The guard's own weight and momentum did the rest as Mallund forced the arm down to knee level, throwing him off balance. From this position Mallund was able to drive his elbow into the man's face, causing him to drop the knife. He manoeuvred the guard to the side of the boat.

'What part of 'bomb on board' don't you understand?' he yelled in the man's ear, as he tipped him overboard. 'Now swim for the tender and get out of here fast!' He swiftly headed along the boat to retrieve his flippers and air tank, but could hear the man coughing and spluttering in the water. He stopped and saw him floundering about five metres from the tender. He stopped.

'Help! I can't swim!' the guard's voice was on the edge of terror.

Mallund checked his watch. The tussle with the guard had taken up too much time. His bomb would detonate in four minutes.

Thou shalt not kill.

There was nothing else for it. Mallund abandoned his gear and dived over the side. His leg snagged on a jagged steel stanchion and he felt a searing pain as it ripped a gash in his right thigh. He rolled on to his back and took the guard in a life-saving grip and swam with him to the tender. It took a superhuman effort to haul the dead weight on to the little boat. Mallund pulled the cord to start the outboard motor. Nothing. He yanked harder, the motor spluttered twice and then died. He yanked again. And again. And again. In his over-enthusiastic pulling at the cord he had flooded the engine with fuel. There was no way it was going to start now. Mallund could not even spare the time to check his watch. The bomb would go off anytime now. He grabbed the oars and fitted them on the gunwales and heaved for all he was worth. Five metres . . . ten metres . . . the little boat was gradually putting distance between itself and the *Black Swan*. Any second now. Mallund ducked down into the well of the boat and waited. The blast lit up the sky. The tender shuddered under the shock wave and Mallund could hear chunks of debris whizzing overhead. He raised himself up and saw the *Black Swan*, a gap blown away in her midships. So much for the little shaped charge. A neat hole? You could have driven a Mini through it. She would slowly break up and begin to sink. He checked the guard, still semi-conscious in the bottom of the boat. He started rowing for the shore, but had not travelled far before he felt an odd sensation. The inflatable boat was wobbling beneath him. When he tried to stand up it felt like he was on a bouncy castle. The rubber had been punctured by flying debris from the blast and the craft was losing air fast. Mallund judged the distance to the shore. About 400 metres, he reckoned. Even without his flippers, abandoned on the *Black*

Swan, he could swim the distance. But what about the guard in the well of the boat, which was now beginning to fill with water? Could he make it to the shore with such a dead weight? Mallund rowed for all he was worth, trying to gain precious metres before the tender went under. He would need every iota of advantage if he was to save the man. Now, the boat had collapsed completely and both Mallund and his passenger were in the water.

'Don't leave me. Please don't leave me!' The guard's eyes were desperate, pleading.

'Unfortunately, I have no option,' said Mallund between gritted teeth. He rolled on to his back and took the guard under the chin, holding him just above the water, which luckily was fairly calm between tides. The gash in his leg was throbbing wildly and he guessed he must be losing blood fast.

'Just try to relax,' he told the terrified man. 'No matter what happens don't struggle, or you'll take us both down.'

They made slow progress, and even after just fifty metres Mallund was feeling the strain of dragging the burly, fully-clothed guard along. How he wished he had not left his flippers back on board the *Black Swan*. Stroke by painful stroke he inched towards the shore, his every muscle aching. He closed his eyes, trying to imagine the pain away.

From time to time he twisted his neck round to check the distance to the shore, which perversely seemed not to be getting any closer. Every few minutes he felt his grip on the man loosening as his arm lapsed into numbness, causing the dead weight to thrash around in panic. He pushed on and on, his breathing becoming more laboured with every metre. The blood loss was beginning to make itself felt. He began to worry about dropping out of consciousness through lack of oxygen to the brain. He knew he was slowing down dangerously, and his thinking was becoming woozy. But all those punishing exercises, the back-breaking mountain hikes, the long distance runs with a fully-loaded pack, the sudden drops into freezing water, the parched desert hikes — surely they had to count for something? They had to. They just had —

A sudden painful jab in his back jerked him alert. Who was it? What was it? He could not understand. He let go of the guard and twisted round. His face scraped against a rough, black, solid surface. Rock. His hand felt a softer surface just below it. Sand. They had reached the beach.

Mallund lay flopped on the sand, gasping for breath. After a few minutes he sat up and suddenly remembered the guard. He was nowhere to be seen. Was he still in the water, perhaps drowned? He was just dragging himself to his feet when a sharp blow to the back of his neck knocked him down again. He turned around and saw the guard above him, holding a heavy rock on high. Mallund rolled round as the rock came down and crashed into the sand a foot from where his head had been. He got to his feet again and faced the man.

'Don't you ever give up?' Mallund gasped, as the guard advanced on him. But his advance was slow; staggering. It was clear to Mallund that his adversary was in no better shape than he was. They locked together in a drunken embrace, waltzing slowly round and round, holding each other up. Then they separated and the guard took a wide swipe at Mallund. Mallund blocked it then fell down. The guard staggered forward and fell over him. Both were now on the ground.

'For God's sake, man — I saved your life!' said Mallund, breathless.

'Fuck you!' said the guard.

Mallund rolled over and straddled him, pinning him down by the throat. 'I'm going now. You'll do the same if you've any sense. And I want you to take a message to your bosses, especially that rat Donlan.'

'Fuck you!'

'Listen!' Mallund shook him by the throat. 'Tell him I want my daughter back. And I'll keep after him until I get her. You got that?'

'Fuck . . . ' The guard gasped as Mallund tightened his grip on the throat.

'Just tell him!'

Mallund gave the throat a final squeeze, got up and half-ran, half staggered into the darkness.

28

The media had a field day with the story.

The Daily Telegraph gave it their page one lead:

MYSTERY OF HUGE DRUGS HAUL FOUND ON SOUTH COAST HOLIDAY BEACHES

The Sun took a more oblique angle on the story:

Holidaymakers were guaranteed a high old time as a massive cache of Class A drugs came floating on to their beaches yesterday.

Sun worshippers at genteel Torquay were stunned as millions of pounds worth of heroin, crack cocaine, cannabis and pills came floating in on the surf as they dipped their toes in the water.

Police were baffled, but were linking it to an explosion on board a yacht in the bay which later sank. A spokesman would neither confirm nor deny that the explosion could be the result of a battle between drugs gangs . . .

Mallund smiled with satisfaction as he read the headlines and watched the news on television.

'That should shake them up a bit,' he muttered, and took a satisfying sip of his cocoa.

★ ★ ★

Donlan was furious, kicking antique chairs across the room in his rage. 'You're sure he mentioned me by name?'

'Yes, Boss,' said the guard.

'Me? Personally?'

'He said you especially.'

'Who the fuck is this joker? Had you ever seen him before?'

'No, Boss.'

'But you'd recognize him if you saw him again, right?'

'Oh yes, Boss. No doubt about that.'

'Then you can thank your lucky stars. After that massive fuck up with the boat I would have had no further need for you — if you take my drift. I would have cut off your balls and hung you out to dry.' He glared at the guard in a way that left no doubt that he really meant it. 'Instead, from now on you'll be working directly with me. We're going to find this shit. Now get out!'

When the guard had left the room Donlan turned to the only other occupant, Mike Handley, his second in command.

'What's this guy got against me, Mike?'

'We have lots of enemies, Pat.'

'This is different. This isn't the usual grief we expect from our competitors. And our friends for that matter. This is personal. After that business with the girls at the warehouse I put it down to some nutter with a grievance. It was small time, way down the line, a handful of girls. But this is major. He knew all about the operation. This is no ordinary bozo. And what's all this shit about his daughter? It doesn't make sense.'

'Maybe she's one of the girls we've got working.'

'How do we know who *she* is when we don't even know who *he* is?'

'Would you hand her back if we found her? Get him off our back?'

'Hell, no. I want him! The bastard has cost me dear and made me look stupid. Nobody does that to Pat Donlan.'

'There's the other thing to consider, Pat. This means we've got a big leak in our security.'

'I haven't forgotten that. We've got a grass somewhere. I'm going to find that bastard too. And when I do . . . '

29

Robin was almost speechless with excitement as he tugged at Mallund's sleeve.

'Jack, you need to hear this.' He held up a digital voice recorder.

'Let's go through the back,' said Mallund, ushering him through to the campaign room.

'I've been monitoring Donlan's phone and guess what I picked up? Listen.'

Robin started the machine and Donlan's voice came over the speaker, talking with Mike Handley.

'So how many have we got?'

'Twenty-six illegals altogether, Pat. Mostly fit young girls who think they've got shiny new passports and respectable jobs in Britain.'

'Don't worry,' Donlan chuckled. 'We've got work for them all right. And you're sure they can get the container into the country no problem?'

'No probs, Pat. We've greased a few palms. The container will come through Customs and border control at Harwich. The driver will park up at the assembly point just outside the port and wait for our man to take over.

The driver speaks little English, so he'd be useless if stopped by police. Better to have a Brit at the wheel on UK roads. The password is 'Have you seen the BBC weather forecast?' He will reply, 'It looks like being good tomorrow'. When he gets the password the driver will uncouple the container trailer. Our own tractor unit will take over the trailer. It's on British plates, so it won't stand out. Right. Here's all the details you need to know. The container number is 241, the . . . '

Mallund listened with increasing interest as the entire plan to import the trafficked women unfolded, marvelling at the attention to detail and ingenuity of the criminals. He immediately began forming a plan of his own. First, a phone call to an old pal.

*   *   *

Tony Small was surprised when he answered the phone to Jack Mallund's voice.

'Well, well, well, Jack Mallund, as I live and breathe.' Small's voice, small as his name, was still the hoarse rasp that Mallund remembered from their years in the SAS.

'How are you, Tony? A long time, eh? Seems like only yesterday we were racing through that blazing Kuwaiti oil field in a stolen artic with half of Saddam's army chasing us. You scared the living daylights out of me. But your mad driving got us through in the end.'

Small chuckled at the memory. 'It wasn't the ideal getaway vehicle, but it was the only thing going when we hijacked it. Thirty tons of turbo-charged diesel going like a bat out of hell. Even the armoured vehicles were getting out of the way sharpish.'

'And the load we were carrying — how about that!'

Both men guffawed at the memory.

'Twenty-thousand toilet rolls! They might have been needed, because we scared the shit out of half of Saddam's crack troops.'

'Changed days, eh?'

'Changed days.'

A silence while both men drank in the memory, each reluctant to let go of this remnant of their adrenaline-charged existence.

'So what do I call you nowadays, now that you've gone all respectable?'

'Jack will do. As usual. So, Tony, how's the haulage business?'

'Oh, you know . . . tough. Too much competition. Cut-throat prices, crippling legislation, red tape. But you don't want to listen to my moaning, do you?'

'I always figured that our mad charge

through the desert gave you a taste for big trucks. Only natural you would go into the business when you left the regiment.'

'Big boys' toys.'

'That's it. Listen, Tony, I need a big favour from you.'

'Thought it might be something like that.'

'I want you to teach me how to drive an artic.'

★ ★ ★

They were approaching an uphill stretch on the M6 motorway. A mere flea bite for the Jaguars and Mercedes flashing past them; but for the huge, heavily loaded articulated lorry it might as well have been Annapurna.

'Get right down the gears well in advance,' said Tony. 'You've got lots of power here, but we will struggle on this hill. Keep the revs up no matter what. Don't let your speed drain off — you'll never get it back and it will drop further away. Keep pushing.'

The mighty diesel whined as Mallund revved it. Cars were speeding past as the thirty-eight tons of tractor and container laboured to the crest of the incline, then slowly regained its pace on the level.

'Well done, mate. You're a quick learner,' said Small.

'Had a good teacher,' said Mallund, grinning.

The day had begun with instructions vital to Mallund's plan — how to couple and uncouple the tractor unit to the trailer section carrying the container. After half-a-dozen goes Mallund had the hang of it.

'I won't ask what this is all about,' said Small. Fishing.

'Then don't.'

'But it would be a hell of a lot easier if I did the driving for you. That way nothing can go wrong. If you're caught driving these monsters without an HGV licence you're in deep doo doo.'

'Thanks again, Tony, you're a mate. But, no thanks. You're better off not knowing. It's something I must do on my own, and do it my way.'

'As you wish. But why have I got a deep down feeling of relief that it's not one of my rigs you'll be driving?'

'That's something I meant to talk to you about . . . '

'Uh oh.'

'Do you know where I can beg, borrow or steal one?'

30

The mission had to be timed to the minute. The container would be parked in a compound approached by half a mile of narrow road in, and another half mile out. The rendezvous would be at 9.30 p.m. The switch-over needed to be accomplished in no more than ten minutes to avoid prying eyes. Also, the occupants of the container would be getting panicky and might start creating noise. The driver of the new tractor must time himself to arrive at 9.30 p.m. sharp, no sooner, no later. If he was ahead of time he must slow down or wait before proceeding. The narrow window in the timings was a godsend to Mallund.

'So here's the drill,' said Mallund. 'I've recce'd the area and there is practically no late-night traffic on that road. I'll take up position on the approach road out of sight of the parked container. Further behind me, Spency will have my old car stalled in the middle of the road, blocking the new tractor unit's arrival. He will delay them long enough for me to get to the container spot on the nine-thirty target. I do the switch and beat it down the exit road. Spency, I need to rely on you. No funny business, you know what I mean?'

'No worries, Jack. I'm clean,' Spency sniffed.

'Robin, you will monitor Donlan's phone, and alert me to anything that might impact on the mission. Especially keep a close track on his whereabouts. Understood?'

'Gotcha.'

'Ros, you will be responsible for finding and getting us to a safe haven for the illegals.'

'That's in hand.'

'Right, so I suggest we all take some R and R time, as our American military cousins say. Rest and Recreation, we need to be at the top of our game for this.'

Spency raised his hand.

'Yes?' said Mallund.

'You forgot to say 'dismissed'.'

'Sod off, Spency.'

As they left the room Mallund took Ros aside and asked, 'Are you OK with this, Ros?'

'OK with what?'

'The whole business. Me, this madcap battle. I fear for you. We're cutting close to the edge and anytime now it could backfire on all of us. I don't want you hurt.'

'You mean it's no place for a woman?'

'No, it's not that — '

'Yes, it is. You're going to give me all your reasons why I should quit. Some of them will be strong reasons only a fool would ignore. Some of them will be lame reasons dreamt up by your own perception. But when you boil them right down, all the good reasons and the lame ones, it comes down to one thing: woman. So let me tell you this, Jack Mallund . . .'

She advanced on him, wagging her finger an inch from his nose, the Medusa hairdo coiled and ready to strike.

' . . . Let me tell you one thing and don't you forget it. I went into this with my eyes wide open. Not just because of you or your daughter, but because it's a chance to rid us of at least a few of these monsters. I've seen the results, Mallund, I've *lived* with the horror these girls have to endure. It keeps me awake at night and gives me bad dreams when I do sleep. Oh, I've done my bit, my little social worker bit. For what it's worth. But it's just a flea bite on the back of a rhinoceros. I'm stuck on the outside, helpless, counting my meagre successes. But this! This is a chance to strike at the heart of the dragon and bring the whole beast down. Frankly, as far as I'm concerned you and your daughter are just a vehicle to help me to get a crack at them. If you gave me a gun I'd even start shooting. So don't ever, ever, underestimate me.' Her eyes were furious, her cheeks crimson.

Mallund held up his hands. 'Phew!' he breathed. 'That's me told!'

She was trembling with rage, pacing the room.

Mallund let her calm down a little, watching as she vented her frustration. He sensed there was something more to her fired-up hatred of these criminals than even her tirade had made out. Something deeper. Something darker.

'Look, let's go and have a drink,' he said.

'Here?' she said, nodding at the Buddies tea bar on the other side of the door.

'No, the pub,' he said, taking her by the arm.

31

Ros cast her eyes around the best room of the Red Lion. If this was the best, then God only knows what the other rooms were like. The banquette seating round the walls was of dark-brown Rexine, cracked and bulging in places, stuffing poking out like weeping sores. The floor was linoleum, but probably had a posh name like 'Cushion Tread' or 'Symphony' when it was laid in — when? . . . the 70s . . . the 80s? It had lost its sheen, and around the bar area and the route to the toilets, little islands of wear revealed the wood of the floor underneath. At the last count, Mallund had read somewhere, eighteen pubs were closing down each week in Britain through lack of trade. It was painfully obvious that the Red Lion would soon be joining the swelling ranks of the dear departed. There were just two other customers, both elderly men silently holding their pints in front of them at the bar as if they were afraid somebody would steal them.

'I didn't think you approved of places like this,' she said.

'You mean tacky inner city pubs on their last legs?'

'No, I mean dens of iniquity. The whole alcohol thing.'

'I'm not that kind of vicar. People should be free to indulge themselves. In moderation, of course. Which is why I'm about to do a very vicarly thing and have a small sherry. What about you?'

'A large gin and tonic. I need it after that scene earlier. I kind of blew up at you, didn't I?'

'You sure did. I don't know where all that came from. You really do feel strongly about it, don't you?' He rose and went to the bar to get the drinks. He returned with the two glasses and set them down on the wet table, picking a dry spot. There were no beer mats, even though they would have been provided free by the brewery. Nobody could be bothered putting them out — or, heaven forbid, even wiping the tables. Morale in this pub had sunk to zero, waiting for the crunch.

'You know what impressed me most?' he said, taking a delicate sip of his sherry.

'What?' said Ros, gulping down half of her large gin in one go.

'That you're not motivated by personal reasons. You genuinely care for all these girls. It's a vocation, an unselfish dedication.'

'Now you're patronizing me.' She downed the rest of her gin. 'Hey, I'm a social worker. It's what we do.'

'Yes, but most of the social workers I know don't threaten to get a gun and go out and shoot the baddies.'

'You want another? My round.' She gestured at his almost full glass.

'No, thanks. I'm fine with this.'

'Mind if I do?' She headed for the bar and returned with another large one. Mallund raised his eyebrows.

'The thing is,' she said, 'I'm pretty sure that you're not doing it just for your daughter alone. Somewhere in there behind that gung-ho façade is a caring man who is fighting on broad principles. A man who won't sit back and let injustice rule. Am I right?'

'Of course there's a little bit of that. I'm a man of God, after all.'

'Hmm. More than a little, I suspect.'

'Make no mistake, Ros, I am driven by the need to save Alice. That alone. Nothing will be allowed to get in the way. I'm totally focused on that. It's the only way to win. If Donlan and his empire fall in the process, then that's just a bit of lucky collateral damage.' He tried to take a determined gulp of his sherry to emphasize his point. Pity it wasn't a large Scotch; it would have added more clout.

The two men at the bar finished their pints and left. The girl behind the bar suddenly switched off the TV and shouted across to Mallund and Ros, 'Sorry, folks, that's it. We have to close now.'

'At this hour? It's only eight o'clock.'

'No trade these days. Hardly nobody through the door since you came in. Boss says it's not economic. Sorry, but take your time finishing your drinks.'

'We can come back in a couple of months when it'll probably be reopened as a gastropub,' said Mallund. 'Look, it's still early. Why don't we finish this conversation at the vicarage? Believe it or not, I do keep a small selection of drinks for special occasions. Might even be some gin, but we could be struggling for tonic.'

'Good idea,' said Ros.

32

Mallund returned from the kitchen with two glasses; a lemonade for him and a gin for Ros.

'I hope soda water goes with gin,' he said.

'It'll do.'

'So, Ros, if we come through this in one piece and Donlan and his cronies are all washed up, where do you go from there?'

'Never thought that far ahead. Too fixed on just getting Donlan, I guess.'

'You have to bear in mind that my game plan is to spook Donlan into handing over Alice. I'll negotiate with him if I have to, but the minute he hands her back, I'm out. Finito!'

'I don't believe that, Jack. I think you will see it through to the end. You are a man of conscience. You won't sit back and let evil have its way.'

'Conscience, eh? My conscience has got me into a lot of trouble in the past, let me tell you. You see, Ros, there's more to this than just the fight with Donlan. I have a battle of my own going on inside me. I have taken vows, and the longer this assault on Donlan goes on, the closer I come to breaking them.

That cannot happen. My vows mean everything to me.'

'You're a strange mixture of emotions, Jack Mallund. If you ask me, you're a powder keg waiting to explode.'

'That's what I'm afraid of.'

He poured Ros another gin, and watched her sip it in the insubstantial light of the room's economy bulbs. They were first generation bulbs, and the cold yellow hue cast a jaundiced shadow under her eyes and nose. It did nothing to detract from her features. If anything, it seemed to enhance her attractiveness, accentuating those rosy cheeks — crimson when she got angry, he had recently learned — and lending a hint of Pre-Raphaelite mystery to the rounded face framed in red hair. But that coiled hairdo! He banished the picture from his mind. He had not looked at her closely before — at least he didn't think he had — and was suddenly taken by how attractive she looked, curled up on his sofa like a contented cat. She was wearing jeans and trainers, which seemed to be her everyday uniform. But he vaguely remembered noting her slim waist, a dim vision of her pert breasts under a tightly fitting dress at a Buddies party, a hazy picture of her shapely legs gliding across the floor in high heels; the graceful way she held herself.

Well, maybe after all he had *looked closely at her before.*

'How's your drink?' he asked, dragging his mind back from the edge of a dangerous precipice.

'Fine. In fact I think I've had enough. I feel quite tiddly. Is that horrible?'

'No, not at all.'

'I don't usually drink this much. It's just that . . . well, sometimes I get so . . . well, things get on top of you.'

'You know what I think, Ros? I think you're a bit like me as far as this crusade of ours is concerned. You're not entirely truthful when you say you're motivated just by the big principle. I think there's something personal in it. Just like me.'

He stared at her, directly in the eyes.

She turned away.

'Am I right?' He softened his voice. 'I *am* right, aren't I?'

She made a soft whimpering noise. He could see that she was weeping.

'Ros . . . ' He crossed over to the sofa, sat beside her. 'Ros. C'mon, let it all out. Whatever it is it can't be all that bad. Let it out.'

She was sobbing, shaking her head violently, dabbing at her eyes with a tissue.

'No, I'll be all right in a minute.'

But she wasn't. A fresh outburst sent her into body-racking sobs that stung at Mallund's heart. He put his arm around her shoulders, comforting.

'You can tell me, Ros. It's my job — even though I'm not very good at it,' he said, trying to raise a smile.

'No, it's too terrible,' she said between sobs. 'Too . . . '

'It's only terrible as long as you keep it bottled up. Once you let it out it's gone. You can lock the door and not let it back in.'

She took a deep breath, steadied herself, wiped her eyes with a fresh tissue.

'No. I can't.'

'Ros . . . '

'I've never told this to a soul before. You wonder why I'm so het up about these girls? Well I'll tell you: it's because I was one of them.'

33

Mallund was struck dumb. Ros paused to let her words sink in. 'Yes, I was one of those poor wretches driven to the edge of suicide by the ordeal. Yes, Jack, it's personal. Personal, personal, personal. I was once groomed, believe it or not. You think all this is new, just because it's all over the papers and the TV? It's been happening for years. Generations. The difference then was that it didn't get reported to the police, and if it did it wasn't taken seriously. And without the back up of police or court evidence the media couldn't risk exposing it. But the Jimmy Savile case changed all that. Then the social media took over and now it's a pandemic. So don't look at me like that, Jack — I was once a naive teenager like everybody else. You can't imagine that, can you? I can tell by your face. But believe it. I was as vulnerable as any of these girls today.' She tried to take a swig of her gin, but choked as it went down the wrong way.

'Ros — '

'No, hear me out, Jack. I need to tell you this and if I stop I'll never get started again.

So, to the beginning . . . '

'I was fifteen when I met him down at the café where we girls used to gather after school. He was twenty-five, or so he said, but I never really found out if that was true, and had his own car, a bright yellow Audi Quattro. He walked into the café with his mate like they owned the place. They turned their chairs around so that they were leaning on the backs, arms folded. 'So this is where all the best-looking talent hangs out in this town,' he said addressing us; then, turning to his mate, 'We've been missing out, wasting our time in those classy night clubs when all the time the real beauties were right here under our noses.' Some of the girls started giggling, but I kept a straight face. He looked us up and down in turn. 'What have we got here?' He turned to Suzie, 'Why it's Julia Roberts.' And to Charmaine, 'And Demi Moore too. Hey, we've really struck lucky here, mate.' He winked at his companion. 'And who's this? Why it's only Sharon Stone, that's who.' This was to Catherine. 'And Kate Winslet.' Jane blushed and stared down at the table. All the girls were giggling except me. Then his eyes settled on me. 'And who do we have here, so quiet and so proud? Surely it can't be Helen of Troy, the face that launched a thousand ships? Hi there, Helen, how ya doin'?' I tried to ignore him. There was a long silence. I didn't know where to look. 'Well, Helen, not very talkative, are we? That's all right, after all you don't know us from Adam. Anyway, I'm Gary and this is my mate . . . Adam.'

'The girls giggled, all except me.

' 'Well, ladies,' he said, rising to go, 'we'd love to stay and chat, but we have business to attend to. Maybe see you next week. 'Bye for now . . . and cheer up, Helen, it might never happen.'

'We watched them drive off in the yellow Audi with a screech of tyres. And he was as good as his word. The following week they were already seated at a table when we arrived at the café.

' 'Come and join us, ladies. The coffees are on us.' He was looking straight at me.

' 'No thanks,' I said. 'We have our own table.' But the other girls were already grabbing chairs to sit beside them. I felt a fool. I had no option but to join them. I must admit, Gary and Adam were great fun. They came by the week after that too. We sat enthralled as they talked about the posh clubs they visited and the bands they knew. They told us about the Blue Parrot Club, which we all knew had a bit of a reputation. A reputation for what none of us was sure, but the mystique and the edgy danger conjured up by the name kept us wide-eyed with wonder.

''The boss is a big mate of mine,' said Gary. 'Just mention my name and they'll see you right. Everything on the house, you won't have to pay a penny.'

''Oh, I don't think we would ever go there,' said Jane. She was the most straight-laced of the girls.

''Why not? It's a fun place. We all need a little bit of fun sometime, what do you think, Helen?'

'I shrugged. I was feeling uneasy about the way he paid all his attention to me. But at the same time I guess I was flattered.

''He fancies you,' said Stephanie.

''Don't be daft,' I said.

''It's obvious,' said Catherine.

'And it was obvious. As the weeks passed he smothered me with attention. There were little presents at first . . . perfume . . . earrings . . . lipstick. Then one day he took me aside as we left the café. 'This is a special present,' he said, handing me a slim package. When I opened it my jaw dropped. It was the latest mobile phone.

''One condition,' he said. 'This is ours and ours alone. So we can talk to each other in private.'

'I protested, but he insisted so strongly that in the end I accepted it. We talked and texted a lot, nothing serious, just good fun. I felt privileged to be his friend. It was my secret. I had this admirer, witty and handsome, treating me like a lady. Slowly, I began to detect a change in the tone of his calls and texts. They were beginning to get suggestive, but in a playful manner. Then they got more serious and for a couple of days I switched the phone off. But curiosity got the better of me and I switched it back on. I didn't know it, but I was getting hooked on this flirtation with danger. Even the way he still called me Helen instead of Ros seemed like some kind of secret code, adding to the thrill. One day I was on my way home from school when the yellow Audi pulled up alongside.

' 'Jump in, I'll take you home,' he said.

'Looking around to make sure none of the girls could see me, I slid into the passenger seat.

' 'Listen, Helen, I'd like to take you out to dinner on Saturday. Signature, do you know it?' Of course I knew it. Everybody knew Signature: the poshest, most expensive restaurant in town. 'Then we can go on to a party at a friend's place. It's her birthday.'

'I was reluctant and told him I couldn't get to stay out that late, but he had the answer to that. I told my parents I was staying overnight with Stephanie.

'During dinner I had one glass of wine, then stuck to mineral water. But, as we left the restaurant, I began to feel a bit queer and told him I'd better not go to the party. He said I'd be OK after a bit of fresh air. We got to the flat but there was no one else there. I remember saying 'What's happened to the party then?' before everything went woozy. When I woke up in bed I was naked. It was morning. He was shaving in the bathroom.

''Morning Helen,' he said. 'That was a good night, huh?' He was grinning at me.

''But I didn't . . . '

''Oh yes, you did. You were good. Bloody good.'

'I was still feeling woozy and light-headed. And, as the realization of what had happened slowly began to sink in I began to feel sick. I couldn't understand why I had blanked out on just one glass of wine.

''You bastard, you took advantage of me while I was helpless! You dirty rotten bastard!' My eyes were filling up and I could hardly speak.

''Don't worry about it, Helen, I'm sure you would have enjoyed it if you'd been there.' He laughed at his joke. A cruel laugh that sent a shiver up my spine. 'Now get dressed and I'll drive you home.'

'On the way he talked as if nothing out of the ordinary had happened. I just stared out the car window, mind blank, taking nothing in. He pulled up around the corner from my home. I couldn't wait to get out of the car, and snatched at the door handle as soon as it came to a halt. He grabbed me by the arm and held me in.

' ''So, Helen, see you next week. Same place, same time.'

' ''You have got to be joking.' I couldn't believe what I was hearing. 'After what you did, you swine? Go screw yourself!' I tugged but he held me tighter.

' ''You still don't get it, do you, Helen? Let me spell it out to you. You're mine now. You'll be there, and I'll tell you for why. Because if you're not, your mum and dad will be getting a little note telling them what you've been up to. What a slut you are. Staying overnight at Stephanie's? They can easily check that, remember. So think about it. Same place, same time.''

* * *

'Well, I did think about it, and the more I thought the more trapped I felt. There was no way out. It would kill Mum and Dad if they found out what I had done — what *he* had done. And I could never hold my head up high again. I felt like dirt. And I *was* dirt as far as Gary was concerned.

'So I turned up, same time same place. We met up two more Saturday nights, went to restaurants and clubs, and I slept with him. I could see no way out. He treated me well and to all intents and purposes I had become his girlfriend. I was beginning to accept the situation. After all, it could be worse, or so I convinced myself. Then one night as I got in the car he asked, 'Did you tell anybody where you were going?'

'I said, 'No'.

'He pulled up outside a pub, a swish new place on the bypass, and said we were going to have a drink.

'I said, 'I thought we were going for dinner?' He just laughed. 'No, a drink first.' He went to the bar and got himself a pint of lager and a mineral water for me. I was certainly not going to touch any alcohol. We finished our drinks and got back in the car. I asked where we were going, but he just said, 'You'll see'. We drove for about half an hour. It seemed as if he was going nowhere in particular, just killing time. We drove into a run-down area I had never seen before. I was starting to feel funny, just like the last time. My head a bit woozy. His voice seemed to come like an echo, saying, 'We're going to have a good time, aren't we, Helen?' I heard myself say, 'Sure thing, a good time. Yes.'

'I woke up feeling dopey again, my eyes refusing to focus. I shifted my weight and the bedsprings jangled. The room was dingy, peeling floral wallpaper, stained and worn carpet. I was aware of a body beside me, a man leaning over me. I said, 'Gary? Where am I?'

'The man grinned. 'Beautiful,' he said, and reached over to touch my hair.

'In the dim light I caught a glimpse of his face. It wasn't Gary. It was a fat man, bald, and sweaty, wearing a dirty white vest; hairy arms.

'I screamed blue murder, my lungs fit to burst. I'm sure they must have heard me out in the street. The door burst open and Gary stormed in. He slapped me twice across the face. 'Shut that racket,' he yelled. 'Now be nice to this gentleman or there's plenty more where that came from. You do as you're told and don't talk back. You're my bitch, remember? I own you.' He slapped me again three times, so hard it brought tears to my eyes and I couldn't see.

'He held his hand up to slap again. 'You're

my bitch. What are you?'

'I heard myself whisper, 'I'm your bitch'.'

Ros's voice had faded away to almost a whisper as she related the story. Mallund sat listening with a heavy heart.

'I think I need another drink,' she said. He fetched her a gin, a small one this time. She gulped it down. 'I don't think I can go on.'

'Try, Ros, it's the only way to lay this ghost. Let it all out.' He rubbed her arm up and down, his other arm round her shoulders.

'I eventually learned that I had been doped with Rohypnol, what they call the date rape drug. But that was only the beginning . . . '

Mallund sat in shocked silence as she related a grim catalogue of abuse, finally telling how she was freed by a pro-active social worker who had infiltrated the racket.

'I had to bite the bullet and tell my mum and dad everything. They welcomed me home with open arms. But I was permanently damaged. I vowed I would do everything in my power to help these girls. That's probably why I became a social worker. So you see, Jack, I have a personal interest in this just like you.' She turned and looked him in the face, tears streaming down her cheeks. Then her body dissolved into racking tremors, and she clung to him as if she were drowning. She *was* drowning. Drowning in misery.

He wiped tears from her cheek with his finger.

'Ros . . . oh, Ros,' he said.

He kissed her tenderly on the forehead.

★ ★ ★

Who can say how these things happen? A burden shared. A common enemy. A mutual sense of loss and desperation. A binding of two empty souls. Wordlessly, they had climbed the stairs and wordlessly they had climbed into bed, as if it were the most natural thing in the world. As if they were a long-married couple. Mallund felt no remorse as he awoke to her face on the pillow beside him. Had he taken advantage of her? No, he decided. They had taken advantage of each other. They both needed the closeness, the warmth of human contact. It had been a long time since Mallund had known the intimacy of a woman and he felt somehow cleansed, invigorated with a brightness that lifted his spirits and spiced up his view of the future. But he wondered what demons she must be battling this morning, after reliving her trauma. She was stirring now. She rubbed her eyes and reached out to him.

'I'm starved,' she said. 'If you show me where things are I'll make us some breakfast.'

'Breakfast can wait,' he said, and moved over to hug her.

★ ★ ★

She was frying eggs and bacon, while Mallund was in the bathroom shaving. In just two days he would be in the front line again, the plan to hijack the trailer-load of trafficked people swinging into action. He looked at himself in the mirror, staring to harden his features, for there had been a sea change in his attitude to the campaign since hearing Ros's story. It wasn't just all about Alice: it was about striking a blow to end human misery, if only in some small way. He stiffened his resolve.

'This is one I have to win,' he told the mirror. 'Failure is not an option.' He resolved to double his fitness regime . . .

34

'Ninety-four . . . ninety-five . . . ninety-six . . . ' His voice came in rasping gasps, barely audible as he struggled for breath. His arms felt like jelly. His shoulders burned fiercely under the strain. 'Ninety-seven . . . ninety-eight . . . ninety-nine . . . one hundred . . . ' This would be a good point at which to stop, yes? But no, must push on. 'One hundred and one . . . one hundred and two . . . '

A time was when Mallund could have done 200 press-ups without flinching. But now it was an uphill struggle. Time and disuse had taken its toll on his muscles, and the long road back to supreme fitness seemed to go on forever. But he needed to be ready for the task ahead. If he was to save Alice he would need every advantage in physical and mental strength. As he pumped away at the press-ups his mind slipped back to a drill square in Hereford. He had just turned 23, young and eager and bullish, cock of the midden, anything was possible. Fail? Me? Don't make me laugh! He had just finished his hundredth press-up.

'OK, soldier, that's enough. Now pick up your Bergen and strap it on.'

Young Pte Jack Mallund smiled smugly at how well he had accomplished the press-ups, and hoisted the heavy Bergen on to his back and secured it.

'Now, soldier, let's see what you're made of. Down you get. Pushups . . . one, two, three . . . '

He knew the SAS selection training would be no picnic, but he never dreamt just how body and soul-punishing it could be.

★   ★   ★

A black, black night. He was on the run. His pursuers were closing in. He had a painful blister on his right foot and was hobbling and stumbling across ditches high up in the Welsh Brecon Beacons. He had been running and hiding for nearly three days. The men chasing him had all the hi-tech devices of modern warfare to their advantage, including night vision glasses through which they could see him clear as day. Even low-tech, too — he could hear the distant barking of tracker dogs. He had nothing, just the shabby clothes he stood in. He had hoped to grab a few hours' sleep this night, but instead he was up and running again.

Stumbling and cursing. They had dumped him in the wilderness in ragged clothes and told him to run for his life. Then, at their leisure, they pursued him with their all-terrain vehicles, like some bizarre blood sport. They were the hounds; he, Jack Mallund, was the fox. He had needed the cunning of a fox to get this far — dodging and ducking, laying false tracks, living off the stingy landscape. But it was not enough. Inevitably, they caught up with him, cornered in a rocky valley. A hood went over his head, tied tightly round his neck, and they roughly marched him for half a mile then threw him into the back of a truck. The ordeal was just the beginning. They tossed him into what seemed like a cell but he could not tell for sure since the hood was still over his head. Only the metallic echoing clunk of the door closing betrayed the sinister purpose of the room. They tipped ice cold water over him while he was still shivering from his exposure on the mountainside and left him. Then the noise started. Nonsense noise, howling like a badly tuned radio only ten times worse. 'White noise', the hellish anthem so beloved of the interrogator. A mind-destroying cacophony composed to wear you down, soften you up for all the dirty tricks to come. There followed a relentless interrogation, hard man-soft man, that went on for days, just how many days he couldn't remember. Terrifying role playing; a gun to his head, the cool of the muzzle against his sweating temple . . . *let's finish the bastard off now, he's no use to us* . . . the surge of relief as he heard the empty click of the firing mechanism. You'd tell them anything if only it would stop. Just stop. But he didn't. He didn't tell them.

They removed the hood from his head.

'A nice cup of tea for you, soldier.'

He accepted the tea warily. *You don't catch me out that easily. This just another ploy. Give me a sense of false security. I know your game.*

'Relax, soldier, it's all over.' A warm, friendly smile on the face of the officer. 'Drink the tea. It's safe.'

Safe? Safe? Who could tell what safe was? Still wary, he took in his surroundings: the drab grey/green MOD paint, the steel industrial shelving, the utilitarian desk and chair and the plaque on the wall, the all-too-familiar winged dagger with the legend *Who Dares Wins*.

Yes, he was back in the real world at last.

They call it escape and evasion, a seven-day ordeal of survival in the wilds with elite SAS hunters snapping at your heels. Seven days.

That's a laugh. Mallund had never heard of anyone lasting that long. Most were captured within a couple of days. It was the culmination of a rigorous training and selection process faced by every hopeful soldier aiming to wear the winged dagger beret.

'Selection?' one recruit had moaned to Mallund. 'This isn't *selection* — it's *rejection!*'

True, from each intake of about 200 top class soldiers from regiments throughout the British Army, most will drop out within the first few days, leaving only thirty to forty successful candidates.

The trial begins with a series of marches — called TABS — in the Brecon Beacons by day and by night, carrying heavy Bergens. They march against the clock. Day by day the distance and the weight of the Bergen is increased to the limit of endurance. It culminates in a sixty-five kilometre TAB carrying a fifty-five pound Bergen and an assault rifle which must be accomplished in twenty-two hours. Several candidates have died during this ordeal over the years.

And then there is escape and evasion, the final hurdle. Mallund was supremely confident he had checked out well in all the stages of selection, and stood beaming as he awaited the official result.

FAIL

The word branded itself into his brain. There had to be some mistake. But no. He, Jack Mallund, had failed the SAS selection.

Jack Mallund, cock of the midden.

★　★　★

When an SAS man shoots to kill, he fires two rounds in quick succession. This is known as the double tap. The rationale behind it is that you might not get a second chance. Your target might only be disabled by the first shot and could come back at you. So you take your second chance in advance just in case. It is a philosophy rooted in the ethos of the SAS — no second chances. Make sure you get it right first time.

Therefore how ironic that such a no-nonsense organization as the SAS should break with its own sacred tenets and offer a second chance to the most unlikely individuals — the candidates who failed its own selection training. But such a mechanism exists, and it was a humbled, more balanced Jack Mallund who took advantage of it.

No more cock of the midden.

He passed with flying colours.

35

The sun was going down as the powerful tractor unit sped along the country lanes, Mallund at the wheel. He was surprised at how lively and responsive the cab only unit was without a trailer. Almost like a rally car, he thought, then told himself to slow down, avoid drawing attention. Five hours earlier, Tony Small had dialled 999 and reported the tractor unit stolen.

'The cheeky buggers uncoupled it from the trailer and left the container stranded. They obviously just wanted the cab.'

★ ★ ★

Mallund pulled up at a spot well out of sight of the parking area where the container with its human cargo was parked and got out of the cab. He cast his eyes around the darkened fields. Once more he felt it: the nagging feeling that he was not alone; that someone was watching him. Could it be Donlan's men? Could he be heading into a trap? He pushed it to the back of his mind. He had no time for that now. *It's just pre-mission nerves,*

258

he concluded. He checked his watch. Nine o'clock on the dot. Spency would be taking up position on the narrow road a mile behind him in Mallund's old Kia, waiting to block the way for the genuine tractor unit. Robin was by his phone and computer, monitoring Donlan's calls and tracking his whereabouts. Any second now, he would call Mallund's mobile. Sure enough, it rang.

Robin's voice: 'Nine p.m. check. Donlan is in Manchester. Nothing to report.'

The walkie-talkie on the seat beside him crackled into life.

Spency's voice: 'I'm in position. No sign of them yet.'

Ros's voice: 'In position, no problems.'

Ros had been delegated to wait on the escape road until Mallund was safely past with the container, then drive an old banger across the road and block it. She would throw the keys away then join Mallund in the truck. The car blocking the way would be a time-consuming obstacle for any pursuers.

Mallund checked his watch. Time to go. He rammed the rig into gear and headed for the rendezvous. There was no more than a handful of trucks scattered around the park, so it was not difficult to recognize his target, parked on its own with no others within fifty metres. The driver was leaning against the container smoking a cigarette. Mallund walked up to him and said, 'Have you seen the BBC weather forecast?' The driver responded in a guttural East European accent, 'It looks like being good tomorrow.' Mallund tapped his watch, meaning there was no time to lose. The driver tossed his cigarette at his feet and ground it into the dust. He uncoupled his own tractor from the container and drove it to the side. Then he stood behind Mallund's vehicle, directing him as he manoeuvred it slowly backwards to link up with the trailer. As he made contact there was a loud bang followed by a metallic grinding and squealing. The cab started to shake. The cab unit did not want to mate with the trailer.

'Damn!' Mallund was pulling forward to try again. 'These things are supposed to be international. If there's a mismatch in the coupling we're sunk!' Keeping a close eye on the driver's hand signals, he inched the cab back towards the trailer. Again there was a bang and the screech of tortured metal. He was beginning to panic. He checked his watch. The criminals' tractor unit was due at the rendezvous in ten minutes. He hoped Spency's part in the mission was going well.

★ ★ ★

A mile further back along the approach road, Spency could see the headlights and hear the heavy diesel engine as the tractor unit approached. He got out of the Kia and waved it down. It pulled up a few feet behind the car stuck in the middle of the road. The driver leaned out the window and shouted above the noise of the engine, 'Move your car, will you? We're in a hurry.'

'Sorry, pal. She's stuck. Just packed up in the middle of the road. No warning, like.'

The driver and two other burly men descended from the cab. Spency recognized them as three of Donlan's henchmen. But had they recognized him? He tried to keep his face out of the headlights, moving into the darkness as much as possible.

'Just get it off the road and let us through,' said the driver.

Spency took his time getting into the car and fitting the key into the ignition. He wound away at the starter for a good minute, even though he knew it would never start — he had disabled the ignition system. He needed to play for time, so he wound away at the starter for another minute. Then another minute, until the battery began to run down. The minutes were slowly ticking by.

'Stay at the wheel. We'll try a push start,' said the driver.

Spency waited until the three of them were bent over the boot and pushing to no avail. The car refused to budge.

'Oh,' he said. 'Forgot — it's automatic. Can't bump start it.'

'Jesus wept!' said the driver.

'Look at the time, Steve,' said one of his companions.

'I can see the bloody time. C'mon, we'll just have to bounce it.'

Each of the men took a corner of the car and pressed down sharply with their weight on it. Spency was still sitting in the driving seat.

'Come on, get off your arse and grab a corner,' said Steve.

Spency made a big production of getting out of the car as slowly as possible.

'Come on, step lively — we're in a hurry.'

Spency took hold of the nearside wing.

'Now bounce the fucker . . . one, two, three.'

They pushed down together on each corner of the car until it was bouncing lightly on its springs.

'Lift!' shouted the driver. With the car almost airborne they hauled it a foot to the left. They repeated the process five times until the vehicle was clear of the road. Spency was now in the full glare of the truck's headlights.

The driver was peering at him curiously.

'Have I seen you somewhere before?'

'Naw, I don't think so.'

'I'm sure I've seen this fucker before.'

'C'mon, Steve, we're going to miss the rendezvous. He won't wait.'

'Seen the fucker before,' said Steve, as he rammed the truck into gear and tore off down the road.

★   ★   ★

At the parking area, Mallund was on his fifth attempt to marry his tractor up to the trailer. He could hear faint noises, muffled voices, from within the container. The occupants were getting restless, and no doubt afraid. He appealed to the driver in sign language. *What's wrong? Why won't it fit?*

The driver replied with a shrug and lit another cigarette. He bent over the coupling mechanism and scratched his head. Then he dipped his arm into the works. There was a clank and a clunk. He looked at Mallund and grinned.

This time the tractor and its cargo were firmly locked together. Mallund could see the lights of what must be the other tractor about half a mile off down the approach road. This was going to be closely run. He gunned the engine and sped off down the exit road. When he saw Ros waving him down he came screeching to a halt. She disappeared into a gap in the hedge and a minute later came driving out in the old car and parked it sideways across the road.

'Get in quick,' said Mallund. 'They'll be right behind us.'

He was gambling on the fact that the driver's limited English would delay his pursuers while they struggled to understand what had happened. He pressed the throttle to the floor and roared off into the darkness.

For Steve and his two colleagues it was a toss-up which emotion came first. Anger or fear. Anger because of how they had been hood-winked; fear of what would happen to them when Donlan found out. He was driving the tractor unit flat out despite the narrow road with its blind bends and unpredictable surface. He had to stand on the brakes and come skidding to a halt when he rounded a bend and found the old banger blocking his way.

'We'll need to get out and bounce it, Steve,' said one of his companions.

Steve heaved the rig into first gear. 'No time,' he said simply. He crept the vehicle forward until it made contact with the car. Then he revved the engine and gained speed.

The car's tyres screeched as they slid sideways along the road, until the car finally overturned on to its roof. From then on it was easy going, and within seconds the car had been pushed into the undergrowth by the side of the road. Steve now had the blood thirst as he raced off in search of his quarry.

Mallund was throwing the juggernaut around like it was a rally car, skidding round blind bends and tearing along narrow lanes at high speed. Ros was clinging to the grab handle for dear life, and could only imagine what it must be like for the poor souls in the container, being tossed around and bouncing off the steel walls. Their pursuers were catching up rapidly; the ploy of leaving the old banger in the road to slow them down had not delayed them as much as expected. They had lost no time at all in pushing it off the road with their truck. Now, they were just 500 metres behind and closing. The road was clear ahead for a long straight stretch, so Mallund pushed the juggernaut up to its limit. Still, the headlights in his mirror were getting closer by the second. Suddenly the road ahead burst into a blaze of light. Red lights. Flashing red lights.

'Damn, said Mallund. 'A level crossing. We're sunk.' He began to ease off. Then suddenly rammed the throttle pedal to the floor. The turbo-charged engine roared.

'Jack! No!' screamed Ros.

'The barrier's only just come down,' he said through gritted teeth. 'The train's still a way off.' To the left, he could see the lights of the approaching train.

Ros closed her eyes.

36

The juggernaut arrived at the crossing at 60 m.p.h. It burst through the barrier, ripping it off and tossing it into the hedgerow at the side of the tracks. From the corner of his eye Mallund glimpsed the train. Almost upon him now. The locomotive filled his entire side window. The wail of its warning klaxon vibrated through his bones. He felt the judder as the wheels of his cab rumbled over the tracks. In a tiny fraction of a second the six wheels of the trailer would do the same — he hoped. Yes! The pitter-patter of the trailer wheels over the rails confirmed the rig was clear of the crossing. Glancing in his mirror, he could see the train rushing past.

'That was close,' he said, letting out a gush of held breath. 'Let's hope it's one of those really long goods trains. That should buy us time while they're waiting for it to pass through.'

They raced along the country lanes, kicking up dust and shaking pretty cottages in their wake. Donlan's men were now right up behind them, popping in and out of Mallund's driving mirror as they attempted to overtake.

'So long as we're on these narrow roads and don't stop we're OK,' Mallund told Ros. 'They can't get past. If we have to stop for any reason we've had it. They're sure to be tooled up for a job like this, and we won't stand a chance against guns.'

No sooner had he finished speaking than the narrow road suddenly widened out. It was a stretch of about 300 metres. In his mirror he watched as the other vehicle slipped out from behind and came alongside the trailer. Up ahead the road narrowed again. There were large trees on each side of it, leaving space for only one vehicle. They were both racing flat out to be the first into the gap and it seemed neither was going to back down.

'Oh, no! Not again!' whimpered Ros, closing her eyes.

Just thirty metres to go. Mallund kept his foot flat. He could see Steve at the wheel of the other vehicle, right alongside him, his face set in a grim mask of determination. Mallund thought briefly of swerving to run his opponent off the road; but with an articulated lorry at this speed there was too high a risk of jack-knifing and sending his own vehicle into the trees.

So it came down to a matter of who was going to blink first.

★ ★ ★

It was Steve. Mallund saw the other vehicle disappear from alongside, and watched in his mirror as it braked hard, zig-zagging in a cloud of dust. He thought he saw it clip one of the trees, pieces of bodywork flying high into the air as it spun around and came to rest. After a few seconds it righted itself and came after them once more.

'Yes, size does matter after all,' said Mallund, nodding. 'You OK, Ros?'

'I'm fine,' she said, though her face was drained of blood. 'But I don't know about the cargo.'

'They'll be fine. There's no way we're going to make it all the way with them chasing us.' He drove in silence for a few minutes, thinking. Then, 'Ros, check that map and tell me how far to the next biggish town.'

'There's one on the main road in about four miles,' said Ros. 'We join the main road in a mile.'

'Good.' Mallund swung the rig into a sweeping curve at 50 m.p.h., his mirrors full of Steve's headlights. Gaining rapidly on him again. He joined the main road, braking hard into the roundabout. Angry horns from his right blared at him as he sailed round and out the other side, taking one of the illuminated bollards with him. Steve's cab was now right on his tailgate again. Luckily the main road was twisty, with oncoming traffic which frustrated Steve's attempts to overtake. The lights of the town came into view as they crested a hill, and soon they were rushing past the 30 m.p.h. speed limit sign at 60. The road took them through the main street, which Mallund entered at a sober 30. It was unlikely that Steve and his mates would try anything here. He cruised the main street, looking right and left until he spotted what he wanted.

'Hand me that fire extinguisher,' he told Ros. 'And get ready to jump when I tell you. Then run like hell.'

Mallund placed the heavy extinguisher on the seat behind him and brought the truck to a halt outside the building he had chosen.

'The police station?' said Ros, bewildered.

'That's right. Now jump. I'll be right behind you.'

Ros leapt from the cab and sprinted down a side street. Mallund manoeuvred the fire extinguisher through the steering wheel until it jammed against the horn, then jumped from the cab and set off after Ros. Donlan's men had stopped fifty metres away, but sped off when they saw two constables rushing out of the police station. The policemen stood scratching their heads at the sight of the driverless juggernaut pulled up on the pavement with its engine running and its horn blasting away into the night air. One of them switched off the engine and removed the fire extinguisher from the horn. Later, a mechanic forced open the doors of the container and one of the constables peered inside with a flashlight.

'Bloody hell, Darren,' he said. 'You're not going to believe this . . . '

BATMAN AND ROBIN THEORY IN MYSTERY OF ILLEGALS DUMPED AT POLICE STATION

Police were today baffled by a bizarre incident in which twenty-eight people, thought to be trafficked from an Eastern European country, were found in a container parked outside a police station.

The 'cargo', mainly young girls, were last night recovering in hospital following what one of them described as a nightmare high-speed journey in which they were thrown around in the container. None was seriously injured.

A police spokesman said: 'It's a complete mystery. The driver parked the truck outside the police station, set the horn, then he and his companion ran off.

271

We are working on the theory that it could have been some kind of vigilante operation.'

Already dubbed the 'Batman and Robin' operation, the drama began when residents along a twenty-eight mile country route reported two trucks racing at high speed through sleepy hamlets late at night. It came to a head in the quiet market town of . . .

★　★　★

'So now he's a fucking hero!' Donlan threw the newspaper across the room and kicked a chair after it. 'Batman and fucking Robin! Jesus!'

He was in such a rage that none of the other three people in the room dared to speak a word. 'He's making a mug of us. Me. We have got to nail the bastard and nail him good. Once and for all. I'm getting bad signals not just from our partners, but from above too. There are rumours about my competence. You know what that means. There's plenty would dearly love to step into my shoes. They must be rubbing their hands with glee. All this just gives them more ammunition and more confidence. Shit!' He kicked another chair across the room. 'What's this cat and mouse game he's playing? If he really wants his daughter back then why doesn't he tell us who she is? Look, we need to find a way of contacting him. Tell him I'm willing to negotiate.'

'Negotiate?' It was Mike Handley, his number two, who dared to speak first.

'Yeah, negotiate.' Donlan let go a smile which he intended to be mischievous, but to those present appeared as simply evil. 'Then I'll nail the bastard.'

'Pat, I don't think he's even ready to talk. He knows he's got you on the run — '

'I'm not on the fucking run!'

'Hear me out, Pat.' Handley raised his palm in the air. 'I know you won't like to hear this, but you've always valued my judgement. I think that the reason for this cat and mouse game is that he knows he can win every round so long as he has the information. He's trying to squeeze you to the max so he can end up holding the strongest hand when you do come to negotiate.'

'So what do you suggest we do?'

'Take the hit.'

'I can't take any more hits.'

'Take the hit. I think he's getting ready to talk soon. Don't worry, he will contact *you* when he's ready. He'll do one last big one just to finally soften you up.'

'What's the next big operation coming up?'

'Nothing spectacular until the event next month.'

'Christ, Mike, if he blows that it will be a disaster. I'll be finished. We can't let him do it.'

'Exactly. So we double up on security. Put a tight lid on it. In the meantime we redouble our efforts to plug the leak. Find the mole and deal with him. And Pat, don't go off half cock when we do find him; we need to keep a calm head. Our enemy is Mr Cool. We need to play the same game.'

'You're right, Mike. I don't know what I'd do without you. Let's have a drink. A toast. To friendship. We've been together now for so many years I can't remember.'

'Forty-two.'

'God, is it that long? Ever since we were ragged-arsed youngsters nicking hub caps in Dublin, eh? We've sure come a long way.'

'A long, long way.' Handley gestured round the room.

'And we've done it together. You've been my right hand, Mike. I don't think I've told you enough how much I value you. So I'm telling you now.'

'We're mates.' Handley shrugged.

'And I can't think of anybody better to get us through this mess.'

'Now you've got me all embarrassed. We're supposed to be tough guys.'

They both laughed.

★ ★ ★

'Mr Cool, eh?' Mallund switched off the recording taken from Donlan's phone. 'So we've definitely got them running scared. Spency, just how safe is your contact?'

'As safe as anyone can be, working for Donlan.'

'We need details of this 'event' whatever it is. If Robin doesn't pick up anything on the phone we'll be relying on your man. And, Robin, how long can we keep up this monitoring of Donlan's phone? They're talking of doubling security.'

'How long is a piece of string?' said Robin. 'I'm amazed it's gone on this long. It depends on when or if they change the phone as a precaution — which quite frankly any security consultant worth his salt would have done long before now.'

'Maybe there's a natural reluctance to bother the boss — we know the kind of temper he's got,' said Mallund. 'They're looking for a traitor, the last person on their mind is the boss. Is there any way at all they can detect if the phone is infected with your spyware?'

'No way. The software copies all the data and sends it to an innocuous data-receiving website that any member of the public can access. Then it erases all evidence of itself on Donlan's phone. As far as anyone can tell, it has never even been there. Totally untrace-able.'

'So what would you do if you were them?'

'First thing, I'd replace all the mobile phones without exception as fast as possible.'

'Then we must assume that is what they'll do. So our happy electronic snooping days are numbered?'

'Very numbered, Jack.'

37

Donlan was eating lunch alone at his desk when there was a knock at his study door.

'Come!'

He looked up from a bowl of lobster bisque to see the squat figure of Ralph Edmondson, his security consultant, entering. This was unusual; Edmondson was a habitual delegator, leaving the day-to-day running of his company to his lieutenants. Donlan couldn't remember the last time he had seen him in person. He watched in silence as Edmonson swept in and went straight to the music centre built into the bookshelves and switched the radio on. It was a classical programme, playing the finale to Tchaikovsky's 1812 Overture, just coming up to the passage with the live cannons. It couldn't have been a better choice if he'd picked it himself. He turned the volume up to an almost deafening level. He put his finger to his lips to signal Donlan to be quiet. He strode up to his desk and snatched his mobile phone. He pushed the button to switch it off.

'What the fuck . . . ?' Donlan's first

reaction, as always, was anger.

Edmondson went back to the radio and switched it off.

'Sorry about that, Mr Donlan, but I'm afraid I need to ask you to hand over your mobile phone. We're going to destroy all the mobiles and replace them.'

'What, even mine? No way, pal. It never leaves my side. I've got a lot of very sensitive information and numbers on this phone. Replace the others if you must, but mine doesn't get taken.'

'Sorry, Mr Donlan, but we need to get rid of them all because we don't know which one is being hacked. Don't worry, we can copy all your sensitive data to your new phone. We've thoroughly checked all possible sources of electronic vulnerability and the phones are the only thing left. Unless you can find a mole in your organization, then everything points to the phones. So it's safer just to replace them.'

'Are you seriously suggesting that my own phone could be leaking information?'

'Not necessarily, but it's as vulnerable as any of the other phones. We're just trying to close all the stable doors.'

'But my own phone . . . how could this happen?'

Edmonson explained how the spyware

could take over his phone, plot his where-abouts, and even transmit his conversations.

'So they could even listen in on my meetings?'

'Yes, so long as your phone is switched on.'

Donlan sat looking at the dead phone on his desk, thinking, then picked it up. 'If I switch it on now could they hear me?'

'Only if it's your phone that is hacked. As I say, we can't be sure.'

'There's one way to find out.' Donlan switched the mobile on, despite frantic gestures from Edmondson trying to stop him. He waved Edmondson aside, and stood with the phone in front of him as if making a speech into a microphone:

'Listen, you bastard. I've had enough of you, you meddling son of a whore. You stop what you're doing and stop it now! You hear? Because we're on to you and when we catch up, boy oh boy am I going to have some fun. I'm going to boil you alive and have your balls for breakfast, you piece of shit. And your daughter can rot in hell — after she's had a taste of what we've done to you. So go and take a giant, leaping fuck at yourself! Keep this channel open, because I'll be giving you instructions. You hear that? It's me who'll be giving the orders. Over and fucking out!'

He switched the phone off and turned to

Edmondson. 'I want to keep this in my personal safe. You never know when it might come in useful.'

'Just so long as you keep it switched off until you want to use it.'

★ ★ ★

' . . . Over and fucking out!'

Robin switched off the recording. 'So that's it then, the end of our little caper.'

Mallund sighed and flopped back into his chair. 'Their next monthly meeting is on Wednesday. If only we'd been able to hold out for a few more days we might have got details of this big event they're planning. Now we're back to square one. Spency, I afraid it's down to you, old son. We desperately need this intelligence.'

'It's going to be really difficult, Jack.' Spency was chewing at a fingernail. 'I've been sailing too close to the wind already. If they're doubling their security it will make it very awkward for my contact. Everybody will be under surveillance. I've been thinking, Jack. Maybe this is the time to talk. He might be willing to negotiate now. The feedback is that he is getting a very hard time from the organization. He just might try dipping a toe in the water with a view to settling. Just a thought, for what it's worth.'

'Thanks, Spency.' Mallund touched him on the shoulder. 'But I think he needs to be softened up a bit more. You heard that foul-mouthed tirade on the phone. He's fighting mad. A bad time for negotiating. I don't want him fighting me. I want him begging to talk to me. Believe me, I'd like nothing better than to settle it all right now, but that ain't gonna happen. And I think one more big operation will do the trick.'

'OK, but you might think of moving things on a bit. Why don't you give him some details about Alice? At least that way we might get to know if she's even alive. If she's not, then there's no point in you taking any more risks. You could just walk away.'

Ros glanced sharply at Mallund. He took her meaning.

'No, Spency, this is no longer just about Alice.' Now it was his turn to return the glance to Ros as he spoke. 'It's got bigger. The more I learn about how these people operate, the untold misery they cause, the more I see that they have to be stopped. I'm going to see it through to the end, whatever that end might be.'

'Batman and Robin, eh?' Spency smiled his reluctant smile.

'Keep me out of it,' said Robin, his first

281

joke. Everybody smiled.

'Right,' said Mallund, 'I think we're all finished here.'

As they were leaving the room, Spency took Mallund aside. 'I'm really glad about what you said in there, Jack. About fighting on. It means a lot to me. Just wanted to say thanks.'

'Let's have a drink,' said Mallund.

38

They went to the same pub as Mallund and Ros had gone to, simply because it was the nearest. The same indifferent blonde was behind the bar. The same two men as before were in front of it, nursing their pints. Mallund ordered his small dry sherry and signalled to Spency, who had sat down on the banquette.

'Just water,' said Spency.

Mallund joined him and held up his sherry glass. He nodded at Spency. 'Changed days, eh? You on water, me on a clergyman's temperance sherry. Whatever happened to the old Special Brew?'

'That's all behind me — behind *us* — now. I never touch alcohol these days. Not even a clergyman's small sherry.'

'And the other thing . . . ?'

'The other thing? — Oh, you mean drugs? You can say it out loud Jack, the words won't choke you. Well, I'm still clean. Can't guarantee how long it will last, they say you're never really free of it, but we'll see.'

'How long?'

'Ever since I joined your mad crusade. That

time I met you — when you were doling out the grub at the soup kitchen — I had just come out of rehab. I would probably have slipped back by now if it hadn't been for you. You got me all fired up. I had been working on my own, playing the harmless streetwise junkie, keeping my eyes and ears open, gleaning information and making dangerous contacts, playing one side against the other. But it had achieved little more than a handful of serious beatings-up. Then you came along. Suddenly there was an organization. And I was part of it!' He stopped talking, and sat in silence, sipping his mineral water.

'What I still don't understand, Spency, is what your interest in all this is. I remember at the beginning when I asked you that question you more or less told me to mind my own business. Now, you turn up like an entirely different person. You even talk proper. It sets off warning bells in my head. You're a loose cannon. Spency, if we're to win this we need to level with each other. No hidden agenda. When I think how much time and effort you've put into this in the past I can't help but conclude you are driven by a deep compulsion. My worry is that it could jeopardize the mission. So long as we know what it is then we can work with it, simple as that. Just keep us in the picture is all we ask.'

Spency sat immobile for a few minutes, then let out a long sigh.

'All right, Jack. The full facts. The story of Jonathan Albert Spencer — that's my real name, by the way. I was a promising car salesman — top end of the market, none of your Arthur Daley trash — Ferrari, Bentley, Aston Martin, that sort of thing. Just twenty-one and salesman of the year. A brilliant future lying in wait, with talk of a move to head office and deputy head of sales. Not bad for a lad brought up in an orphanage and a string of foster homes. I had a sister, Stacey. Our parents died in a bus crash in Switzerland. Their holiday coach went off the road and plunged down into a gully. Turned out the driver had had a heart attack. So I had to watch out for Stacey. She was six years younger than me, and we really loved each other because we were the only things in the world we each had. Not just your usual brother and sister love: this was something special. I know what you're thinking, Jack, but there was nothing unnatural about it. The psychologists might try to say differently, but Stacey and I shared a pure and natural love born of necessity. They allowed us to see as much of each other as possible. I adjusted well to the foster homes, but Stacey could never settle. She was strong willed and rebellious. Three sets of foster parents had to give up on her, because of her 'disruptive attitude'. By the time she was fifteen, the social services were having trouble finding foster homes willing to take her in. She ended up in a home where the foster parents were more interested in the income they got from the authorities than in the welfare of the child. She started running wild, staying out at night. Then one day she went out and never came back. Just like your Alice, Jack. The police investigation ended up a blind alley. Then, one day, they found her body in a dingy bedroom in a building known to the police as a brothel. She had taken an overdose. A verdict of suicide was brought in even though the Coroner remarked on signs of violence, especially severe acid burns to one side of her face — '

'Acid burns?' Mallund butted in. 'Wasn't there something about that . . . a story Ros told me . . . something about a brother . . . ?'

'Yes, Jack, I was that brother. She wrote me a letter begging me to help her, gave it to a girl to smuggle it out and deliver it to me. The girl double-crossed her for favours. When the pimps read the letter they were furious. The acid was their way of making an example of her. She couldn't take it anymore so she lay down on that dirty mattress in that dirty room and stuffed herself with sleeping pills . . . ' He choked up and had to take a swig of water before continuing.

'I was devastated. I can't explain the depth of the grief I felt. Our love was something special, so the grief was special too. I went completely off the rails. Had a breakdown. Lost the job. Lost the brilliant future. Started drinking heavily. Then drugs. Living on the streets . . . well, I don't need to tell you of all people how easy it is to end up on Skid Row.' He looked Mallund in the eye, sensing the bond between them.

'But even then there was still some fight left in me. I could not desert Stacey's memory. So I reasoned: if I'm on the streets I might as well use it to my advantage. I was down among people at the sharp end, the prostitutes, the addicts — people who knew what was going down. I gleaned the stories, the rumours, the names. Yes, the names. People could be careless about what they said in my presence . . . old junkie Spency was invisible, even when standing next to them. The road led me to Donlan, but he was invincible. Anything I did would be a flea bite on his back. Then you came along and it all changed. Now he's hurting, like he hurt my Stacey.'

Mallund put a firm hand on his shoulder.

'Thank you for telling me this, Spency. It has put my mind at rest.'

'And mine too. I've never told anybody this before.'

'It won't go any further than me.'

'I don't care now. Somehow all that matters is to get Donlan and bring his empire down.'

'And we will. I promise,' said Mallund, but had to back up his promise with a silent prayer.

Spency jumped up straight in his seat and shivered, like a wet Collie shaking water from its coat, steeling himself with a new resolve.

'Anyway, down to business,' he said after a while. 'Now that the phone scam has been rumbled I guess it's up to me to get the information on the big event. I have to warn you, Jack, that my mole is very vulnerable, and with the tightening of security he might even refuse to meet me, let alone talk. All I can say is I will do my best.'

'That's all we expect,' said Mallund.

Lying in bed that night, he took stock of the situation, talking to the ceiling. 'We've slain Robin's dragons; we've laid Ros's ghost, and now we've cast out Spency's demons.

'My four-man patrol is now all present and correct . . . '

39

The orang-utan was sitting quietly as he peered through the bars of his compound. Spency pulled faces at him, waggling his ears and stretching his lips wide with his little fingers. He scratched his head. Then he adopted the stereotyped stances of the primate, beating his chest with his fists and flapping his hands under his armpits, trying his best to make the beast copy him. The huge face simply stared back at him blankly. Spency gave up after a while. He turned his back on the cage. His contact was late. He checked his watch. Unseen by Spency, the orang-utan lifted his own left arm and stared quizzically at his wrist. The zoo was the latest in a line of meeting places chosen by his contact. Always in open spaces which were public but not too busy. The zoo at ten in the morning suited his purpose.

Twenty minutes later he saw the tall, stooped figure approaching him. They both stood facing the orang-utan, six feet apart.

'This is definitely the last time,' said the gruff voice. 'It's getting too hot. Donlan's going ape-shit and suspecting everybody. His hotshot security adviser is putting everybody under the microscope. So you'd better make this one count.'

'Tell me about the big event that's happening soon.'

'Oh, that? Forget it, kid, you'll get nowhere near it. There was a tight lid on it before, but now . . . well, you might as well try to sneak into Fort Knox.'

'Try me anyway.'

'OK. It's one of Donlan's proudest creations. You'll have heard of his special parties, the wild, anything-goes orgies for the super rich and super-notorious? Well, this one is to be the daddy of them all. He's gone over the top on it to try and rescue his damaged reputation. He's even taking over a Scottish castle. They'll be jetting in from all over the world . . . Arab sheiks from the Middle East, mobsters from the States, Russian Mafia godfathers . . . you name it. Plus some very prominent individuals on the world stage. They love Donlan's weekends. They can play out their fantasies in total confidence. He guarantees complete discretion, total iron-clad secrecy, and he enforces it with an iron fist. It's what they pay for. Wrecking this event would surely be a massive blow to Donlan. But, as I said, you won't get within a mile of it.'

'Still, can you give us details?'
'OK. They'll be at the usual drop-off.'
'Will we meet again?' said Spency.
'I very much doubt it,' said Mike Handley.

40

Mallund studied the Ordnance Survey map of a remote patch of coastline in Scotland's Western Highlands. He located the castle, overlooking a wild stretch of rocks and caves etched by the sea on one side, and a steep gradient sloping away on the other sides.

'Couldn't have picked a better spot myself,' he said to Spency, Ros and Robin bent over the map beside him. 'Those ancient chieftains knew what they were doing. Impregnable. Easily defended all around. Donlan's big do certainly won't be at risk of getting disturbed there. It'll be a big problem for us. I'll need to recce it first, so time is short. I might even have to spend a week or so hiding out. I've arranged to take an early sabbatical. The earthly powers-that-be have been getting a bit twitchy about my absences. During the sabbatical you're supposed to do something constructive that will improve you. I don't know if this counts.' He ended with a wry smile.

'So where do we fit in?' asked Ros.

'Not sure yet. Robin will, of course, keep monitoring the phone in case Donlan honours us with another courtesy call. I'll call on you two as and when needed. But on this mission I will be working alone.' He waved down protests from Ros and Spency. 'It's the way it has to be.'

★ ★ ★

The brooding landscape of the glens slid by slowly as Mallund wound his way westwards towards the coast, water flooding his windscreen as the wipers fought a losing battle against the persistent mist. His lights were on full beam. 'Good grief,' he muttered, 'it's midday and dark as Hades. Scotland!' He reckoned he had about fifty miles still to go, so he stopped at what was laughingly described as a 'viewpoint' and stared at the mist. It stared back at him. He poured a cup of coffee from his flask and slid the seat back to stretch out. It had been a long drive, giving him plenty of time to think. This would be the most difficult mission of all. He had thought of everything he could possibly think of to ensure its success. But there was always the buggeration factor, wasn't there? The tiny missed detail that could snowball into catastrophe. He dismissed it from his mind. It could drive you mad thinking about it. He replayed his preparations behind closed eyes, leaving nothing out.

It had begun two days earlier. There was very little public information about the castle other than that it was in private ownership and available for hire. When not in use it was looked after by a caretaker. Anticipating that he might have to rough it in the wild for some days, he packed a typical SAS survival kit. Then he remembered the simple escape and evasion emergency kit that most SAS soldiers carry, so compact it could be kept in a tobacco tin. Didn't he have one somewhere? He had kept it as a souvenir when he left the regiment. He rummaged among the drawers and pigeon holes of an old oak writing bureau and found it under a pile of dog-eared notebooks. He blew the dust off the top and opened it. The materials inside the box were so strategically packed that it held an inordinately large amount. One by one, Mallund extracted them:

> A thin serrated wire that could be used
>   as a saw that could cut through the
>   toughest steel
> A button compass that could be sewn
>   on to a uniform, or swallowed if nec-
>   essary (and recovered later)
> Wind and waterproof matches
> Flint and steel for fire-starting

Safety pins
A small candle
A mirror for signalling
Basic fishing kit
Water purification tablets
Condoms (placed inside a sock they
    make excellent lightweight emergency
    water carriers holding two litres each)
Snare wire
Razor blade
Lock picking tools
A polythene survival bag
A tampon

In training Mallund had questioned the tampon, then learned that Special Forces had discovered at least ten emergency survival uses for it. It weighs next to nothing and is a valuable source of compressed cotton wool. It can be used to start a fire; it provides an emergency medical dressing; it expands on contact with blood, making it ideal for plugging bullet wounds; it acts as a fletch for a blowpipe arrow; as a water filter; as a wick for a makeshift candle; left in its sheath, it becomes a bob for a fishing line; the outer wrapping makes a waterproof container for matches; the plastic sheath doubles as a blowpipe for nursing a fire into life and, with some of the cotton wool plugged into it, as a safe drinking straw-cum-filter.

Mallund carefully packed the contents back into the tin and slipped it into a pouch on his Bergen along with the rest of his survival gear. Sentimental.

Now, sitting in the car in the swirling mist, he turned his thoughts to the day ahead. He needed somewhere fairly near the castle to leave the car, somewhere it wouldn't attract attention. Up here, he reckoned, any stranger's face attracted curiosity. He got out of the car and stretched his legs, glanced at himself in the side mirror, and wondered if he had chosen the right image for this encounter. Stout walking boots with plus fours tucked into thick woollen socks. A sober black jacket and a straw hat. Then there was his dog collar, something he had worn only rarely for the past several months. He would carry a selection of brass rubbings under his arm. The image was supposed to say: *Slightly eccentric vicar on walking holiday.* A last minute doubt flickered in his mind: brass rubbings. Does anybody still collect brass rubbings? Or did all that die with Agatha Christie? He decided to keep them, a good talking point if ever he was stuck for something to say. After all, he's eccentric, isn't he? He checked himself in the mirror once more.

'All I need now is a set of prominent front teeth to complete the picture,' he muttered.

He took his time driving the remaining distance. There wasn't much point in rushing through the mist. Then, suddenly, it cleared, and he found himself looking down on a deep glen with a river running through it. He hadn't realized how high up he had been, and the altitude came as something of a shock when it jumped out at him without warning. There was a long winding descent into the glen, at the far end of which he could vaguely make out some buildings, one of which he assumed would be the bed and breakfast cottage he had booked. He parked behind the cottage and explained to his host and hostess that he would be staying the night, but might go walking for a few days, and would it be too much of an imposition to leave the car there until he returned?

'It'll come to no harm there, Minister,' said the husband.

41

In the morning he asked directions to the castle. 'I'm told it's worth seeing,' he said. 'Especially the unusual chapel.'

'I'm afraid it's not open to visitors,' said the wife, as she placed a massive plate of fried eggs, bacon, sausages and black pudding in front of him.

'Don't you worry about that,' said the husband. 'There's a caretaker, wee Andy McFadden. Just tell him Robbie Hepburn sent you and maybe he'll give you a wee tour.'

'How extremely kind of you,' said Mallund. He had been fretting all morning about how he was going to con his way into the castle. Now he had a personal recommendation. It was too good to be true.

The mist had disappeared and the sun was shining as Mallund approached the castle. Even from a distance it presented a striking sight. It was built high, on seven storeys, with sheer walls topped by turrets and conical roofs; its fairy-tale appearance suggested it might be more at home in the Black Forest than on a bleak Scottish promontory.

McFadden was outside dabbing paint on a

wooden bench as Mallund came striding up. 'Good morning, sir,' he said cheerfully, waving his incongruous rolled-up umbrella.

'Mornin', Minister.' McFadden was a short wiry man with a jowly face and silver hair cut short. 'A fine day for your walk, is it not?'

'Gorgeous, one of God's blessings on us all.'

'That it be.'

'Robbie Hepburn in the village told me to remember him to you.'

'Robbie? Oh aye.'

'Said you might be able to let me have a look at the chapel. Brass rubbings, you see . . . ' Mallund gestured at his knapsack. 'But I wouldn't like to inconvenience you.'

'Well, I'm not supposed to . . . but if Robbie says it's fine, then it's fine by me.'

McFadden led him through the arched main door, across the Great Hall, through a maze of minor rooms, a vast kitchen, along interminable corridors and finally to the chapel. Mallund's eyes were registering the multitude of nooks and crannies that might serve his purpose. He also took note of the quite sophisticated alarm system; he doubted whether he would be up to disabling it.

'Do you sleep in the castle?' Mallund asked, offhand. 'I must admit I would find it quite scary.'

'Oh aye, but it disnae bother me. You get used to it, and I'm a good sleeper. A clear conscience will always be rewarded by a good night's sleep. Well, this is the chapel. I'll leave you to it and get on with my work.'

Mallund unpacked his brass-rubbing equipment and started going through the motions. When he was sure McFadden was busy outside, he poked around as much as he could on his own side of the castle, checking rooms, corridors and stairwells. While the layout was still fresh in his mind he hurried back to the chapel and jotted down a quick diagram. After half an hour McFadden came into the chapel.

'Are you all right there?'

'Capital. Capital,' said Mallund. 'Nearly finished.'

'If you find your way back to the kitchen, there'll be a cup of tea for you.'

'Thank you. I hope I don't get lost,' said Mallund with a chuckle. 'This place is so huge.'

'You'll find it easy enough.'

Mallund grabbed the opportunity to get 'lost' and checked out several more rooms in the process.

Seated at a long oak table in the kitchen, Mallund sipped his tea and asked idly, 'So how many rooms do you have here? Must be dozens.'

'A hundred and three, if you include them all, large and small. The castle can accommodate eighty guests overnight, but it costs a pretty penny, I can tell you. The company that owns it spent a fortune on making the rooms the height of luxury. Maybe you'd like a wee look at them?'

Mallund was astonished at the unashamed opulence of the rooms he was shown: beds big enough for four, square beds, round beds, semi-circular beds, antique furnishings, windows dripping with silk blinds, silk Persian and Chinese rugs over polished oak floors, magnificent fireplaces of mahogany and marble, and — the epitome of extravagance — gold-plated taps in the bathrooms.

'This is truly a wonderful place you have here, Mr McFadden. I wonder — I'm a bit of an amateur artist too. Nothing special, the Lord has gifted me with a small talent. Would you mind if I did a few sketches for my portfolio?'

'No, not at all. I'll be working outside if you need me.'

Mallund ambled round the building in a wide circle, rapidly sketching diagrams of strategic areas.

'I don't suppose you get many takers at the price they charge?'

'Oh, you'd be surprised. There's a lot of

people with money to spend. Mind you, it makes you wonder the kind of things they get up to when they're here. But I mind my own business. The good Lord did not give me eyes and ears to meddle in other people's affairs. In fact, there's a big do next weekend. They'll be arriving in their helicopters and fancy cars. Important people, who don't like to be seen. They're sending up their own security experts to go over the place on Tuesday and Wednesday.'

Mallund thanked McFadden and waved a cheery goodbye.

★ ★ ★

Back home in his vicarage kitchen, Mallund was cooking a variety of ingredients which to the uninitiated would have suggested he was baking a cake. A pound of sugar, half a cup of baking soda, and one other white powder, saltpetre soil treatment bought from a garden centre. He had mixed five parts of saltpetre to three parts of sugar, and was slowly heating it in a large pan. He turned the heat off once the sugar had turned dark brown and was beginning to caramelize. He added baking soda and gave the mixture a final stir and, while still liquid, poured it into four cardboard boxes which he had lined with aluminium foil. He pushed a length of fuse, gleaned by dissecting a box of fireworks, into each box, then he set it aside to cool and harden.

At a separate table he attached the ends of each fuse to a home made igniter made up from match heads which were in turn connected to the terminals of a battery. To complete the detonation sequence he added a tiny radio receiver and actuator bought from a model aircraft shop.

He now had four very potent smoke bombs.

It was a simple technique gleaned from the explosives course during his cross-training. He could, of course, have bought over-the-counter smoke bombs from a joke shop, or from a pest control outlet, but they would be far too puny for his purpose. No, he needed a vast, spectacular amount of smoke. A veritable Vesuvius of smoke.

Enough to smoke out an entire castle.

42

It took Mallund very little time to set up an ideal observation post half a mile from the castle. It was a slash in the landscape just over six feet deep and four feet wide, running like a trench for 150 yards. He noted gratefully that there would be no digging-in involved. He checked his position relative to the horizon. It was low. The last thing he needed would be to find himself silhouetted against the setting sun as he moved about. Remembering his training, he prepared to scan the terrain before committing himself to the location. He pulled out his binoculars. Rather than sweeping them willy-nilly across the countryside, he adopted the standard procedure. First, he briefly paused his preliminary scan at five selected distances between himself and the horizon, noting each distance. Then he did a more detailed search, starting with the distance closest to himself and working out towards the horizon, systematically covering the terrain from one side to the other in overlapping strips. It was all clear.

He had spent several hours covering a wide

semi-circle on three sides of the castle to find the best position for his observation post. He wore a camouflaged combat suit which he had customized by sticking and pinning tufts of heather and local grasses to give him an edge. He did the same to his bedroll, and even the green tarpaulin that would cover his 'den'. After all, what had McFadden said? *Helicopters and flash cars.* So he would need to be invisible from the air, just like on a real military mission.

His Bergen contained all he needed for up to five nights — food rations, water, flint and steel for fire-making, water purification tablets, night vision glasses, a mobile phone, and a hand-held radio to contact Ros and Spency who were staying at the B&B in the village. The phone and radio turned out to be next to useless because of the high peaks and deep glens. He would be on his own. In separate waterproof compartments in his Bergen were his four large smoke bombs. He had come early in order to be ahead of the security team. He needed to be sure that they had finished checking the place before he could plant his devices.

For three days and nights he monitored the activity around the castle. He counted the security men as they arrived and, two days later, as they left. Good. They had not left any member of the team behind. He paid particular attention to McFadden's routine. Two factors worried him, each involving a gamble. First, the alarm system. He had established that it was off during the day while McFadden was around, but did he switch it on again when he was inside in the evening, or did he leave it off until he went to bed? Mallund would have to gamble that McFadden would take the easy option of leaving it off so he could move around all areas of the castle without the fuss of having to keep switching the system on and off. Then there was the CCTV scanning the area around the castle. No way to avoid that. But again, he could take a gamble. Most CCTV systems are passive, silently recording events, and the recordings tend only to be looked at *after* there has been an incident. In fact, all they do is confirm that you have already been robbed and with luck show the perpetrators in action. Very different from live CCTV which is constantly monitored by a team on shifts. Mallund could hardly imagine McFadden sitting glued to the TV monitor all night. It was a calculated risk. Even if the alarm was zoned so that only his living area was deactivated, leaving the rest of the castle live, he would still likely have to do regular rounds which would necessitate switching the entire system off. Mallund had noted that on two successive evenings McFadden took a stroll around the outside of the castle and took his fishing rod to the shoreline where he spent about an hour. But the castle was always within his sight.

On the third evening Mallund was ready, his smoke bombs packed in a separate rucksack also containing essentials, including his tobacco tin escape and evasion kit. True to form, McFadden emerged and began his circuit of the castle. As soon as he was sure the caretaker was on the blind side of the building, Mallund moved swiftly, covering the ground in running leaps, from time to time diving flat on the ground to check around. He had already selected his entry point during his unofficial tour of the castle. A low window just off the kitchen area could be forced open from outside and then made good again when he left. He opened it and climbed in. He located the hiding places he had selected for his devices — two on the ground floor, one on the first floor and one on the third. He stashed them and quietly made his retreat down the stairs. As he passed a mullioned window on the stairs he glimpsed McFadden. No fishing rod in hand, the caretaker was just about to enter by the front door. Mallund retreated back up the stairs and cast around for somewhere to hide. He found a large, windowless room with the door open. He slipped in and waited. He could hear McFadden clumping around. He heard the massive front door shut with a resounding thump. Then other doors and windows followed suit. McFadden was locking up for the night. Mallund could hear him in the corridor outside, closing doors. He pressed himself back into the darkness of the room and pulled the door shut after him. Two minutes later there was a scratching at the door. Then a metallic click as the door was locked from outside. He heard the rattle of a bunch of keys as McFadden made his way along the corridor, securing the castle for the night. Then came the high-pitched beeping as the alarm was activated.

'Damn!' he muttered. His escape now firmly blocked, he sat down to take stock of the situation. By rights he should have been out of the castle and sprinting across the heather by now. Instead, he was trapped. In the morning McFadden would open the door and confront him. Even if he made a run for it then, the incident would result in a return visit by the security team who would surely discover his smoke bombs. Mission failed. Groping his way in the total darkness, he tested the door with his fingertips. Probably solid ancient oak, thick, with stout steel hinges, it might as well have been in a prison cell. He rummaged in his rucksack for anything to aid his escape, tracing the shape of things with his fingers in the dark, but there were no tools. Then he found it. His fingers swept over the shape of his tobacco tin containing his mini escape and evasion kit. He prised it open and felt the contents one by one until he found what he was looking for: the thin steel blades of the lock-picking kit, simple tools like a dentist's probes.

When he probed the lock with his fingers, his heart sank. His picking kit was designed for delicate surgical work on sophisticated modern locks, not on this Gothic relic of the Age of Chivalry. It felt as if it was carved from stone. He tried his picks. They flopped around in a void, rarely making contact with any metal. If he could only get out of the room after McFadden deactivated the alarm and before he came to unlock the doors, he might have a chance to sneak out unseen. But first he had to get himself out of this dark room. He sat down to think. He took stock of every item on his person or in his rucksack that could be of any use. One small penknife was all he could find. In the total darkness, he groped around the room on hands and knees, bumping his head on the walls. It was empty, probably been cleared out to serve as storage. So it all came down to the penknife. He sat, focusing his mind on the lock. What would it look like inside? It would be a simple 'skeleton' lock, he reckoned. It was too old to have barriers like the spring-loaded pins and tumblers used in Yale type locks. In a smaller version, such as in an antique wardrobe, it would be simple. You could do it with a paper clip and a tiny screwdriver. The problem here was the sheer weight of the internal components. Add to that the stiffness that comes with age, and his puny picks would be fighting a David and Goliath battle. But the penknife . . . could it be used as a backing to provide extra leverage? It was worth a try. He inserted the penknife blade, then one of his picks, using the knife blade to fill much of the vacant space and give him a solid platform from which to work his picks. He tried one pick after another, trying to locate the bar mechanism, wiggling and jiggling in the hope of catching the mechanism.

Four hours later he was still at it. The SAS might teach you how to escape from an up to date lock-up, but there was nowhere in the brief about medieval castles. He fiddled and scraped, but could not get the pressure points just right. He threw his tools down in frustration. 'It's like trying to knit a sweater and eat spaghetti at the same time,' he said to the room. He rested his aching wrists and began all over again. An hour and a half later he felt something move. No more than a tiny tremble. He paused and held his breath, commanded his fingers to be still. His pick had kissed the bar. Slowly, he began to move the pick and the knife blade together and —

'Damn!'

It slipped away again.

The luminous dial of his wristwatch told him it was ten to six in the morning. No doubt McFadden would be an early riser. In fact, he thought he could hear faint stirring noises coming from downstairs. Time was running out. He resumed his task with fresh fervour, attacking the lock in his panic. *Slow down*, he ordered himself. *Easy. This needs a cool head and calm hands.*

Half past six, and no further forward. He tried to remember the exact position he had been in when he last touched the bar, and tried to replicate it. He tried every combination of pick and knife, to no avail.

Seven o'clock, and now there were more definite noises coming from downstairs, doors banging, windows opening. Locks opening. Mallund put his ear to the lock and gently paddled his pick and knife, stirring, hoping for the chance in a million contact. It announced itself with a spongy feeling from the tip of his pick. Movement. He shut his eyes despite the total darkness and focused his mind. *Keep pushing in the same direction. Easy. Don't lose it.* CLICK. The lock sprung open.

As he sneaked the door open he could hear McFadden trudging up the stairs. He cast around for somewhere to hide, but the corridor was empty, except for a large suit of armour at the far end. He padded along the corridor and squeezed in behind the suit. He felt like he was in a scene from an Ealing comedy, but it was his only option. With luck, McFadden would not come right to the end of the corridor, where there were no doors to unlock. Mallund watched him stop at the room he had been in and insert the key in the lock. Looking puzzled, the old man shook his head and moved on to the floor above. Mallund squeezed out from his hiding place and raced down the stairs. He slipped out through the window he had used to come in, pausing for a minute to remove all signs of his entry, and sprinted back to his observation post. He stayed there all that day, from time to time checking the area around him. At sunset he glimpsed a movement on the horizon against the light. A man? A deer? By the time he got his field-glasses it had dropped out of sight. He needed an early night, a good untroubled sleep, but his head was awash with troubled thoughts and fears; fears for Alice if he failed; thoughts of how much longer his faith could hold out against the storm of troubles assailing it. Dawn was almost breaking when he finally dropped off, only to wake again at full light.

43

The helicopters and the cars had been coming and going all day as Mallund watched from his observation post. Long, black limousines and a handful of Ferraris, Aston Martins and Maseratis were parked in a compound away from the castle. Their occupants had arrived in the ultimate designer clothing, many of them wearing dark glasses. There were a lot of women among them. Two coaches drove up and disgorged a load of beautiful young girls, who filed through the main door by pairs in an orderly queue. Well disciplined. The security heavies, in the regulation black suits and designer shades, pony-tails and earrings, were either milling around or standing quietly watching. Mallund made a mental note: eleven of them. He rolled back into his gully and waited. He wondered if he had made the right decision over the detonation of his smoke bombs. He had rejected a much easier method which would have used a simple battery-operated digital timer bought from Tesco, instead of the less reliable radio set up. That way he could be safely at home when the bombs went off. But he wanted to be on the scene where he could set them off in stages whenever the time seemed right for best effect. At least that was the argument he put to himself. There was another reason, though.

He wanted to see Donlan's face.

★ ★ ★

Mallund waited until almost midnight to give the festivities time to get well under way, then gathered his four tiny radio transmitters, each set to different frequencies to match the receiver in the corresponding bomb, and crept towards the castle. He hid the transmitters among some rocks about fifty yards from the walls. Stooping low, he edged up to a window and peered in. The scene was like a Roman orgy. Fat men in togas were frolicking with beautiful young slave girls. In another scenario Viking invaders were grabbing 'virgins' and dragging them upstairs. In another, Little Bo Peep was being paid attention by a grizzly farmer. Mallund did a double take to make sure he was seeing right. Yes, he wasn't wrong. This Little Bo Peep was a man. Truly, Donlan had delivered on his promises to his punters. Anything goes, provided you can pay for it. The room must have contained a large slice of the international underworld, with a smattering of entertainment and political figures. Mallund gazed in disbelief; short-lived disbelief as it turned out, for everything suddenly went black as a solid object made painful contact with the back of his head.

★ ★ ★

He awoke to find himself being dragged along a corridor and thrown on to a stone floor. His vision was triple; his head pounding and throbbing where he had been hit by a guard. He cursed himself for having been so engrossed in the 'entertainment' not to notice the man creeping up behind him. From another planet he heard a voice. 'We thought you'd want to see this, Mr Donlan.'

'You're damned right I do.' Mallund felt his hair being tugged to lift his face from the floor. 'It's got to be *him*! But he's too out of it to talk now.'

It was Donlan's voice, close to his face. But was it really Donlan? Mallund was aware of a face ringed with voluptuous curls, wearing a curly moustache and a huge hat, like one of those old French kings.

'You want we should take care of him, Mr Donlan?'

'No. I'm keeping this one for myself. It's

got to be him! I feel it in my water.'

'Where do you want us to keep him?'

'We're in a castle, for Christ's sake! To the dungeons, of course, to the dungeons!' He laughed heartily at his little irony.

'But, Boss, there's no locks on the dungeon doors. They're only for show.'

'Just make sure he's well trussed up. I'll deal with him at my leisure. I don't want this to spoil the party.'

Mallund was vaguely conscious of being tossed into a dank stone cell. He imagined he heard a metallic click as somebody roughly grabbed his wrists. Handcuffs? Then somebody was messing with his feet, winding and tugging. A rope? He had an overpowering desire to sleep. He dropped out of consciousness.

He awoke to a blinding headache, feeling nauseous, but at least things were a bit clearer now. He checked his body and all his limbs. Nothing damaged. Good. His brain was beginning to clear by the minute, but it had nothing but bad news to report. He was handcuffed and his feet bound by thick rope. Gaffer tape across his mouth. He was helpless, well and truly bound. His only hope was to escape somehow, but he had a snowball in hell's chance of doing that. He tried not let his mind drift on to what would happen to him when Donlan eventually got to him. But willy-nilly the mental images broke through. And when he thought of what would become of Alice, it renewed his vigour. He struggled furiously until exhausted, and had to rest.

Calm down, man, he told himself. *Save your strength. Think, damn you! Think!*

He ran through all his training over the years, looking for something that would aid him. Then it came to him: he had been too woozy-headed to remember it. Stupid! A Special Forces training video he hadn't paid too much attention to at the time came to mind. By an American instructor breaking out of handcuffs.

He checked the handcuffs. Smith & Wesson 100s, standard issue for US police and many other forces around the world. It was all coming back to him now. He was relieved to see they were the regular cuffs with a four-link chain, and not the solid high security rigid bar type such as those used at Guantanamo Bay. How he wished he had paid more attention to the video at the time, but the basics were clear enough. The object was to manoeuvre the chain so that the links became tangled up and locked on themselves. Then, using the two cuffs as levers in a pincer movement, with enough pressure and leverage, either one link would snap, or the steel pins securing the end of the chain to the cuffs would break. It was lucky they had cuffed his hands in front of him and not behind, which would have made the procedure much more difficult.

Still, it was easier said than done. Even the instructor had taken ages to free himself. It was hit-and-miss getting the chain links to snarl up sufficiently. There were countless combinations that would bamboozle even the chaos theory practitioners. It involved pushing the elbows out and rapidly winding the cuffs round the chain in the hope — and that's what it amounted to, hope — that the links would lock. Mallund lost count of the number of tries before he finally got a stable lock-up. But as soon as he put pressure on the links they slipped apart again and he sagged into exhaustion. The cuffs were too new, that was the trouble. The links were shiny and slippery. He remembered a tip from the instructor. Try to rough them up a bit. He wriggled his way across the floor to one of two rough stone pillars from which, no doubt, hundreds of poor wretches had hung in agony over the centuries, and started rubbing the chain against it. After half an hour of scratching, the metal had lost its sheen and was less slippery to the touch.

He tried again. And again. Over and over. An hour later the chain locked up again. This was it! He carefully raised his hands up to head height and manoeuvred the cuffs into a V-shape over the locked chain. He pushed on the cuffs trying to close the V, straining till his wrists felt fit to break. His head was bursting with the effort, his face purple, his chest aching. Then . . . *ping*. The chain snapped in two. Mallund painfully ripped the gaffer tape from his mouth, picked up the broken link and examined it.

'You little beauty,' he said.

He undid the rope round his legs and edged out of the cell, heading up several flights of stairs. He heard a door slam ahead of him and footsteps coming down the stairs. It could be a security man. He needed somewhere to hide. He tested the handle on the first door he came to, opened it and slipped inside. It was dimly lit by candles. He could hear a voice murmuring low: 'Hmm . . . Hmm . . . Hmm.' When his eyes adjusted, he saw a dark-brown man at the other end of the room. He was naked on a bed, spread-eagled, handcuffed to the bedposts. A slim, naked blonde was covering him in what appeared to be chocolate and was licking it off his chest.

'Oops! Sorry!' Mallund whispered as the

man raised his head off the pillow.

'You're welcome to watch,' said the man.

'Sorry, not my cup of tea,' said Mallund. 'By the way, I can show you a good way of breaking out of those cuffs! That's if you ever wanted to,' he added in a whisper, as he slipped quietly out of the room. On the way his hand found a garment hanging behind the door. He unhooked it and took it with him. He realized he would be sure to attract attention dressed as he was in simple black jeans and a black polo neck. Any kind of disguise would help. He found a dark corner in which to slip the garment on.

'I don't believe this!' he said under his breath, as he emerged.

No one took any notice of the clown making his way down the staircase. Mallund, inside the costume, wished he had a clown face mask to complete the picture; as it was, his face was in plain sight. He gambled that no one would be interested enough to scrutinize him closely at that time of night.

. . . Unless, that is, you happened to be a keen-eyed security heavy. Especially one who had seen Mallund's face before, albeit many years ago.

44

Mallund found himself staring into the face of Don, one of the two henchmen who had abducted him and taken him to Donlan's home during his time living on the streets. Mallund immediately started to walk away, but too late. One by one the lights were coming on in Don's brain. His face registered a faint glimmer of recognition, then it all came together.

'Hey, you!' he yelled across the throng of noisy revellers filling the Great Hall.

Mallund broke into a run, dodging among the bodies, across the room and into a corridor.

'*Stop that clown!*' Don's voice cut across the hubbub. Some of the partygoers burst out laughing.

Don gave chase, following Mallund into the corridor. Mallund immediately realized that he was at a huge disadvantage owing to a necessary item of clown fashion — namely shoes that were two times the normal size. The huge comic boots were slowing him down, but he realized that stopping to take them off would cost him even more time, and he could hear Don's rapid footsteps closing up on him. A door ahead led to a flight of stairs going down. Mallund dodged behind the open door and waited. As Don appeared running in the doorway, Mallund stuck out his oversize shoe. Don tripped and went head over heels down the stairs, cursing all the way. Mallund retraced his steps, looking for a way out. He came to a glass door leading on to a terrace at the rear of the castle. A handful of partygoers were smoking and chatting on the terrace. They didn't even look at him as he walked casually across the lawn and into the darkness. He found the radio transmitters he had hidden among the rocks and he immediately activated numbers one and two on the ground floor and waited. Nothing happened for a minute as he held his breath. Slowly, at first, wisps of dark-grey smoke began to curl out of the castle walls, seeking out gaps. He activated number three on the first floor and number four on the third, and watched as the smoke invaded them too. Two minutes later the entire castle was enveloped in a thick pall of smoke. He listened for the alarm. Somebody would be sure to break the glass and press the red button. He waited.

Come on, where are you?

Another two minutes and the shrill ringing

of the alarm sounded over the moor. He had established from the type of alarm that it would be connected directly to the emergency services. In the town, bleary-eyed members of the part-time Fire Brigade would be pulling on their socks, rudely awakened from their slumbers. In the police house, Constable Geordie McDowell would be grudgingly gathering his boots and wondering if he had time for a quick mouthful of tea first.

Mallund waited and watched as the smoke engulfed the building. He felt confident enough to venture down to the front entrance. Exterior floodlights had come on to reveal a bizarre sight. There was total panic. People were pouring out of every door into the night, naked and half-naked, dressed for fantasy. There were Nazi officers, both male and female, the women officers in stockings and suspenders; there were characters from fairy-tales and nursery rhymes, slaves in chains, a French maid with his seven o'clock shadow already showing, men in rubber head masks, some with their hands still bound. One man had lost his mistress, but was still bound into a crawling position on all fours. He was scrambling around like a pitiful stray puppy, the lead dangling from his steel-studded leather collar. Mallund's first reaction would have been to burst out laughing, but just then he saw it, bobbing about in the crowd, that huge French king hat. Straight out of his semi-conscious dream. Donlan. He kept his eyes on it as it moved among the crowd. There was such a panic and noise that he might not be noticed if he slipped himself in amongst them to get close to Donlan. Dare he try it? Was it worth the risk? He joined the mass of screaming and shouting bodies and shadowed Donlan at a safe distance. He saw his chance when Donlan broke away from the crowd as if looking for someone or something, and went into a dark corner. Mallund swiftly stepped up behind him, put him in an arm lock and dragged him further into the darkness. He wrapped his arm tightly round Donlan's throat, muffling him.

'Not a sound!' Mallund hissed. 'Just listen. I've got this close to you and I can do it again. I could have a knife to your throat. If you want to deal use the old phone you kept.'

He put a sharp extra pressure on Donlan's windpipe and kicked his feet away so that he fell to the ground, gasping. As Mallund slipped away into the darkness surrounding the castle, Donlan was lying on the ground trying to summon his men, but no words would come.

When Constable McDowell and the Fire Brigade arrived, the place was still in chaos. McDowell surveyed the scene in awe. He needed to take statements. But how can you get a sensible statement from a man in a rubber head mask with a ball gag in his mouth and his hands bound behind his back? Besides, the witnesses were fleeing the scene in a mass, uncontrolled exodus. Exotic cars and limousines full of half-naked and bizarrely dressed men and women sped past in a flurry of flying gravel and screeching tyres. The sound of helicopter engines winding up drifted over from a nearby field. McDowell corralled half-a-dozen people in a corner and ordered them: 'Don't move until I get to the bottom of this!'

The fire-fighters quickly established that there was no fire, only smoke from four devices they had uncovered. 'Looks like a gigantic practical joke,' one fireman told the media.

The Sun was the most up front:

SMOKED OUT!
Kinky revellers flee castle in midnight fire scare

A picture snatched by one of the fire-fighters on his phone appeared in most of the national dailies. It showed a bizarre carnival of guests fleeing the scene in panic, many of them covering their faces.

★ ★ ★

Donlan reviewed the unwelcome media attention his event had received.

'The bastard had me by the throat, Mike. He could have done for me there and then.' Donlan was kicking furniture again. 'By the fucking throat. I don't mind telling you I was scared. Really scared.'

Mike Handley nodded in sympathy. 'He is one cool operator, Pat, that's for sure.'

'The roof has fallen in on me this morning. Nobody's returning my calls. Not only am I a laughing stock, but important people want my blood. It will cost me dearly to clean up this mess. And then who knows what will come next? He's got to be stopped.'

'I think the time has come to negotiate, Pat. Find the girl and hand her back. What's one little trollop compared to losing everything? It's only your pride that's standing in the way. Hand her back, then you can deal with him at your leisure. Deal with both of them, if you want.'

'But we still don't even know who or where

327

she is. Christ, she could even be dead for all we know.'

'Then talk to him, Pat. Use your old phone like he told you to. And be quick. The sooner this is over the better.'

45

As Donlan's second in command, Mike Handley was in a position of great power. Donlan trusted him and valued his advice. In fact, all the sensible moves that had led to the flourishing of their crime empire had come from Handley. His cool head and analytical brain were in sharp contrast to Donlan's volatile temper and bog Irish pig-headedness. Everything was simple to Donlan. If something or somebody gets in the way, just steamroller your way through and over them. Handley, however, took a more oblique approach, asking how it could be accomplished with less disruption — and perhaps gain some extra advantage on the way. Handley was a thinker. And first among his thoughts at this time was the downfall of Patrick Edward Donlan.

They had partnered together since their teens when Handley, the streetwise Dublin con artist living on his wits, and Donlan, the bluff petty thief straight from the bog, bumped into each other while leaving the Probation Office. They immediately established a bond — after all, didn't they share the same probation officer? This simple commonality was to tie them together as inseparably as man and wife as they moved up through the underworld. Nicking cars and smuggling sheep across the Irish border led them into the lucrative drugs market. And when Ulster erupted in the late 1960s, drugs and gun-running became the golden goose for the duo. They had stuck together through thick and thin, and had to disappear to Australia for two years after falling foul of the IRA in an arms deal that went wrong. They resurfaced in the UK and muscled in on some established rackets which launched them on their way to creating the international criminal organization that they headed today. Donlan regularly proclaimed his eternal brotherly love for Handley with a slap on the back, especially in drink, but Handley accepted it with a long-suffering kind of smile. Even after all these years he had not come to share Donlan's sense of brotherhood. They were a business unit that worked well, a yin and yang that got results and prospered. A long time ago Handley had tired of the relationship; tired of Donlan and his crass ways. This had eventually led him to a stark realization: he did not even like the man.

★　★　★

When Mallund started his one man vendetta against Donlan, Handley had seen his chance. No more Number Two. He could be Number One. He had sent out feelers which led him to Spency, to whom he began feeding the information vital to Mallund's campaign. Now, as he entered Donlan's study carrying a large brown envelope, he could see his ambition becoming a reality.

'This is it,' he said, waving the envelope above his head, 'the goods on the girl.' He slapped it on Donlan's desk.

Donlan opened the envelope and extracted a colour photo of a pretty young blonde, studied it for a few seconds, then read the writing on the back aloud. 'Angela Mallund . . . father Jack Mall — Jesus Christ, Mike! He's a vicar! You mean to tell me this slime ball who's been giving me all this grief is a fucking God-botherer?' Donlan's eyes lit up when a sudden realization came home to him. 'We've got him, Mike! We don't need to find the girl. We can grab the bastard right now!'

'Slow down, Pat, slow down,' said Handley. 'That's easier said than done. There's a problem.'

'How can there be a problem? It's dead simple. We just pick him up.'

'He's disappeared.'

'Jesus! Why the hell didn't you grab him

straight away as soon as you got this?'

'He timed it well. By the time this came into our possession he was long gone.'

'Well, find out where he is! Put every man on it. Put the screws on his friends and family. Somebody somewhere must be harbouring him. Tear the fucking city apart if you have to.'

'Won't do any good, Pat. Turns out he's some kind of SAS veteran. He's probably on some remote moor living on cow shit and rat piss. And he'll stay there until you decide to talk to him.'

Donlan sighed the sigh of a man who had run out of options. 'All right. All right.' He rose and opened his personal safe. He pulled out the phone with Robin's software buried deep within it and switched it on. He almost yelled into the phone.

'Listen, you bastard! You win! We'll meet and I'll have your daughter. Just make the arrangements.' He disconnected.

'Now we need to find this girl. Fast.' Donlan sat gazing at Alice's photograph. 'Tasty little thing. Let's just pray she's still alive.'

★ ★ ★

Dinner for Mallund was in fact a step up from cow shit and rat piss. Earlier he had snared a rabbit using the thin wire saw from his escape and evasion kit as a noose and wire. He decided he was remote enough hidden in a crease in the barren moor to risk a Dakota fire hole over which to cook it. He dug a hole eighteen inches deep and another similar hole a foot away. Then he dug deep into them and carefully scooped out the soil until he had created a connecting tunnel between the holes. He lit his fire in one hole, relying on the vacuum downdraft from the second hole to feed the fire, keeping smoke to a minimum. It was four days since Robin had relayed Donlan's message to him by satellite phone, and he had exhausted his rations. From now on he would have to live off the land, boosting his strength with edible wild plants, snails and insects. That didn't worry him. But with each passing day he became more dejected as his hopes for Alice rapidly faded away. What if she was dead after all? It was the cold, lonely nights huddled up in his dugout that were the worst. He feared going to sleep for that was when the nightmares came. He found it easier not to sleep, but the lack of it was beginning to play havoc with his senses. He chewed on a tough piece of rabbit leg and wondered about quitting and heading back to civilization. But Donlan's vast network would have been alerted to him. It was too risky. So he lay on his plastic groundsheet and willed himself to sleep.

The grey, damp dawn was eating its way into his bones as he awoke from a fitful sleep. There was a distant beeping. He rubbed his eyes and shook his head to clear away the fuzz. The beeping was closer now, coming from inside his dugout. An alarm clock? No, he didn't even have an alarm clock. Beep . . . beep . . . beep . . . then it dawned on him. His satellite phone. He snatched it up and heard Robin's voice deliver a simple message.

'They've found her!'

* * *

'So where the fuck is she?' Donlan's voice was impatient.

'In the Middle East. Lucky for us she was one of the favoured few.' Mike Handley was reading from a blue-covered file. 'Thanks to her good looks she was spared the local flesh mill. She went straight to auction and was snatched up by a sheik for his 'collection'.'

'Collection?'

'That's what it says here. Jesus Christ! — get this! He's eighty-two years old. Just likes to be surrounded by beautiful young women, apparently. Like pets, I suppose.

'Window dressing', is the phrase my informant uses. He says she is 'in very good condition'. Sounds like a used car, if you ask me.'

'Spare me the wit, Mike. What does he mean?'

'Means she will have been well looked after, clean, no rough stuff, although she's likely to have a drugs habit — it's their way of keeping her under control.'

'So how do we get her back?'

'It'll cost you big, in both cash and favours, but it can be done. A lot of palms will have to be greased. In the end, the old boy probably won't even notice she's gone.'

'Right, I'll leave it to you. Get on to it right away, there's no time to lose.'

46

The arrangements for the handover of Alice were dictated by Mallund.

'Is he taking the piss?' Donlan was reading Mallund's instructions with a frown on his face. 'He wants me to wear tight *Lycra* cycling shorts? And a tight matching jersey? This can't be for real!'

'He obviously wants to make sure you're not concealing a weapon,' said Handley. 'Even at a distance a gun would show up as a huge bulge.'

Donlan read on. The handover would take place at a large clearing in a heavily wooded area six miles from the city. Donlan was to come alone, bringing Alice with him. He would leave Alice and walk away. Simple, no complications.

Mallund had chosen the spot because the open area afforded a safety zone in which he would be out of range of normal weaponry. He would be able to check round the wooded periphery before the meet in case Donlan had concealed any of his men. Double-cross was second nature to Donlan, so Mallund would need to be on his toes. He went over the plan with Spency, Ros and Robin.

'There's not much for you three to do,' he said. 'Ros will be standing by a good distance away with an extra car for a swift getaway in case anything goes wrong. Spency and Robin, well, you two just keep your fingers crossed and pray for me.'

'I still think you're mad going alone and unarmed, Jack,' said Spency. 'You'll be a sitting duck. Let me help. Even if he hands over Alice and you both get away you'll be looking over your shoulder for the rest of your life, no matter where you hide. Donlan must be taken out if you are to have any peace.'

'You know my rule, Spency: no killing. My way is the best way. I'll take my chances.'

Spency shook his head in exasperation and stormed out of the room. Outside, he found a quiet spot, took out his mobile and speed-dialled a number.

★ ★ ★

The night before the rendezvous with Donlan, Mallund knelt alone in his church and prayed silently.

Lord, help me be true to your teachings in the task that lies ahead. Forgive me for the lesser transgressions that have brought me to this stage. Give me strength to resist the temptation that will surely assail me, and support me in my hour of need. Amen.

He rose from his knees, and felt the cold steel of the Browning Hi Power automatic, a dead weight against his thigh. It had taken an agony of soul-searching before he had finally decided to open the drawer containing the Browning that Ben Yates had left with him. As he unwrapped the weapon from its oiled rag and weighed it in his hand, he felt a sudden urge to put it back. But he didn't. *You're not thinking straight*, he told himself. He was only too aware of the folly of meeting with Donlan unarmed. But he was certain that if it came to an unarmed tussle between Donlan and himself that he would gain the upper hand and be able to free Alice. He was satisfied that with both Donlan and Alice dressed in the skin-hugging clothes there was no way Donlan could conceal a weapon. He had reasoned that he could take the gun along as a scare tactic, use it to bluff his way out of a difficult situation if Donlan tried any tricks. It would also lend a bit of clout to his rather tenuous position. Of course, he would never dream of firing it. It was simply a prop. *Then why have it loaded with a full clip of bullets?* Well, he reasoned, he might need to use it to make some noise, or provide covering fire. Every advantage would help.

But what if the need to shoot to kill becomes too compelling? He closed his mind to the matter and packed the gun among the things he would need the following day. In his bones he felt that he would face yet another crisis of conscience before tomorrow had run its course.

* * *

At the appointed hour Mallund drove his Kia into the clearing, switched off the engine and waited. He had already checked the wooded periphery on foot. Ten minutes passed and he saw Donlan's white Range Rover enter the clearing and stop fifty yards away as instructed. Mallund got out of the car as Donlan opened the door of the Range Rover and stepped down. He led Alice by the arm and began to walk her towards Mallund.

'That's far enough,' said Mallund. Donlan looked faintly ridiculous in his skin tight cycling outfit. Alice's outfit simply pointed up her perfect figure, following every curve, creating a stunning picture with her long blonde hair piled up over her head.

Donlan came to a stop and grinned. 'I suppose you think you've won, Vicar?' he said.

'Just leave her and walk away,' snapped

Mallund. 'I promise I won't give you any more trouble.'

'Do you think I'm stupid? I'm holding all the cards here.' Donlan reached into Alice's piled-up hair and pulled out a knife. He held it to her throat. 'Suppose you just stay put where you are, Vicar. My men will be here soon. So. Now I've got both of you. Father and daughter. Two for the price of one. I'm going to have some fun, I can tell you. After all the trouble you've caused me.'

Mallund cursed himself. He had been so overwhelmed at seeing Alice that he had overlooked the possibility of her hair as a hiding place for a weapon.

Now it was a stand-off. There was nothing else for it. He reached behind his back and pulled the Browning from his waistband. He aimed it straight at Donlan.

Thou Shalt Not Kill.

Mallund's brain felt like it was at the centre of a tug-of-war. This wasn't supposed to happen. If he gave in to Donlan and surrendered then both he and Alice would end up dead. And Donlan would live to prosper in his evil empire. It had come to this. His faith was being tested to breaking point. His finger found the trigger.

Thou Shalt Not Kill.

Beads of sweat broke out on his brow. *His sacred vows. Oh, his sacred vows.* He had a clear sightline for a shot at Donlan's head.

Donlan was leering at him. 'Go ahead, Vicar,' he taunted. 'You don't have the balls to pull the trigger.'

Thou Shalt Not Kill.

Mallund was aware of his finger increasing the pressure on the trigger. As if it had a life of its own. His finger versus his conscience in a fight to the death.

$\star$ $\star$ $\star$

The shot took away half of Donlan's head. The report went echoing through the woods, sending flocks of frightened birds high into the air. Alice was standing screaming as her captor lay at her feet in a pool of blood.

Thou Shalt Not Kill.

Mallund was confused. Where was the acrid smell of gunsmoke? Where was the hefty kick of recoil as the Browning launched its deadly cargo at the target? There had been nothing. Slowly, it dawned on him.

I didn't shoot! I didn't pull the trigger!

He looked around, dazed. *But if I didn't shoot, then who did?*

$\star$ $\star$ $\star$

From behind a hillock among the distant trees, Corporal Ben Yates packed up his long-range sniper rifle and silently melted into the green of the forest. 'God sure moves in mysterious ways,' he said to himself as he ran, crouching through the undergrowth.

Epilogue

They were walking in the park on a crisp and cleansing autumn morning, kicking at the leaves in their piles of gold, russet, olive and mustard: Mallund, Ros and Alice.

Just like a real family, thought Mallund. He was in the middle, his arms around their shoulders.

It had been a long, hard road back for Alice, helped largely by Ros. Counselling and drug rehab had gone a long way. Everyone was hopeful for the future.

The police investigation concluded that Donlan's death was a gangland killing. Mallund, too, thought it the most likely scenario. He never did find out that Spency had been tipping Ben Yates off about his missions, and that his old buddy had been shadowing him in case he got into trouble. Mike Handley achieved his ambition of stepping into Donlan's shoes, but the organization was on a downward spiral to nowhere as confidence slumped owing to the glare of publicity, with nervous partners and backers withdrawing their support.

As they crunched through the carpet of

dead leaves, Alice suddenly broke away from under her father's arm and started walking backwards in front of him.

'Dad? Can I ask you a question?'

'Sure. Anything, sweetheart.'

'That time in the forest clearing.'

'Yes?'

'When Donlan had the knife to my throat.'

'Yes?'

'Would you have pulled the trigger?'

Other titles published by Ulverscroft:

LIVING DANGEROUSLY

Dan Latus

When old friends Anne and Josh Steele ask Frank Doy to look after their son, Tom, Frank can't say no. But he is in terrible danger. After a drink-driving incident that took Tom's friend's life, the victim's gangster father holds him responsible and wants him dead. Frank takes his charge to an isolated cottage in wintry Northumberland, but trouble soon follows. As the lonely village is held siege during a blizzard, Frank unravels a story at odds with the Steeles' version of events — a story of a dangerous business partnership turned sour, and a young man placed in jeopardy by family loyalty.

We do hope that you have enjoyed reading this large print book.

Did you know that all of our titles are available for purchase?

We publish a wide range of high quality large print books including:
Romances, Mysteries, Classics
General Fiction
Non Fiction and Westerns

Special interest titles available in large print are:
The Little Oxford Dictionary
Music Book
Song Book
Hymn Book
Service Book

Also available from us courtesy of Oxford University Press:
Young Readers' Dictionary
(large print edition)
Young Readers' Thesaurus
(large print edition)

For further information or a free brochure, please contact us at:
Ulverscroft Large Print Books Ltd.,
The Green, Bradgate Road, Anstey,
Leicester, LE7 7FU, England.
Tel: (00 44) 0116 236 4325
Fax: (00 44) 0116 234 0205

DARK POWERS

Raymond Haigh

When special agent Samantha Quest frees a young girl from a secure children's unit, she's taking on the most powerful people in the country. Annushka Dvoskin, daughter of a Russian oligarch, has used her mobile phone to video an incident which could prove disastrous for the government, especially if information of her affair with an older man also gets out. And enemies of Annushka's father have dispatched a team of hitmen to murder her and Samantha. As they flee from danger, they search desperately for the phone — using the footage as a bargaining tool may be their only hope for safety . . .

A KILLER PAST

Maris Soule

Seventy-four-year-old Mary Harrington doesn't want to revive her past. She certainly doesn't want her son and granddaughter to know exactly what she was doing forty-four years ago. But when two teenagers from a local gang attempt to mug her, old habits prove hard to forget. Sergeant Jack Rossini — Rivershore, Michigan's lone investigative detective — initially doesn't believe an old woman could have put the youths in hospital. But once he meets Mary, he becomes curious; and his interest is piqued further when he discovers that there's no record of her existence prior to 1944 . . .

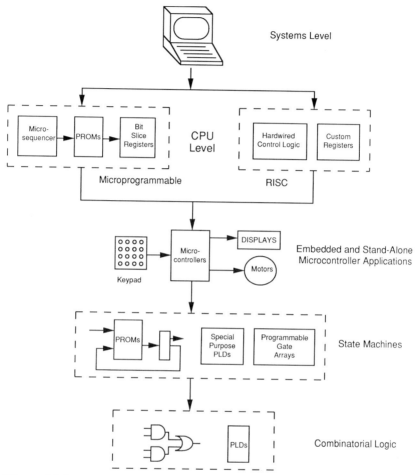

Figure 14-1
Programmable Circuits Hierarchy.

The last level in the hierarchy is the simple combinatorial circuit. These are the devices that glue the more sophisticated chips and assemblies together. While conceptually simple, these combinatorial circuits often have the tightest speed constraints and are critical in determining the overall system performance.

At all levels of this hierarchy, programmable circuits play a key role. This book has started at the bottom and worked its way up the hierarchy. The modern design engineer and those who support and coordinate design activities must understand the spectrum of options that programmable circuits provide. Currently, programmable options must compete with alternative approaches: stock chips, such as RAMs, UARTs, and timers; custom ICs; standard cells; and gate arrays.

For many applications these alternatives to programmable logic will enjoy price and performance advantages for many years. Ultimately, however, the margins will decrease in magnitude. What are called programmable techniques today will be considered the standard design methodologies of tomorrow.

In the upcoming years, the digital designer's role will be much more *descriptive*. CAD tools will allow the designer to start at the top level of the design and then work down. At the uppermost level, the design will be described in block diagrams with signal routing shown.

The designer will then push down into each box, describing its operations in whatever form is the most applicable. More block diagrams, function tables, state tables, or logical equations are only a few of the options. High-level design description languages, similar to today's VHDL, will be directly available as part of the design environment.

The actual function of the various blocks might be described algorithmically, using such common languages as C, ADA, FORTRAN, or the new and friendlier object-oriented languages. The programming will be an integral part of the design process.

Simulation will also be an interactive part of the design process. As the design moves toward completion, a full suite of test inputs and expected outputs will be generated. Performance models, parameter sensitivities, and required tolerances will be calculated as an ongoing part of the design.

Only when the design has been warranted to perform as intended will it be committed to actual hardware. The functional blocks will be automatically partitioned into realizable slices of silicon. The actual chips used and the silicon technologies will be independent of the design process. For initial testing and limited production runs, programmable architectures will be used. For higher volumes, the data base will be compiled down to standard cell or gate array implementations.

This process will be transparent to the designer. The important operation will be the design. The translation of the design to silicon will be handled by specialized post-processors. These post-processors will insure that the chip set will meet the performance requirements regardless of how the chip set is realized.

Such a design will be virtually self-documenting. Another engineer will be able to follow the design trail smoothly. There will be no guessing, which is so common in many labs today, as to the function of a particular device. Changes and updates to the design will be possible with both ease and precision.

This scenario is only somewhat futuristic. Even today, design environments exist that demonstrate many of these capabilities. Several vendors are working on processes that will allow PLD-based designs to be translated directly to gate arrays. High-level design and simulation languages are adding abstraction to circuit engineering.

Currently, the use of programmable circuit elements, PLDs, microcontrollers, PROMs, and microsequencers exceeds one billion dollars per year. For the foreseeable future the trends are clear. Programmable circuit design techniques will account for an ever-increasing percentage of successful designs.

These trends will change the nature of electronic engineering. The successful engineer will be more verbal and less visual and will be able to accomplish more powerful and cost-effective designs in ever-shorter periods of time.